BEAUTIFUL
ANIMALS

BEAUTIFUL ANIMALS

A NOVEL

LAWRENCE OSBORNE

HOGARTH

LONDON · NEW YORK

Published in the United States by Hogarth, an imprint of the Crown Publishing Group, a division of Penguin Random House LLC, New York.
crownpublishing.com

HOGARTH is a trademark of the Random House Group Limited, and the H colophon is a trademark of Penguin Random House LLC.

Library of Congress Cataloging-in-Publication Data
Names: Osborne, Lawrence, 1958- author.
Title: Beautiful animals : a novel / Lawrence Osborne.
Description: First United States edition. | New York : Hogarth, [2017]
Identifiers: LCCN 2017019236| ISBN 9780553447378 (hardback) |
ISBN 9780553447385 (ebook)
Subjects: | BISAC: FICTION / Literary. | FICTION / Psychological. |
FICTION / Action & Adventure.
Classification: LCC PR6065.S23 B43 2017 | DDC 823/.914—dc23
LC record available at https://lccn.loc.gov/2017019236

ISBN 978-0-553-44737-8
Ebook ISBN 978-0-553-44738-5

Printed in the United States of America

Book design by Lauren Dong
Jacket design by Evan Gaffney
Jacket photograph by Panagiotis Kostouros/Millennium Images, UK

10 9 8 7 6 5 4 3 2 1

First Edition

For Kelley

There is no ship for you, there is no road.

As you've wasted your life here, in this small corner,

you've destroyed it everywhere else in the world.

—CAVAFY

HYDRA

ONE

HIGH UP ON THE MOUNTAINSIDE ABOVE THE PORT, the Codringtons slept through the dry June mornings in their villa shaded by cypresses and by awnings rolled down over the doors. They lay in pajama-clad splendor among their Byzantine icons and paintings of Hydriot sea captains, unaware that their daughter Naomi had taken up early swims, that she dressed in the cool of her own room an hour before daylight, half reflected in a wishbone mirror. She put on a cambric shirt with French cuffs and a leather thong necklace, slung a small denim beach bag over her shoulder, and then made her way down the whitewashed steps that ran below her father's house. She walked to the port along a narrow helix of steps, through landings with iron grilles and sudden views of the sea where the stone arches retained the nocturnal cool; the wild lots with their signs reading *Poleitai* and the marital bedrooms now open to the sky and filled with motionless butterflies.

Down by the town Naomi passed the Hotel Miranda with its chained anchor strung against a wall and a door that opened into a secret garden sunk in a blue glow of plumbago. A priest sat on the step as if waiting for something, and he gave her a nod. They knew each other without knowing each other's names. The holy beard that remained the same, the girl who walked with silent steps summer after summer as if she couldn't hear anything around her. At the toy port she walked around the over-priced yachts without stopping at the cafes. She climbed above the tourist harbor and out onto a path above the sea, silent in her espadrilles at first, then singing and counting her own steps. She passed a row of cannons set into the wall, the monument to Antonios Kriesis, wind-shredded agaves leaning like totems out of the hillside. She went around the island northward on a track that led to the little bay called Mandraki, a place where her Greek stepmother often said the waters never moved. She had never discovered why piles of rusted machinery lay by the side of the path, boilers and girders, cement mixers long ago pitched among the flowers.

At the crest of the hill above Mandraki there were a few im-posing villas with long walls around them, their door knockers shaped as heads of Athena. Below it the bay held a run-down little resort called the Mira Mare where, on the beach, a small seaplane had been dragged up and its windows covered with screens. Frames of parasols with no straw lay in disorder in the lot behind the beach, but past Mandraki the path was uncon-taminated. It wound toward Zourva through scrubland hill-sides, and there great fields of stones swept down to the water in a blistering wind. The water was almost black before the sun rose high enough to lighten it. This was where Naomi always swam, sometimes half hoping to die, until she was too cold to continue and her fingers went numb.

She never told her father and Phaine about her morning swims and there was no need for them to know. What would they have said? Solitude was a value that meant nothing to them. They wouldn't have understood that every morning she felt the same listless and vague expectation, the same dis-satisfaction with the tempo of the world as she knew it. She

4

sometimes thought that she had internalized this perpetual disappointment since childhood, though she could never quite put her finger on her unconscious reason for doing so. Or perhaps it was the island itself. The summers that went on forever, the afternoons too hot for purely animal activities. And worse even than these, the ancient bohemians whom her father and stepmother mingled with. The stunning emptiness of it didn't even bore her; it made her feel superior to the island's hedonism but without being able to suggest an alternative to herself.

Afterward she dried herself on the stony slopes among the wasps. She wrote in the small diary she carried with her while across the straits lay the low and promising shadow of the mainland. Beyond the haze lay the Argolid and the jetty at Metochi, both too far off to really see. It was usually eight or so by the time she had walked back to Mandraki and wandered into the resort looking for a coffee. High above the cove, raw mountainsides held up a white sanctuary in the first sunlight. She had always, during her childhood, imagined saints living there, hermits beaten by winds. But they had never appeared. The boys laying out the umbrellas and regimented loungers on the strip of sand knew her by now. The flirtations had subsided and they regarded her increasingly with a sullen skepticism because she had, a hundred and one times, rebuffed their advances.

Before long, her eye was drawn to the lines of navy towels spread out on the sun loungers in the heat. It was shabby but secluded; sometimes the former was the price for the latter. The bay was so small that the ocean in front of it possessed a wide-angle immensity in comparison with the cramped beach. There, in any case, two women had already arrived, clambering down from the path with their beach bags, straw hats quivering as they moved, with the prudent agility of beetles.

They lay on two loungers and the boys came down to them with trays of iced water, and it was clear that they came there every day and that the staff knew them well. They probably ordered breakfast and lunch with plenty of alcoholic drinks in between, because there was a familiarity in the manner of the Greeks. The resort was dying, paying non-guests were as vital as guests. It was an older woman and a young one, perhaps a mother and daughter. But Naomi didn't recognize them from the endless parties to which her father and stepmother were invited and to which she also subjected herself since there was nothing else to do on the island. They weren't famous, then, and they weren't the Beautiful People and Jimmie and Phaine probably didn't know them either. Nevertheless, here they were, drinking their coffee out of big blue cups and flicking away the flies with—of all things—a pair of tropical-weather fly whisks. The girl was remarkably fine, slender, spun-gold hair, too white for that sun, which made her eyes look even more desperate and avid. When the light hit them they gave off the inhuman glow of blue gemstones. The whisks were amusing and she inwardly approved, even when the accents floated over and seemed to suggest they were American. So they were, and before their coffee was consumed they had looked up at the British girl with her yogurt and honey on a wooden spool and their eyes filled with a light and homely curiosity. You too, at Mandraki?

THE FEMALE HALF of the Haldane family had discovered the cove the very first day they arrived on the boat from Piraeus. They had gone on a long walk around the island themselves, without Mr. Haldane, and if Amy thought about it she would have had to admit to herself that she always made the best discoveries when her husband wasn't around to spoil it.

"It was Samantha who found it—she asked the cleaning women at the villa, which was very clever. But I think you got here before us."

"I've been coming here for years," Naomi said with deliberate weariness.

"So you know—"

The other girl was younger than Naomi, maybe nineteen or twenty to her twenty-four, with eyes that were steady and cool: perhaps like herself a student of human beings and their calamities.

"You live here?" she said, calmly interrupting her mother.

"My father has a house. He's had it since the eighties."

"Lord," the mother said. "We've stumbled on an expert. He's really been here that long? So you must have grown up here."

"Summers."

"Summers on the island. We have a summer house on an island in Maine almost as nice as this one. But we're New Yorkers. Maybe we know your father?"

She was a little eager, and Naomi had to tamp her down.

"I don't think so. My father and stepmother are quite odd socially."

"My husband, you know—he's recuperating from an injury. He came here to heal, and it didn't seem like a bad idea. He's recovering already—wouldn't you say, Sam?"

"He's already walking around on his bad foot."

Naomi moved to the lounger next to theirs. She stretched out, and there was something in the unfurling of her body that drew attention to itself. A narcissist, the mother thought.

"I speak Greek," Naomi said, smiling. "I can order anything you want. They have a lot of things off menu."

The mother looked up at the waiters by the bar, and her mouth wavered.

"What about yogurt?" she murmured, pointing to Naomi's abandoned breakfast. "I wouldn't mind some yogurt."

"*Yaourti*," Naomi called over sharply. "*Me meli.*"

The heat crept to the back of their necks, and when it settled in behind their ears it refused to relinquish its quiet grip. Two trees hovered at the crest of the hillside, burning in their own gray light. They could sense dogs still asleep beneath them though they couldn't be seen, and Naomi asked quietly what was wrong with Mr. Haldane.

"He went into a cage of monitor lizards at the zoo," the girl said without expression, "and one of them bit his foot. It severed the tendons, and they have bacterial agents in their saliva."

"Sam, really."

The truth was he had fallen off a ladder while painting a greenhouse near Blue Hill.

"It's embarrassing. Jeffrey is such a fool with ladders. But he broke his hip *and* his foot."

"No lizards?"

Amy turned to her daughter. "I don't *think* there were any involved."

"He was in a wheelchair for a month," Samantha said, "and now he's on an island with no cars or bikes. He said that was the whole point—it would force him to walk. But now that we're here—"

"He just sits in his chair painting all day."

"Well," Naomi said, looking up at the sky. "It's kind of hard to do much else here. It's what I do." It was a lie but, as far as she could tell, they didn't spot it and she didn't care if they did.

THEY TALKED FOR a while. It was the banter of people of similar social standing subtly divided by a common language. Seabirds circled overhead and there was no music; the bouzouki for the tourists was not yet necessary. They could hear only the water moving against the rocks and the first cicadas stirring as the sun encroached upon the hillside. The heat rousing all living things. Amy finally lay back and sank into her comatose sunbathing, and the two younger women decided to swim out together to the rocks of the outer cove. They went down to the water in a sun that now burned their faces and slipped in together. They swam very quietly, and it seemed to Naomi as they paddled with their hands below the surface that they had rubbed up together companionably in some unconscious way from the very first moment. One never knew why that was, but Samantha—she might as well call her Sam since her mother did—was cool and dry in a new way to her. She was the elder child of a wealthy father who, apart from his inherited money, was a retired journalist. Her fifteen-year-old brother was also back at the rented villa, playing chess with Mr. Haldane. Sam admitted she hadn't really wanted to come but, as always, her mother had insisted. They had found the perfect house through friends in New York.

"It's near Vlychos, but I guess you know it. There's a donkey in the garden. Which I think is cool."

"A donkey?"

"Well, it comes and goes."

"I think I know the one—it's Michael Gladstone's house."

"Then you do know it. He's had it for years. Dad says it's the best house he's ever seen. But I think he means it's the best house he's ever been an invalid in. You?"

"We're high up above the port. My parents bought it when they were young and Leonard Cohen was still living here."

"That was smart of them."

"They calculated it," Naomi replied. "That's the way my people are."

They swam past a jetty tilted sideways into the water and surrounded by flotsam: iron posts with elaborate moldings, bright green fishing nets and wire racks. It was as if whole villages had been smashed by violent winds that winter and their debris scattered over the coast. Where the path turned the first corner, there were piles of discarded machinery. They got out here, lay on a small protuberance of rubble, and looked back at the beach. The sullen rows of sunloungers looked like discarded toys or mechanical refuse identical to the debris accumulated behind them. It was curious, as if the place were about to be abandoned forever. The signposts knocked flat, the mineral orange stains in the surfaces of the rocks. Even the reconstructed fort above them—if that was what it was—had the look of something thrown to the winds. And yet above, the white abode of saints shone in sunlight.

Sam's mother had finally been approached by one of the boys and was talking up to him with unnecessary smiles. One never knew about mothers. Naomi's own was long dead and the woman asleep at this very moment in her father's arms far up the mountain was a different matter. But Amy had seemed normal at first, and now here she was flirting with the beach boys in aprons. Was it because her husband had a crippled foot for the summer?

She turned to Sam.

"You get on with your mother—I'm jealous. Mine is a stepmother. She's not bad, but she's not mine. Sometimes it's a drag having to deal with her."

After Sam had obliged with an "I'm sorry," Naomi told her the story in a few sentences. Her father was an art collector and a philanthropist. Since he knew many people and bought a lot of art, he was the center of many people's agitated attention. Her stepmother was Greek, from Kifissia in Athens, but the Kyriakou family had always been domiciled in South Kensington.

"She's younger than yours," Naomi went on, "and comes from an illustrious line of military fascists. I like your mother. She says what she thinks."

"That's a good thing?"

"It's not a bad thing. There are worse things. Do you say what you think?"

"Not always. Don't military fascists say what they mean?"

Naomi's smile was easy to provoke, but it never developed fully. She controlled it in the way that a child manipulates a kite.

Sam looked up at the sky's featureless zenith. In this place you could hear the tiniest noises from afar. The stirring of a cicada in a wall's crack a mile away, waves echoing from an unseen cove. But when the wind suddenly rose it obliterated everything else and there was just the melancholy hissing of the sage carpeting the hillsides and shivering as if moved by a fear of its own. The Haldanes would stay here till summer's end, and through all that time Sam would be counting down the minutes, and for that matter the sunsets. Maybe she would even find a boyfriend, a summer fling. Such things usually happened. Or else, if a friendship with Naomi didn't blossom, she would just be alone and read a hundred novels in her little white room beyond Kamini. If it turned out that way she wouldn't mind. Anything was better than a summer in the city, a visit to the grandparents in Montauk, the drifting from day to day that free time in libraries always induced. She rarely made new friends in the city, and she was already tired of the old ones. What she never found there, in any case, was a friend with any edge to her. The girls her own age were tiresomely uniform, as if a human-production plant in the center of the country had churned them out according to an approved paradigm. Suddenly, she had found someone different.

Eventually they got up and strolled back down to the cafe under the palapa, where a table had been laid out in the shade with a bottle of Santorini wine and a tomato salad with black olives. The mother had arranged it. The wind, again, made it slightly sinister. Sam, with some fuss, refused the bread that was offered to her. She said she was gluten-intolerant.

"*Eviva*," Amy said, and raised her glass. "I learned it yesterday down in the port. Cheers, right?"

"*Eviva*," Naomi said, and tapped her glass and then Sam's. "There's also another one you should know. *Na pethanei o charos*—may death die. Death to death!"

They ate some baklava with black coffee and then agreed to walk together back to the port. By now, in fact, the shadows around the cypresses had begun to shift, and when they set out they were content not to say a word until they turned a corner and saw the first houses of Hydra.

TWO

I WAS NEVER SURE ABOUT THIS VIEW," JIMMIE CODRING-
ton said to his wife as the maid came out onto the terrace
with their gin and tonics and a bowl of Kalamata olives in oil.
You never heard her until the very last moment, and then her
charm appeared suddenly, as if by accident, and you had to take
notice. "Don't you think it's gone downhill over the years? The
funny thing is, I can't say why. It just seems to have become
smaller and shabbier."

"Maybe we've grown bigger and more magnificent."

Jimmie liked the idea, but it wasn't true. The port was still
there, as in their shared past, the sea still sparkled all the way to
Thermisia, the captains' houses with their palms and toy cannons and painted wardrobes still belonged to socialites, and the
bells from the churches high up above the streets sent down
their music to disturb the squares where decrepit cats gathered
to witness every dusk.

"Or we've become smaller and shabbier as well. But it did
occur to me. Funny, it did occur to me. You may have a point
there."

Phaine spoke to the maid in Greek.

"Are you making something for tonight or should we eat
out?"

"As you wish, madame. I can make *psarosoupa*."

13

"Oh, not that again. We'll eat out, Carissa. You can leave after you've cleared up the drinks."

"Very well, madame."

Phaine turned back to her husband as the girl walked off, her black uniform cutting a sexual dash against the whiteness of the terrace.

"Shall we go down to the port and eat octopus? I want to."

"I got a call from Nobbins." It was his pet name for his daughter. "She says we should meet some Americans at the Sunset. She's made a new friend."

"Oh?"

"Some journalist and his family. I've never heard of him."

"How tedious. Shall we tell them we have heartburn?"

"No, I think we should go. I'm tired of upsetting Nobbins. I think we should try and be jolly, like a family, don't you? Besides, it's good that she's meeting people."

"Well, *meeting* people was never her problem, Jimmie."

"It's not always a question of problems. Even if she has a few, she's hardly alone. Everyone has problems."

"That's like saying everyone gets headaches."

An old conversation, many times repeated, and it could rile him easily with its obvious futility.

"Don't be so hard on her," he protested. "She's had some tough times. I don't suppose anyone takes their mother's death easily at that age. But enough of that. Let's go to dinner."

She acquiesced but felt intensely annoyed.

"All right. Can I get drunk?"

"Not at all, monster. Best behavior, if you don't mind. When they ask me your name I'm going to say Funny and see what they say. It'll be very telling."

"I really don't care. I'll be going to bed early anyway."

He snorted and reached for the olives. The former owner of Belle Air airlines had a way of knowing what his tempestuous wife would or would not do at the end of an evening. Sleep was the last thing on that extensive menu, and in that spirit they made a customary toast:

"Who's better than us, Funny?"

"No one!"

The maid hovered in the center of the vast terrace, listening for a cue, semi-invisible. It was she alone who was aware of the martins whistling as they swooped around the stone posts that marked its outer perimeter. They were almost alone out here in the mountains, the very last villa of the port at the top of its own vertiginous set of steps and walled off from the rest of the species with graceful emphasis by ancient padlocked doors and iron grilles. From there the sea felt closer and more real than the houses below them. The only other villa across from the gully was closed down, the Greek owners bankrupted by the financial crisis. Paid gardeners groomed the cypresses and olive trees in its garden, but otherwise it was a ghost house. On the island it was mostly the foreigners who had remained solvent, who stayed on for their summers and kept their doors freshly painted. Carissa was a native who had watched them evolve all her life. First the poets and writers renting fishermen's houses for ten dollars a month. Then the prosperous middle-agers from the cities, then the airline entrepreneurs with a taste for art. She regarded them all as barbarian intruders.

Codrington had even named his house Belle Air, which was rather lame as well as misspelled (Bel Air, however, would not have evoked his airline), and he had filled it with art made by people who had, over the years, become his friends. The maid had no idea why he valued them, these objects that littered every room. There was a ceramic bust of Hitler smoking a cigarette in the front room that always made them laugh. It was famously ironic. But what was the joke? Her father was a Communist who had always told her that the British were not to be trusted.

"Even so," Codrington was saying as he held his wife's hand, "the summer isn't so bad this year. I only wish Naomi would enjoy it more."

"Where does she go every morning? She gets up at dawn and disappears. I asked Carissa, but she said she didn't know."

She turned a second time to the maid and spoke again in Greek.

"Where does Naomi go in the morning? Do you make her coffee?"

"Yes, madame."

"She doesn't say?"

"No, madame."

Phaine returned to English.

"She's only here for the free rent anyway. What happened in London?"

Jimmie confessed that he was not entirely sure.

"She left Fletcher and Harris, and she's only said something about a disagreement. She doesn't tell me anything. Hasn't since she was fifteen."

It was the hour of the swallows. Codrington always fell into melancholy when he thought of his daughter. Perhaps it was because in her there remained some beautiful trace of his first wife. While Naomi was still alive, Helen was not yet dead. There was the lingering vestige of the mother in the daughter. But a broken home disrupts the continuities, in ways that he had not foreseen, that no one ever foresees. Naomi, he thought, being a teenager at the time of Helen's death from cancer, had never recovered. The broken teenager never mends. The law, in any case, had been a bad choice for her; it didn't suit her temperament. He suspected that being in litigation for a large firm had been playacting for her, a form of impersonation. But can you make your own children authentic against their will? It was never clear, after all, why the young adopted liberal or leftist positions that clearly had nothing to do with their own material conditions and in fact undermined and contradicted them entirely. At first you could put it down to youth itself. If you weren't a socialist at twenty you had no heart—and so on. But what if they now had a generation that sailed into their thirties without this deranged view of the world being challenged by anyone they could respect? Not because such people didn't exist—they were easy to find—but because they were effectively screened out of the person's consciousness by peer pressure and conformism. It was, he had decided, because they were a spoiled, soft generation who had never experienced anything in the real world. Indeed, they didn't really believe in a real world in the first place. Their consciousness had been created by the media, not by life.

The Codringtons made their way down the steep steps to the port. Dusk enthralled Jimmie. The houses had high walls, relics of a time when feuds and vendettas raged, and even at high noon the calcimine squares could be empty and guarded, as if they remembered the plague. The fuchsias and cicadas and blinding whitewash, the donkeys toiling up the stone steps with their bells, felt removed from the modern world by the simple application of nostalgic stubbornness.

The Codringtons moved slowly because of Jimmie's age—he was almost seventy and not as stable as he had once been—

and on the way down they met another exile, an old American struggling upward in the opposite direction.

"Look," Phaine whispered, "it's the Ancient Beatnik!"

"Evening, Jeremy," Codrington called out to him as they crossed a white square at the same time. The American raised a hand and there were no other words necessary. So it was after a few years. You simply raised a hand and that was enough. The semaphore of the tamed.

They came down into the port just as the last ferry back to the mainland was leaving. A few soldiers stood around the harbor with slung weapons, inactive and mute, staring at the Hellenic ship as it pulled out with its lights ablaze and the tourist music animating the decks. Up the little hill to the left of the harbor, Jimmie's walking stick tapping the cobbles, they came to the first bend where cliffs plunged down to the water, young people clinging to the slabs of rock below like prehistoric animals. There were terraces with tables of dark blue cloth, bronzed Slavic women with oiled hair laid out on sofas with their drinks. Above the restaurant's terrace stood one of the old island windmills, aloofly superior to the frustrated and harassed waiters in aprons. Sloping pines like giant bonsai would have shaded the terrace in sunlight. By the outer wall with its row of cannons, the Haldanes were already seated with Naomi within a glow of pleasurable energy and they had a startling arrangement of shellfish laid on ice between them. Jimmie's rapid eye spotted the young girl seated next to his daughter at once: the friend, the Huckleberry friend, he thought at once with a quick approval and a nod to himself.

The tables around them were filled with British and French families. Here and there were wealthy Athenians escaping from their national tragedy, and perhaps relieved to be back among their true peers. The couples who came every summer, the men with the yachts who docked for a month and then disappeared again. Sam caught Jimmie's eye and she wondered about him. He looked like a decaying nightclub singer. Naomi's stepmother was an appalling snob, you could tell at once. The kind of couple who would vet their daughter's prospective friends, even if it was just with a glance. But things soon settled down and flowed on, because it was the law of summers among the rich that the season of leisure should flow like a large and charming river. The imperative was to have a good time and float along on the luminescent surface. You couldn't back down or show weakness. It was not that different from the horror of the Hamptons, except this was less pretentious and slightly less soulless. She was beginning to like these people. At least they were curious about strangers; they asked her questions, they pestered her for insights into her baffling generation. Here being young had a value that wasn't just physical or sexual. Youth became the fount of other people's curiosity—what did she think, what did she want to do in the future, how did she feel about the old? It amused them. It amused them because it mattered.

Sam didn't exactly tell the truth in answer to such questions. As she ventured into a few glasses of wine under the watchful eye of her mother, less comfortable thoughts invaded her head. Even though she was still young, it had occurred to her that if she could relive any moment in the past she would refuse. But why was that so? A thousand summers could be like this, each one as beautiful as the last, and still nothing worth reliving a second time. It was an amazing idea.

Naomi and Sam connected silently through their eyes. The older girl reeled her in in this way, and Sam felt for a moment that she was the kite this time. Jimmie was being a raconteur, that most terrible of things. Naomi half turned to her and there was disdain in her frozen smile. Isn't it awful? the look said to her new friend. Isn't *he*? The two of them enjoyed a moment of contempt, but Sam was not as disdainful. She found the old man rather jolly and gimcrack.

So, she thought, Naomi's like me. She's tormented.

Naomi leaned over and said to her ear, "He goes on like this for hours. Who knows who'll be mown down. It's like a snowplow without gears. Should I say something? Your poor parents."

But Amy was not suffering at all. Fascinating, she was thinking to herself. A man with some force!

After dinner Naomi left her father and Phaine at Sunset and walked the Haldanes home to Vlychos. Just before Kamini the path rose to a series of platforms and steps and a restaurant called Kodylenia's where the terrace was still open and a few old men sat with their shot glasses of ouzo in an aura of timeless patience. Oil lamps hung from the trellis rocked back and forth to the sound of old Tsitsanis songs piped through speakers. During the day, Naomi recalled, it was usually Mahler and sundry hits of Rossini. The Greeks didn't look up. A well-heeled French family did. They came down into Kamini, boats hauled up on the sand. On the far side of the beach stood a ruined cafe, blood red, with shattered windows and an old sign that read *Mouragio Cafe-Bar* in Greek. A half-moon had risen above the dry mountain, and by its light the forms of horses gradually became visible in the fields. They stood perfectly still, attuned to the smell of humans.

The house lay above the path to the left—somewhat before Vlychos—and the fields below it tilted away toward treacherous cliffs and the sea. But even there, on perilous pastures, horses stood quietly attacking the wet grass. It was the usual white house with Aegean-blue frames and pillars, and there were lemon trees outside it. The bloated and neglected fruit lay all over the grass.

"Do you want to come up for some tea?" Amy asked as they came to the villa's wall and the iron gate swung open.

They went up to their own terrace and they saw Jeffrey standing there with his pipe and a box of matches. There was a look of surprise that didn't quite seem to be directed only at them. Perhaps, Naomi thought, that was his default expression all the time. Surprise at life itself, or else an endearing incompetence. He was lighting oil lamps but he also turned on the more efficient orange glass electric lamps as well. There were two rocking chairs and two rattan sofas, and between them a glass table covered with desiccated ornamental sponges. The island had once been the center of the Greek sponge trade. They sprawled into the cushions and it occurred to Naomi that the evening was ending much better than it had begun. The Haldanes were more relaxed when in their own company and away from the intimidating headlights of her father and his overbearing confidence, which had crushed them in subtle and intangible ways of which they were only partially conscious.

Sam sat curled up by the edge of the porch with the wind whipping her hair. Her eyes were slow and absorbent while her father talked.

"Is it true," he said, blowing smoke, "that your father offered a ride on his yacht? I won't go, but Sam and Chris would *love* it."

"Yes," Naomi said, "he offered. We can sail right around the island. We do it a lot. Good swimming."

"I'd love to," Sam said, but without any drama.

"Will you go, Amy?"

"Sure. I want to see the wild side of the island."

"You can't walk to the wild side, can you?"

Naomi shook her head. "Not really."

"I'm not really into the wild sides of islands," Jeffrey said. "Though I like to walk on the wild side from time to time. I'm happy to stay here and wallow with my crippled leg, but everyone else—"

"Then I'll arrange everything," Naomi said.

"Can we go spearfishing?" Sam asked.

"I don't see why not."

But Sam didn't want to go spearfishing, she just wanted to know if it was possible in that unknown sea.

"You'll only see dolphins," her mother put in majestically. "And you can't spear those."

"Why don't you stay the night, Naomi?" Amy finally suggested. "We have two extra rooms, all made up. It's a long walk to your house. Just call your dad and let him know."

"That's a fine idea," Sam said quietly. "Will you?"

Naomi weighed it up for a moment, then let herself slide.

"All right, I will."

Sam took her up to one of the spare rooms. It was on the east side looking over the sloping fields, with the dark blue Greek shutters pinned back against the walls and dried herbs in glasses set on the tables. The owner's books were here: Seferiades and Kazantzakis, in aging English editions. Thistles lay scattered over the ship-timber floors. The bed was iron, creaky and high as in the old days when people died in them with gravitas and in confident expectation of an afterlife. There was a white table with a washbasin and jug, some lemons in the first days of decay. It was a room where Sam sometimes read alone.

They sat on the bed for a while, with their knees curled up beneath them, and gossiped about the evening. Naomi wanted to know about Sam's petulant brother, Christopher, who was in his room. He was entering the moody phase of adolescence and often retreated into his computers and online games. Naomi had always wondered about having a brother. It must be exhilarating occasionally, just because of the competitive hostility.

"He's too gentle for that," Sam said. "Mostly, he's just annoying."

Naomi let her head sink onto her arm. Her eyes were slow and sarcastic, and they never released the object of their attention a moment too soon.

"Am I annoying?"

"I didn't say you were."

"I'm an only child. Only children are always a bit . . . We're spinning tops. You know that."

"Really?"

"Your brother saved you."

"From being a spinning top?"

"We need someone to keep us spinning."

Sam drew her knees up and they began to feel more sisterly. She asked questions about Phaine. Was she really called Funny?

"Of course not. It's a joke."

"So Phaine's a Greek name?"

"Obviously."

"I think your dad is hilarious," Sam said.

"The people on the island like to call him a character. I've always thought that was an insult myself."

Sam rolled onto her back and her limbs were relaxed and loose like those of a child gorged on chocolate cake.

"I liked that he wore a tie. My dad would never wear a tie."

"But I like your father," Naomi said. "Shall we swap? I don't mind if he doesn't wear ties. I think we should get up early and walk to the end of the island. All the way to the end."

It was said more as a piece of firm advice, even as a directive, rather than as a casual suggestion, and Sam was jolted a little by it. However, she said nothing. She couldn't deny that she was attracted to someone suddenly taking control of a subsequent day because such a thing had not happened to her before. Usually people quietly did what *she* wanted rather than the reverse, and now she wondered if she should go along with it or make a petty show of independence. Yet she realized immediately that it was the independence that bored her. Naomi offered something else—a sense of knowing what she wanted long before anyone else did.

"Sooner or later," Naomi now said quietly, "you'll understand that I know everything that you can do on this island and which are the most pleasurable things. I've done them over and over, so I know. If you let me guide you, you'll save yourself a lot of time."

"That's very arrogant, but I don't mind having a guide."

"Guides are worth their weight in gold. But only if you want them."

She looked at Sam archly and the smile was like a rope tugging at a horse's bit.

"Sure I want," Sam said.

"So we're agreed."

After the two had wished each other goodnight and Sam found herself alone, she couldn't sleep for a long while. She lay on the bed with the windows wide open, the rusted hinges creaking as the wind antagonized them. She rolled herself a cigarette and calmly enjoyed it by the window so the scent wouldn't reveal itself to the others. A lot had happened, quite suddenly, but she couldn't say quite what it was. The Codrington family were an event in themselves, but she could already tell that they would never invite her up to tea at their lofty villa. They didn't do things like that. They were planets closer to the sun than her own; their orbits were different. It was Naomi who would come down into the port and amuse her, who would give a meaning to her endless summer. There was something alarming about her, but it was just possible that Naomi herself had been suddenly altered—just a little—by contact with Sam. There is the spinning top and there is the girl who whips it into motion, but the two are merged in the same motion.

THREE

THEY GOT UP EARLY AND, FORGOING THE PANCAKES that Amy habitually offered, walked down to Vlychos to have breakfast at the Four Seasons resort. It was a small place on the beach a mile beyond the village on a solitary path that eventually led to Palamidas. Even by six-thirty butterflies danced around the crooked fence poles, bumbling across slopes of gleaming Hottentot figs and disappearing into thin air when they felt like it. Like primitive armor, prickly pears grew along the low walls and their paddles were finely robed with tiny cobwebs. It was hushed even near the houses. They could smell fresh hay and coffee, and from the coves came the ghostly repetitions of little waves.

They had loose beach bags slung over their shoulders with bathing suits, towels, and sunscreen. Coming through luxuriant century plants to a place called Castello, they climbed above the beach there to a higher elevation where decayed wooden gates with padlocks announced the phantoms of abandoned houses. Where the shallow water suddenly deepened there were irregular shapes of black opal, like the forms of stationary sharks, and farther out dark green masses that suggested a brooding energy that would always remain withheld from the upper air. An episode of malaria, she thought, but didn't know why. A malarial dream made of sponges and submerged rocks. Close to shore a bare islet appeared with a white chapel built upon it, and against it they saw a fragile yacht tacking toward the two humps of Dokos. But the ripples spreading over the sea's surface from the wind were faster than its wake. At Vlychos, they gazed down on a cheerless beach with rows of straw parasols amid a cluster of power lines—the path went right above it—and they could see large Greek men already positioning themselves to catch the first solar rays shooting over the sea. The whole affair was crammed into a cove. They wandered down to an old stone bridge and crossed it. Underneath them a man rode his donkey train, never looking up at the two girls; the fabulous mustache of a past century, the high boots, the hands of a strangler. He spat a *Yassas* to people they couldn't see.

At the Four Seasons, with its shaded terrace covered by low-hanging trees, the Russians for which the place was famous had not yet appeared and the house that formed the main building of the hotel seemed closed up and indifferently idle. Yet the doors were open, and there was a glimpse of a cultured interior consisting of random antiques and a whiff of classical music. The straw parasols were trim and ready, unlike those of Mandraki, and the sand was raked. They sat at a beach table under the shade and ordered black coffee, a bitter *sketos* for Naomi and a sweeter *metrios* for Sam. The sweat began to dry on them, but it was impossible for Sam to imagine what it would be like to take this walk under a noon sun. It would be the kind of torment that only the affluent unemployed would inflict upon themselves.

They drank three cups each and ordered some toast with marmalade for Naomi and bowls of Greek yogurt with nuts. Sam said, without lying, that it was the best marmalade she had ever tasted. Naomi said they could smoke a little too, no one would notice. A little kif in the morning did the trick. She rolled a joint and they smoked it in turns. So she has weed, Sam thought calmly. She knows how to get it even here. She's an operator.

As if reading her mind, Naomi explained.

"I get it from a local girl who rows around the island with a stash. She'll come by later where we're going."

"Are you serious?"

"It's an insider secret here. She has stuff she gets from Turkey. She doesn't sell to tourists unless they're recommended. Don't tell Christopher either."

They got a buzz, but not enough to make them giddy. Then they walked on up the hill an hour later, braving the heat. The path curved against steep hillsides with the sea churning at the foot of cliffs. The road to Palamidas. A power line on poles swept all along it, the poles slightly deranged and angled.

Before they got near Palamidas, they scrambled down a ravine filled with irises. It was a narrow area of stones, where they laid out the towels, stripped, and changed into their bikinis. They lay down and waited. It was like waiting for inspiration. They began to talk, because the silence was conducive to it. Naomi asked Sam about her inability to eat bread. Had she been off it a long time? A few years, Sam said. She'd found that she was intolerant about the time she had started her periods. Luckily, it was a well-known intolerance in her generation; everyone had understood, even her mother. Surprisingly, Hydra was well stocked with gluten-free products. It was the Anglos, Naomi said tartly. They brought them in with them, and now the Greeks too found that they were gluten-intolerant, whereas they had ignored it for three thousand years, which showed you how stubborn they were.

Sam sensed the sarcasm, but she decided to go along with it by changing the subject. She asked if Naomi was seeing anyone, either here on the island or back home.

"You mean a boyfriend?"

"Whatever you want to call it."

"I'm in a bit of an interregnum right now," Naomi admitted.

"A what?"

"A pause between boyfriends. Probably between two uninteresting boyfriends."

Sam felt emboldened to say: "Is the pause better than the guys?"

"In some ways it is. It depends on the guys. I've been alone for a while and I like it. I really can't say why."

"I know what you mean. I haven't had that many boyfriends myself, but sometimes I think thinking about it is better than having it. It's better than *doing* it, no?"

"I wouldn't say that."

"I mean almost."

"I still wouldn't say that."

Naomi smiled up at the sky and her skin, to Sam, was an English mask perfectly modeled to resemble a human face and the smile didn't break its polished surface. And yet she could feel the tensions moving back and forth beneath it, ideas and moods roaming as if from empty room to empty room. It could have been easily mistaken for boredom, but it was more electrifying than boredom. It was like a child looking for a centipede to kill.

"What about Miss Sam?"

"There's a boy I like—he's in Mexico this summer. I didn't want to bring him here anyway. My father doesn't like him."

"He didn't want to come along?"

"He didn't want to be with my family. It's understandable, given the way my family carries on. We're a bit . . . boring."

"That's not very loyal of him."

"Well, I'm not very loyal either. I haven't been thinking about him. I'm not the loyal type."

"I know that feeling."

"I was hoping there'd be some here. Boys, I mean. They say Greece is the place for that. Is it?"

"Sure it is."

An hour later, they heard the slap of oars on water and a small rowing boat swung into view, a young woman of about Naomi's age propelling it forward. They rose up onto their elbows and the visitor looked at them with a surly unsurprise from under a wide-brimmed straw hat, which she took off as the boat floated in toward them.

She was dressed in a swimsuit and a loose pale orange linen shirt, and her hair was knotted all the way down to the waist. She came up to the strand and raised the oars and shot a familiar *Yassou* at Naomi. When the boat was a few feet from the rocks she stood up and lifted a saddlebag, opened it, and took out a small packet. Naomi in turn had taken out a roll of euros and threw it into the boat. Back came the packet. The girl sat down again and the oars rose, dripping, while she scrutinized the American girl. There was no amicality in the eyes, no common cause. "Who is she?" she asked Naomi.

"Don't worry about her," Naomi replied in Greek, "she's a friend."

When the skiff moved off, the girl put her straw hat back on and began singing to herself as she rowed out of view. Naomi waited until she had disappeared before assembling a joint. They smoked it together, still lying on their backs, and then, refreshed, they climbed up toward Palamidas, the dust swirling around them until they reached a point where they could go no farther. The church at Episkipos was too much of a climb, and so they turned back.

AT THE GATES to the Haldane villa Naomi said that she would head home. Her father and Phaine were expecting her for dinner and that night, for once, she would have to be punctual or risk their ire.

"Jimmie just sent me a message—we have to be at the port at seven tomorrow morning for the yacht. Can you do it?"

"We'll be there. What should we bring?"

"Nothing at all. It's butler service."

"Butlers?"

"Well, they're not dressed like butlers."

Sam seemed to hesitate about something. Her words were drawled and almost purring.

"All right. Are you sure I can keep the weed?"

"I bought it for you," Naomi said brightly.

"Cool. I won't bring it tomorrow, though."

Naomi took her hand for a moment and swung it like a jump rope.

"Don't be late, Miss Sam. I hate late girls."

"I'll be on time."

Naomi walked down to the port. She was dreading dinner, but it had to be endured. The swallows massed in the sky, an air of mad poetry and derangement. She had a quick drink at the Pirate Cove to steady her nerves, then climbed up the steps sunk in plumbago to the villa. When she got to Belle Air it was Carissa who opened the door for her, and the expression on her face was somber. The maid was tarted up, the cosmetic polishing almost professional.

"Madame is in a bad mood."

They stood together for a moment in the secluded cool of the vestibule among the old Turkish swords, and Carissa filled her in on the day's observations. They spoke in Greek, and the humor flowed easily between them in that language. They knew each other well. More than that, a calm telepathy existed between them. They had known each other for years, since Naomi was an early teenager and Carissa not much older. That night madame had said that her stepdaughter was a parasite.

"Well, I knew she thought that," Naomi said grimly. "What else?"

"Your father defended you. They had a row."

"That bitch. At least *you* are priceless, Carissa."

"She also said you should go back to London and get a job."

"She did?"

"She did."

But why should it be me who goes back to London? Naomi thought.

"Never mind," she said. "I'll prepare myself for dinner."

She went up to her room. She shut the door and showered for half an hour. It was her childhood room, older by far than Phaine's tenure in her father's heart, and it gave her a reassuring sense of entitlement at the core of the house. Her bed, her old books and childhood things moldering away in the salty air. In every other room the intruder had carefully expunged all traces of her dead mother and replaced their former warmth and coziness with her own chilly taste.

Naomi sat in front of her dressing-table mirror and put on a little makeup. Her father always appreciated the effort at a family dinner; his eyes shone for a second and the compliment was made without words. She put on a simple dress and pulled her hair back and then went quietly down to the terrace, where Carissa had set the table with a touch of magnificence: asphodels in a vase, the family silver from Nottingham. Jimmie and Phaine were already there, with Frank Sinatra from the salon turned up loud and "Fly Me to the Moon" belting out to subdue the cicadas. Jimmie was smoking a stupendous Havana and reading the *Wall Street Journal*; Phaine was drinking a vodka tonic. When she saw Naomi she stiffened and casually shouted out: "So there you are!"

Jimmie looked up over his half-moons and smiled at the sight of his only child looking subtly elegant and, in some inexpressible way, contrite. He put down the paper and playfully hit the side of his wineglass with his spoon, making it ring like the announcement of a toast.

"Let's have Carissa bring out the pâté," Phaine said. "She made some black olive pâté—it's an old recipe, you know."

But in fact the maid was already bringing it out. Jimmie poured the Bandol for his daughter and for a few minutes he was curious about the Haldanes. The old guy was a bit of a stiff, wasn't he? The wife wasn't bad, though. Bit of a looker and light on her feet, eh? The boy had shifty eyes, though.

"What about the daughter?" Naomi said.

"Oh yes. I forgot about her. You've gotten to know her a bit, haven't you? Is she sweet?"

"Of course she's sweet."

"Did you hear that, Funny? She's sweet. But I can't remember her."

"Jimmie, let's face it: you only remember what you want to remember."

Since this was undeniable, he held his tongue for a few seconds and tried to come back with a better line.

"All the same," he resumed, "it's not like me to forget someone sweet. There must have been something ordinary about her. Or something very unsweet. Or maybe I didn't like her."

It was the usual dinner *à trois* at the Codrington manor, with constant small talk about neighbors and commercial developments in the ports (invariably unwelcome) and dishes cooked by Carissa in the vast kitchen brought out on an assortment of antique plates. That night she presented lavish servings of fish oven-baked with lemon and olives, and oily roasted potatoes sprinkled with sea salt and blades of thyme as long as eyelashes.

"We're happy to take your new friends around the island tomorrow," Phaine said. "But first Jimmie and I thought we should have a talk with you about your situation. Your work situation, I mean. It seems to me, anyway, that you haven't been entirely forthcoming about what is going on with you or why you had to leave the firm. You know perfectly well that your father put a lot of effort into helping you get that job—and now it has evaporated from one day to the next without any explanation from you."

She began stabbing at the potatoes with her fork, and this formed an interlude that served as an invitation to Naomi to refute her.

"That's unfair," the girl said weakly. "I—"

"You just show up here saying you've lost your job and expect us to accept it. It's a little baffling. Apart from anything else, we could help you if you come clean and told us exactly what happened. We're not saying that it was your fault—we don't know either way. We can't know anything unless you tell us and stop being so evasive about it."

"I lost my job. I think that's all you need to be aware of."

"It's not the end of the world to have lost your job, it happens all the time. But one thing you can't do is just pretend that nothing happened and then expect us not to ask any questions. We have a perfect right to ask questions."

"I didn't say you didn't."

"Darling," Jimmie said to his daughter, "I'd rather like to know *why* you were fired, if you were fired. Were you fired?"

Naomi put down her fork, and her whole body tensed.

"It's a private matter," she stammered. "I would have thought it was obvious why—" ·

"But if you want me to help you—"

"I don't. I just need a place to think it over."

"You have that and you will always have that. But we need to know what happened so we can help you. Don't you think? Phaine says that honesty is the best principle, and I'm bound to say I agree with her."

"You can tell us," Phaine said emphatically, putting down her fork as well. "We can't be in the dark about things like this."

"I know you were having trouble with your boss—"

"It wasn't that, it wasn't. It's more complicated."

Naomi felt herself crumpling; she wanted to put her hands over her ears and drown out both them and the Sinatra with a long scream.

"Was it the Weaver case?" Jimmie persisted. "You told me about that and I googled it."

"What if it was? The only thing that matters is that they fired me. So yes, they fired me."

"I see." Phaine sighed triumphantly.

"Did they really?"

"Yes, Dad."

"What a despicable thing to do. What was the reason, then?"

"I'm not sure I even know."

"Then it was despicable for them to fire you."

"Is there something you're not telling your father?" Phaine insisted.

"You mean the reason?" Jimmie burst out.

"Do you want me to say it, Naomi?" Phaine said.

"I can say it. Though there's not much to say. They claimed I manipulated evidence to get a defendant off."

She gave up and laid out the details of the crisis that had cost her her job. She had volunteered to defend a Turkish restaurant owner in Dalston who had beaten two men with the butt of a shotgun during an attempted robbery. The case against the restaurant owner had obviously been brought by the two men and the attacks—or self-defense—had been witnessed by two other people who had been in the street at the time. It was politically sensitive, her partners had told her, and they had been inclined to refuse the case. She had made an argument for defending the man and used the two witnesses to great effect. The Turk was acquitted, but one of the men he had beaten suffered permanent brain damage. A scandal had erupted. Attention turned to the two witnesses. A journalist had discovered that they were friends of the defendant and had then gone on to allege that she had known this beforehand. To her father she insisted that she hadn't, but in reality she had known. The partners were given irrefutable proof of this. In the end, it had been an instinctual call on her part: she wanted to defend a Muslim against his tormentors. There was nothing ignoble in that. Just because the three men were friends didn't make the testimony of the two who had been in the street false. It was, she said, a setup and a matter of scapegoating.

"Well," Jimmie said, keeping his voice flat and trying to control his indignation, "misunderstandings and mistakes at law firms happen all the time, if we're to be honest. You made a mistake in good faith. It's a matter for the public prosecutors, or whatever they're called. I simply can't understand why your own firm would turn on you like that, or take such accusations seriously. Were they afraid of another investigation?"

"They decided I'd broken their rules—"

"Had you?"

She was evasive: "In their interpretation."

"But that's extraordinary. We can't have that!"

He threw down his napkin dramatically and stared at his wife as if she would take up the challenge of his exclamation. But she sat back, bit her lower lip, and shook her head.

"Calm down, Jimmie. Have a drink and calm down. I'm glad you told us the truth finally, Naomi. I knew it was more serious than you were letting on."

But from then on Naomi said nothing, reaching for her wineglass. Her father eventually relaxed a little and wiped the unctuous sweat from his forehead—the evening was warm. Then he went back to his fish and potatoes and they let the subject go for a while.

Jimmie was thinking. What was she planning to do with herself now that she had nothing to go back to? He hadn't realized that it was this bad. How could she have got herself in such a stupid position? She had a knack for doing that, he had to admit to himself. It was, he feared, more than a slipup or a personality clash. She had done something she didn't want to fully own up to. It was the damnedest thing, the way she kept secrets about herself. He was sure this talent for secrecy had found its way into her way of handling controversial cases. This time she hadn't got away with it and she had paid the price. It was a bad deal for the Codrington name.

When they were finished, Carissa came in again with three coconut puddings she had made from an Asian cookbook that Phaine had given her. The lamps shook in gusts of wind, they could hear awnings and lines around other houses rattle and snap, and somewhere on the trail to the top of the mountain a flashlight suddenly shot a beam of light into the emptiness.

"Did you see that?" Jimmie said to his wife. "Are they hunting foxes up there?"

He reached for his cigar box again. He called over the maid and asked her to put some Theodorakis on the music system. There was a song called "The One Unforgivable Sin" that he wanted to hear before bed. It would put him in a better mood. Then, like the sudden remembrance of a dentist's appointment, he recalled that the following morning they had to go on a cruise with the Americans. He cursed silently. But then he had an inspiration.

"Nobbins, is it entirely necessary that Phaine and I go around the island with you tomorrow? You can take the boat and the staff—show your friends a good time. We don't have to be there. You've done it a hundred times, so I'm not worried. Just don't end up in Turkey."

Naomi suppressed a wild expression of relief and merely nodded. But she and Phaine exchanged bitter glances.

"Are you sure?" the latter said to her husband.

Naomi accepted a shot of ouzo as a nightcap. The stars had been out for some time, but she had not yet noticed them. Their cold glamour provided a link to forgotten centuries. Her eye, instead, was drawn up to the silhouette of the mountain from where the flashlight had come. For a moment something moved against the darkness of the slopes, a figure scrambling up toward the little church at the summit like a giant cockroach. She downed the ouzo and forced back the tears that threatened the surfaces of her eyes, and held herself steady until it was time for a second shot. There was a brief protest from her stepmother, but father and daughter took the second one and there was a moment of healing between them. Over the years she had discovered from experience that the best moments between them were when they drank ouzo together. That double-edged and flavorless drink was their dark truce, their mutual anonymity.

FOUR

A T THE PORT THE HALDANE SISTER AND BROTHER AR-
rived with only their father and met Naomi at the Pirate
Cove for a coffee before they embarked. Amy had preferred to
stay at home and do some painting and cooking, and even Jeffrey looked as if he had been prevailed upon to come by his
children. He put a brave face on it, however, and drank cup
after cup of *sketos.*

The three-member crew of the *Black Orchid* were also there
and they all sat together. The three Greeks were suddenly interested in the explosive beauty of the American girl, and Jeffrey
bristled with protective annoyance as the caffeine went to his
head. Naomi was observant. The Haldane males were wearing
similar khaki shorts and black-top sneakers, the same University
of Pittsburgh sweatshirts and the same baseball caps. A family whose men had a uniform. It was fantastical—she had seen
such things in movies—and it made them, in some way, easier
to deal with. The boy was in a good mood but said nothing. He
obviously didn't need to. He was doing exactly what he wanted
to do on that day.

"It's a real yacht," he eventually did say to Naomi, his face
bright with appreciation. "Do you guys fish on it? You could
catch bluefins."

Naomi caught Sam's eye at last and there was silent laughter between them. As they walked to the boat along the gang-planks, they exchanged a private *Yassou*, and to Naomi Sam looked exceptionally vibrant, more so even than the previous day. Perhaps it was the dowdy uniform that played to her strengths. There was also a blush from the sun.

They boarded the yacht and the boy rushed around inspecting everything with many a guttural "Wow!"

"There's a bedroom down there," he called up to his father. "There's a sign over the bed that says *Disgrace*."

"That's an artwork," Naomi explained.

She and Sam went out onto the back deck and sat in the chairs there. The sun hit them and the crew set up the awning. The table had been arranged with an ice bucket, a cooler, glasses, and china plates. Sam looked up at the burned brown hills and something in her bristled. It was like the Middle East, a corner of Lebanon or Syria centuries ago. Slaves moving among the saddled donkeys in the caves high up among the glaring rocks. It had its enigma. It wasn't quite what she had expected. As they moved off into open sea the mountain named for Eros rose above the toytown of cafes and discos and scuba shops. She saw people walking along the path above Sunset and the early-morning swimmers on the flat rocks below it. The collective pantomime of a holiday. Then the crew turned up the engines and they moved swiftly along the coast, passing Vlychos and the Haldanes' house. And then Amy was there waiting for them with an energetic wave, like a gaunt lone figure in an Andrew Wyeth painting; the yacht sounded its horn. They went past Molos and the remoter headlands, Cape Bisti and Tsigri Island and the Aghios Konstandinos. Then they turned in to follow the edge of the island as it led to Cape Aghios Ioannis. On this far side there were no houses or roads; the beaches were hemmed in by dramatic cliffs and rock formations. The sea looked darker and more volatile. When they anchored for a first stop the waves came hard against one side of the boat, shaking it gently. Under the awning the group was served with fruit juice and coffee, croissants and *tulumba*. Some music was put on—calypso, Naomi explained, and some Louis Armstrong from the soundtrack of *High Society*. Her father loved it. She took Sam down to the bedroom and they changed into their bathing suits. Sam saw that there was indeed a tubular neon light above the bed that spelled out the word *Disgrace*.

"It's sick, isn't it?" Naomi whispered. "It cost him twenty thousand dollars."

Sam looked around the disorderly melange of art, the bedside lamps made of solid glass and the Keith Haring panels inset into the walls. It could have been so cool, she thought, but somehow it wasn't.

They went back up to the deck and found the crew lowering the steps into the water. Jeffrey and the boy peered over at long thin gar speeding through the blue like animate needles. The shore was about a hundred meters away, a comfortable swim. From the boat the sandy bottom was now visible, a shimmer of dark gold. Sam and Naomi put on rubber flippers and masks but decided to do without the snorkels. They slipped down into the water and quietly swam away from the calypso, the brilliant silverware, and the anxious fatherly gaze. Jeffrey was thinking that, after all, he was not so sure about this self-assured British girl. She had prized his daughter away from them a little, and he and his wife were both aware of it. But it seemed to him that it was not deliberate. Naomi was one of those people who exert an entirely unconscious influence on others and who cannot be held responsible for the effects. It was tropism, not conspiracy.

This, of course, made her more dangerous. His earnest and upright mind was, moreover, ruffled by her ease of movement and her offhand manners—they seemed to him proof of a superiority that he would have to belittle in order to survive.

THEY WERE AT the shore in minutes, hauling themselves back into the air and lying flat on boulders facing the yacht. They could still hear Louis Armstrong and the calypso rhythms, and the crew had broken out a bottle of champagne, probably as much for themselves as for their unknown and unimportant guests. The foam shone for a second as it spewed into the water. *"Eviva!"* Naomi shook out her wet hair and leaned back. Once again, that aristocratic ease of movement and gesture, and Sam did the same, stretching out her toes with their crimson warlike paint. She had painted them the night before. There was a rustle of lizards darting under rocks and she turned, but they were faster than her eye.

After a few minutes they got up and climbed a steep hillside. They had soon reached a platform from where they could look down at the boat and the father and son hunched together playing chess under the awning. Sam thought how restful it was to be separated from them finally, away from the bickering and the family trivia. One of the crew was swimming around the boat, his voice carrying up to them with great clarity. *"To nero einai gamo kryo!"* one of the others called back to him. Their tongues had loosened in the absence of any Greek speakers.

The hillside behind them cast a shadow far out into the water that just clipped the aft of the boat and dimmed the little Greek flag hanging there. Another disheveled slope led down to a cove congested with rocks and rubble, a place that must have been well out of sight of the boat. There was something tempting about it, with the absence of a track and the cactus proliferating across it. They got up. As they slipped out of view of the boat Jeffrey looked up and felt a moment of unease, but the crew didn't notice. A small shadow had suddenly passed across his world. But the crew knew that Naomi was familiar with the island. In reality, the girls were exultant. The opalescent purity of the sky, the absence of cloud and contamination, made them feel secure. They skipped off down the shelving stones toward the second cove and the heat rose up toward their faces.

Sam felt freer as soon as she was out of her father's sight. She remembered the warning her mother had uttered to her earlier in the day about the sun. To hell with her, though. To hell with the family brand. Her skin liked the sun's ferocity.

"What does *skatofatsa* mean?" she asked as she trailed her guide.

Naomi turned and said, "Shitface."

"Is it a useful word?"

"I use it pretty much every day."

"*Skata-fatso*. Fantastic."

"*Fatsa*. You can use it in America."

At the far side of the cove they sat again and caught their breath. The boat had disappeared behind the land's shape, but they could still hear the music from *High Society*. When the wind swept across the hillside, however, it vanished and all they could hear was dust and grit flying.

"Should we keep going?" Sam asked. "Maybe they'll follow us and pick us up farther on."

"I didn't bring my phone. We'd have to wave to them from somewhere."

"Then let's wave."

They turned and climbed up the next slopes until they could see the boat again. They waved, but no one saw them. Forgotten already, Sam thought with amusement and with a certain amount of satisfaction. They shouted and the abrupt echoes came back to them. They wondered what to do next; beyond their vantage point lay ravines and coves, desert scrub shining under dark blue light. It was so still and undisturbed that it provoked in them a childish desire to ruffle it up and make it less pure. Without even talking about it they walked on, plunging down toward the sea a second time, singing as they went, threading their way carefully through prickly pears to the words of "Paperback Writer."

What beautiful animals we are, Sam thought, beautiful as panthers. When they reached the white rocks along the water she saw two red spots as she stepped past them. Blood, she thought at once. She stopped and kneeled to look closer, and there was a sudden bafflement in her face. She had been right. They were two dried spots of blood, like small things that have been casually mislaid. She felt a quick thrill whose root was hidden to her.

"It can't be," Naomi said.

"They have animals here?" Sam wondered aloud.

"No one hunts in these parts."

Something in Sam stiffened and her instincts kicked in. She touched one of the spots. "Just two spots? No, it's a drip. From a height."

"I guess so," Naomi said.

"It must be from a person. Hikers, maybe?"

People did come here on private boats, like themselves. But Naomi was skeptical.

"We didn't see any boats leaving before us."

"Then they must've walked over the mountain."

"No."

They rose and looked around but saw nothing. A mood of doubt went through them, but they said nothing to each other. They merely kept walking, scaling the next rise until they were peering down at slopes thick with glistening thistles. There was a curve of rock and sheltered water beneath it, waves foaming a few feet out on the hidden stone. At first, nothing to see. But here, in the full sunlight, a figure lay stretched out in the thyme bushes, a man asleep on his side in a pile of rags with a plastic bottle on the ground beside him.

The man was half naked, in tracksuit pants, with thong sandals. A tattered sweater was laid out on the cactus a few feet away as if drying. He looked young to them, long-haired, the beard grown out and ungroomed. An exhausted hobo of the sea. Naomi could tell that he was not Greek. It was something about the clothes, the totality of his exhaustion. But Sam was thinking differently. She looked farther down the coast and saw nothing. Not even the flimsiest dinghy or a discarded paddle. She was an avid news reader, being the daughter of a journalist, and something had already occurred to her, and though she might have come to the same conclusion as Naomi she was less moralistic about it. They couldn't now pretend that they hadn't seen him, and they couldn't walk back to the yacht without making sense of it. She was curious for a moment, but she then wondered about the extreme concentration that seemed to have come into Naomi's face.

Gradually, the English girl lost her alarm; it was Sam who held herself tense and wanted to go back immediately. But Naomi calmed her with hand gestures. There was nothing threatening about the sleeper. He was abject and abandoned, self-abandoned even. The two drops of blood were his. A cut hand, a cut foot: his misery had expressed itself. There was a way of telling that he had come from the sea, not from the port, and that he was not sleeping through a surfeit of leisure. Suddenly there was motion in the skies and they looked up. Two huge birds were circling overhead, turning slowly and looking down at the three humans as if there was something in their arrangement that needed to be deciphered. Slowly, they dropped closer. The man turned equally slowly onto his back and his mouth fell open. His naked torso was covered with long weals and scratches, and the skin had begun to darken. They moved back to the ledge from where they had started out, one step at a time, not a pebble displaced.

"He's not dying," Naomi said. "He's just sleeping. He's washed up from the sea."

Sam wondered aloud if they should go back anyway and talk to him. It seemed cowardly to just return without doing anything, without making contact.

"Make contact?" Naomi smiled.

"I didn't mean it weirdly. I meant—just go down and see who he is. He was bleeding."

"Not today. Another time."

Naomi signaled and they set off back the way they had come, but more hurriedly.

When they were close to their original landing, Naomi said, "We definitely shouldn't say anything to your father. Nothing at all. Right?"

"Nothing."

"I'm sure he'll overreact. He'll probably go to the police straightaway. He'll think it's the right thing to do."

She had reached out and gently locked a hand around Sam's

wrists so that the younger girl was forced to look up into her metal-steady blue eyes. There was a quivering little threat inside the pupils.

"He's an Arab, isn't he?" Sam blurted out.

There was a long silence as they worked their way back into view of the yacht, which had not after all dislodged itself in order to find them, and when they scaled the first hill on their itinerary they waved, as before, and the crew, who might have been growing a little anxious at their long absence, made signals in response as if it were they who had gone missing for a while.

WHEN THEY GOT back to the port, Naomi and Sam slipped away by themselves and went to a taverna inside the labyrinth of alleys. It was dusk. The first moment of cool in many hours and they gulped down a carafe of Moschofilero at a table on the street. Around the amphitheater of the port rose the terraced captains' houses of centuries past while, increasingly audible, starlings babbled in the trees of the squares. Birds on the wire, Naomi always thought, in honor of the Cohen song. Sam's hands were shaking; she seemed about to launch into an outburst. But about what? I haven't asked her to do anything outrageous, Naomi thought. I haven't made her do something illicit. She hasn't been forced.

But Sam was not thinking that. She was, on the contrary, filled with an elated trepidation that was shy and quiet. She had the feeling that Naomi was thinking so fast that she wouldn't be able to catch up with her, that she had an idea what to do, but entirely for her own reasons.

"Don't worry," Naomi said now. "It's just between us. You

and me. We can do whatever we want. There's nothing dangerous in it, Sam. We ought to help him."

"Even though we don't know who he is."

"Does it matter who he is?"

"Yes, it matters."

Naomi sighed. "It *doesn't* matter. People like him are coming here on bits of wood. Don't you think it's appalling?"

"Of course I think it's appalling. But so what?"

"Then we have a chance to help. I'm a lawyer—that's what
we do."

Sam rolled her shoulders and her tone was suddenly dismis-
sive.

"Really? I don't think that's your reason. I think you want an
adventure."

"Well, if I did, it's not a crime."

"No, it's not a crime, but you're talking to me like a lawyer.
When in fact you don't know who he is."

More gently, Naomi admitted that she didn't. All right,
she thought, maybe I'm atoning for coming from money that
I didn't earn. But would that be so bad? She lowered her voice
and tried to be more persuasive. "Wanting to help the helpless
is not an uncommon desire, and if you want me to explain it
I'd say that I'm determined to make a difference. It's not just an
adventure. And if it is, it's one with a purpose."

"My ass."

Sam pursed her lips and her face lost its color. She hadn't
really meant it, and she realized that what she'd said a few moments earlier sounded cowardly. Accordingly, she doubled down
in order to disguise the fact.

"It's such a dumb situation to put yourself in. Now I have to
hide something from my father, and I've never done that."

"You've never hidden anything from him?"

"No."

"That's hard to believe. Anyway, I can't see what difference it makes. What's he going to do if you tell him?"

"It just feels gross."

"Trust me," Naomi reassured her. "We should really wait and think a bit before we do anything. I know you're interested to see what happens and you can rise to the occasion if we decide to help a migrant, but it can't be something that's really ours if your father knows about it—admit it!"

"Let me think, then. It has nothing to do with my dad."

"Come on, let's have some tsipouro and go home."

But Sam had felt the needle used against her, and the little wound bled. Before long, however, her mood picked up, spurred by the pomace brandy. Naomi gave her a crash course on this lesser-known Greek liquor. There was anise-flavored tsipouro and the plain kind. There was Tsililis and there was Kosteas; there was Idoniko without anise and Babatzim with it. Unlike ouzo, tsipouro was made from grapes and you could taste the pomace. And the anise here was fruity—Naomi taught her how to say one word for it, *glykaniso*. Tsipouro was also peerlessly alcoholic, it prised apart mind and spirit. They forgot about the Arab on the far side of the island and began talking about upcoming parties instead. Naomi explained to her how the scene worked in the summers: the families who returned every year, the famous artists who set up their studios between June and September, the influx of journalists and interns and hangers-on that made the parties unpredictable and fun. They knocked back three rounds of ouzo. Night had fallen without their noticing it, and the alleys glowed with their creamy whitened walls. Windows opened in the houses; from the upper floors came the sound of pianos and *Tosca* and Greek heavy metal. A smell of booze began to touch the air, but very lightly. The restaurants slowly filled up. The lights grew brighter. Into their own came wanderers and drifters looking for friends and interesting strangers, which meant of course pretty ones. Sam was alert with curiosity. It didn't seem possible that such a social world could exist on such a small island. Many of them knew Naomi. They came up, embraced her, glanced with a smile at the young sidekick and stayed for a drink or two. There were some young Americans, too, boys more cynical and worldly than anyone she knew, and she was interested in the effect they had on her. Even the New York ones were not from her world, they were not what she was used to. Perhaps it was because here they were out of their element and therefore unleashed. Their eyes had a different cruelty and freedom. Their schools and parents were far distant and out of mind, and they were free to do as they liked: on their way to other people's houses, to drinks parties on terraces above the port or yachts stationary for the night in the harbor. That was what summers were for. Soon Naomi and Sam were being whisked up to one of these parties as if it was the most normal thing in the world.

They went to the villa of an elderly American painter whose name Sam should have known but didn't; it was surrounded by one of the island's characteristic high walls, and in the garden behind them tortoises inched their way through a garden of long grass studded with enormous fallen lemons. But why, she wondered, did they have candles soldered to their shells? This was Naomi's world, and nothing about it was obvious. Yet there was an air of madness and fun that would probably last all night and without foreseeing it she had been dropped into that atmosphere at just the right moment.

The painter Ed Milne was there with his wife, both ancient and burned to a handsome crisp by thirty reckless summers, and on the walls were his creations, small oblong abstractions of pale gray and blue with titles in Greek that she couldn't understand. *Oinopos Ponton,* and so on. The rooms looked Ottoman as she wandered through them with her highball—a Turkish official had built the villa at the end of the eighteenth century—and soon she had lost Naomi and was among strangers, innocent and beautiful, as she was well aware, and with the added advantage of being unknown to them all. It was an advantage that might only last a single night, but it was a huge one all the same. But not all strangers enjoyed this privilege. She thought of the other one on his cliff sleeping out in the open, and she wondered whether he did, in fact, enjoy an advantage by virtue of being unknown. She couldn't tell yet because he was not a stranger of the same sort. He was, thus far, almost entirely a creation of her own imagination.

FIVE

OVER THE NEXT DAYS, AS THEY SWAM AND SUNBATHED together on the remote beaches, they talked about what they would do. Gradually Naomi prevailed, and Sam agreed that the humanitarian thing to do would be to go back and bring the castaway a basket of food and some necessities. It was a simple thing to do and it was also a moral thing to do, and being both moral and simple it was an easy thing to do. Easy, simple, and moral: but it had to be planned. Every night Naomi monitored the Greek news in case their charge had been apprehended by the police, but he never appeared in the media and she heard no mention of him in the flow of island gossip, to which her nativized ear was attuned. He remained invisible, and the longer he did the more intensely she felt the emotion of her mission. She didn't believe in signs, but there were surely signs involved here—to her mind, there was no one on the island who would be more sensitive to the issues than she was. She couldn't possibly allow anyone else other than Sam to become involved in this salvation. But that said, she also needed Sam at her side, complicit and eager and docilely attuned to the project at hand. For Naomi, it could not be a solitary endeavor. She needed a platonic lover in her orbit.

At nine one morning, when they should have been snorkelling near Mandraki, they rented a small skiff with an outboard, loaded it with two bags of groceries, and returned to the far side of the island.

This time it was different. When they returned to the same place where they had seen him previously, they saw him at once, washing himself in the cove, using his hands as a little bucket. He wasn't as handsome as Sam remembered, but his relaxed gaze and the body language, his resignation and indifference, served him well. The two women stopped and put down the bags and, with a nervous banality, waved. The man came out of the sea, dried himself, and sat down where he had slept. He dressed, but without hurrying, and Naomi turned to Sam, as if for the last time.

"You see, it's just him. There's nothing to worry about. And there are two of us."

The man turned finally and waved back, a sign that encouraged, and they went down toward the beach with all the calm they could muster.

He had pulled on socks and sneakers and a dark blue T-shirt, tattered and on the verge of disintegration by now, and next to him lay what appeared to be the most precious thing still in his possession, a bar of soap wrapped in paper. It was a scene of quiet ruin, at the center of which sat a man who was unruined. The long hair and beard, even, had been groomed with his fingers and flattened out. He's about the same age as Naomi, Sam thought. A little older perhaps. She was gripped by a sudden doubt, but they had to talk, and as soon as they did the doubt ebbed away and she was left with human immediacies that demanded all of her attention. It was Naomi in any case who asked him if he spoke English or French, or even Greek, and he said, "The first two," in English. She stood about six feet away, and her shadow fell across his face, as she intended. But she spoke as soothingly as she could, because although questions were unavoidable they could be uttered without alarm.

"Where did you come from?"

He pointed to the sea, but without any convincing vehemence.

"You swam from a boat?"

"That's right."

"Where is it now?"

He shaded his eyes to see her better. They were not calculating eyes, and they were not particularly inquisitive. Earth, Naomi thought. He has eyes of earth. His voice was soft, educated, slow in rhythm and the accent unobtrusive. His English was excellent. But that was not a remarkable fact in the world these days; an expensive school evidently underwrote his command of their language.

"Gone—it's just me."

"And the others?" Sam said.

He waved a hand—no others.

She didn't believe him, but she said nothing.

They set down the bags and opened them, and when the man saw peaches he clapped and shouted *"Merci!"*

"We saw you the other day," Naomi blurted out.

It had to be explained, after all.

There was the stilted moment when she had to hand him the little penknife she had brought with her to cut the peaches and the tomatoes. He took it and looked her in the eye; something grated between them. "I saw you too," he said, turning to the peach in his hand. "But then you ran away."

"We came in a yacht—do you remember?"

"I saw it. But you had Greeks with you."

"You don't think I'm Greek?" Naomi chimed in.

He said she had English written all over her.

"What about me?" Sam said defiantly.

"Australian."

Naomi turned to Sam. "This is Sam. She's not Australian. She's American. I'm Naomi."

"And my name is Faoud."

It was only then that Sam thought back to the time she had first seen him and remembered that he had been wearing tracksuit bottoms and thong sandals. The fantastical idea came to her that it was not, after all, the same person at all. We don't know either way, she thought. Naomi doesn't know any more than I do. We're both in the dark.

The dark, however, was not a bad place to be. They sat down beside him and all three cut up the bread and laid chunks of feta on the loaves with tomatoes sprinkled with some coarse salt they had brought with them. It was as if they had just met in a London park, strangers exchanging names and peaches. Faoud didn't appear distrustful or distant; he seemed to have measured the two interlopers and judged them according to his own view of the world. He had been expecting them, or expecting someone. He said he had been considering scaling the mountain and making his own way to the windward side, though he had no idea what might lie there. A village, a town. There was always a village at the very least. There were always houses, places where you could ask for water or help. But it was a gamble to approach a house in the remoter islands, as many back in Turkey had told him. He asked Naomi what the name of this island was. When she told him he rolled the word around in his mouth and considered it. *Hydra*. It didn't mean anything to him. He asked her what kind of place it was, the windward side. She said, "There's a port, many houses, it's a different world."

"Then I got lucky," he said, lowering his eyes.

"You came through Turkey?"

He had, but there was no elaboration on his past. It was as if it was superfluous to make commentary on something so rudimentary.

All right, she thought, he doesn't want to go there.

"When did you last eat?" Sam asked.

"Many days ago," he said.

"It's an abomination," Naomi said, echoing her father's tone.

Seven days before you die of starvation, Sam thought coolly.

There was something about him she didn't accept, a smooth quality that eluded her. Some elusive qualities in a man were acceptable, but others spelled unwelcome outcomes.

"Eat the cheese," Naomi said to Faoud. "Get the protein. I'll bring something better tonight."

"*Merci.*"

A line of vaporous cloud had formed at the horizon. As it spread and turned a hot silver, waves of new heat touched their faces. The summer was ripening into its full delirium. The sea darkened and lost its cool metallic sheen. When they glimpsed it now—suddenly, at the end of a lane or from a high set of steps—it had a feverish depth of color that made them momentarily forget that they were even in Europe. Exposed to the sun all day, and an equally feverous empty sky, the two women began to feel loosened, their consciousness deliciously weakened, and they thought of the cool conveniences of the port, the cafes at midday under the awnings, the iced beers and the siestas that would follow. But none of these things extended to Faoud; inevitably, then, they began to think of where their charity led next. Naomi immediately thought of the abandoned houses in Episkopi. She told him that he couldn't possibly stay here on the beach, that it would be better to move into one of those. He bowed his head and said nothing.

"You have to move today," she went on. "Tonight. I'll come back tonight and take you there."

"Really?" Sam burst out.

She was uneasy and now also a little resentful at the pressure being applied to her. But Naomi was in fervor now.

"There's no other way. He'll die out here. There are only a few shepherds in Episkopi and they use the houses for animal sheds. It's the best place to hide him."

For a moment Sam thought of ditching the charity and simply going back to her family and their afternoon games of chess and backgammon. It would be so much easier than this pointless exertion. She suddenly resented both her own passivity and the relentless charity-worker passion of the older girl, in which to boot she didn't quite believe. Naomi's playful cynicism—the thing about her that most appealed to Sam—seemed to have disappeared in a baffling way from one day to the next. She could understand the logic of it, but why the determination to make a stranger into a moral cause? You could help a stranger without making him into a cause. You could inform people who could help. As far as she could tell from the news, the Greeks had been rather welcoming to the refugees coming from Turkey. But then again, she also remembered the new police who had begun to appear at the port, and it was equally possible that since Naomi knew more about this country than she did, she also knew better what the current climate of fear and paranoia might be. It could go either way, she admitted to herself. But nevertheless a dilemma had been forced upon her and it was one that she had not asked to be a part of.

She looked across at the man cramming his mouth with bread and olives, and of course she felt sorry for him. Days at sea floating on some piece of garbage with a single bottle of water. A flight from war and chaos in Syria, as she had read in the European papers a thousand times. One knew the images. But there had been something vague about his replies to Naomi's questions. Their embarrassment had kept them from asking directly, but there was no reason not to probe any further. She wanted to ask him then, where exactly he was from, who his family were, and why he had had no choice but to wash up on this island rather than one closer to Turkey. But again she failed to make the move.

Naomi turned to her again and her expression was more forgiving—she knew that Sam would play along with it, that she was more interested in this than in silly parties.

"Let's go back soon," she said. "I need a beer. And we need to think. Don't you agree?"

They got up and shielded their eyes from the sun. The man looked up sheepishly and he understood everything; there was nothing to explain to him. He was intelligent at least, the eyes responsive and alert to every human beat. He said, "Will you come back tonight?"

"We'll come back after sundown and take you round to Episkopi if we can find a house there. We'll go to Episkopi now and see."

"It's a great favor," he said. "I can't thank you enough."

She wondered then if he had another plan. They walked back to the boat.

Out of earshot, Sam gave vent to her doubts.

"Oh, don't think so much," Naomi snapped. "He's got a complicated story, so what? How could he not have a complicated story?"

But it wasn't just complex, Sam shot back. It was vague and evasive.

"I didn't think so," Naomi countered. "What was evasive?"

"Do you think he's a Christian or a Muslim?"

Naomi burst into laughter.

"What?"

"I said do you think he's a Christian?"

"I don't really care if he is or he isn't. Should I have asked him? I'm not doing it for religious reasons."

"What if he's a Muslim?"

"I'd be even kinder."

"Is it different if he's Muslim?" Sam said. "Kindness isn't the point."

FROM THE DOCK at the hamlet of Palamidas they climbed for an hour to Episkopi until they were among the ravines and uneven fields where cyclamen flowers survived. They sat on a stone wall and looked down at the sea, at the islands compact and bare, the shadow of Dokos and beyond it the pale mass of the Argolid. Hillsides swept down to a jagged coast met by water the color of gem silica, their steeply pitched surfaces maculate with gray rock and quivering sage. Lone gothic agaves thrust up unexpectedly, their heads torn sideways by the winds, and around them ancient wire donkey fences lay on the fields like tossed sea wreckage, patched up with discarded beds and old house doors. It looked like a land taking its time to die, to revert to prehistory. But its advantage was that there were many lonely ruined houses here which, since Naomi could speak Greek, she could bargain for if she found an owner.

By now the emotions of two hours earlier had dissipated. They were burned by the salt wind and their chattering minds had fallen silent. They walked around looking for people. Climbing to higher ground, they could see flocks of goats, a line of horses. Two men reclined in the wild grass, and it was clear they had been watching the girls for some time. Naomi had always thought that she knew everyone on the island, but these were unknowns, shepherds in their sixties in coarse patched shirts and braces, quietly alive beneath bursts of white hair. She spoke to them, they answered politely. She had to be careful what she said. It was enough to say that she needed a hut for herself and her friends to use occasionally over the summer. They liked to come out here to swim at the Nisiza peninsula nearby. She could offer a ridiculous price that they would never refuse.

They looked at the burnished American girl and something in them softened. It was her air of insolent innocence. One of the men had two huts he used for the animals; they were on high ground but easy to climb up to. He gestured to one of these buildings, a square structure about a hundred meters away, close to the path that ran all the way to the port. It could be hers if she really wanted it, though there was no electricity or water. There was a pallet the shepherd used to sleep on and some tools, including a bucket and a scythe. If she wanted to take it she could pay him later that day and the deal was done.

"All right," she said. "I like the sound of that."

They walked up to the hut together and looked inside it; the door had no lock. It was cool in the heat, and dry. There were no spiders and no drafts—it would do. She took it at once.

The man was pleasantly surprised and did a little dance on his toes. She went over everything with him carefully. No one was to come up there after she had taken the hut. He was to tell no one that he had rented it out either. It was, she said, for social reasons. Her father would disapprove, and she didn't want him to know. To seal the deposit she gave him a fifty-euro note, and she and Sam started back down toward Palamidas. The two men stood and watched them go with slightly mystified expressions. But soon the two girls were out of sight and the world returned once again to its normal state of torpor, heat, and boredom, a state in which they were both perfectly happy, offering as it did no expectations but divine and therefore inexplicable windfalls.

At Palamidas they waited for a while in the shade of a looming hill near the water. It was a desolate place, but lit by the fairy waters. The same pieces of rusted machinery littered the broken-up quay as at Mandraki. A small lamp with a solar panel attached to it, jetties with tires strapped to their sides. The beach was littered with splintered wood, like the scene of an explosion in a matchbox house. It was a place preoccupied by its own labors.

"What did you say to him?" Sam finally asked.

"Just money talk. I'm going to put Faoud in that hovel and the old man is going to rent it to me for the summer. It'll be all right until I figure out something better."

"He'll be expecting a boutique hotel I bet."

"Faoud?"

"He looks a little spoiled to me."

"That's not really the right word, is it? You don't like him, do you?"

Sam shrugged and crossed her feet. She was merely grateful to be out of the punishing sun. She didn't have any feelings about Faoud that weren't physical, instinctual, and unthought.

"I don't care one way or the other," she felt compelled to state.

"I don't believe you. You didn't like him—I could tell."

"But you do," Sam said.

"So now it's me?"

"You were all over him."

"*You* were looking him over. You're not fooling me."

"Come on, I wasn't."

"I saw it all. It doesn't matter anyway. You can like who you want."

Sam looked away for a moment. She had to decide whether to be honest or to spin a tale. In the corner of her eye she had caught the arthritic motion of two old women in the black garb of a previous century making their way across the space behind the landing in the shade of a dark rose parasol. Humans are like spiders in their old age, moving from shadow to shadow in the bright sun, inexhaustible in their way. She would never end up like that, even if she stayed here for the rest of her life, which of course she wouldn't. In New York, she wouldn't age like that. She would rebel. Then she decided not to answer Naomi at all: yes, Faoud was beautiful, but she didn't see any reason to explain being interested in that. It was her business, her weakness, if it was a weakness at all, and it was purely a private crisis. Beautiful things subdue. It didn't concern anyone else. It was a mystery within one devotee. They sailed, therefore, back to Hydra in silence. Sam was happy with that. When they got to Kamini the girl disembarked, kissed Naomi's cheek, and walked off to the family villa alone on the long path to Vlychos. Naomi went back to Belle Air and slept through the afternoon.

THE HALDANES HAD dinner at home that night. The maid made lemon soup and moussaka, and as they ate on the patio, lightning flickered against the edge of the nocturnal sea. Thunder rolled in after it, distant and soft, and the wind picked up; the candle flames guttered. "So it's going to rain?" her mother said, looking up at her and trying to guess where her daughter had been for so many hours earlier that day. After the meal was finished and the plates cleared away, Sam lay on the outdoor sofa and ate *galaktoboureko* with cups of Lipton's doused in sliced lemon. The family gathered around the coffee table with jazz on the record player, and bits of paper flew around the patio on the gusts of wind. Her father, his newspaper open wide—yesterday's *Tribune*—tapped his foot to the Louis Jordan and puffed at his pipe.

"By the way," he drawled, not removing the stem, "your mother and I were stopped by the police walking back from the port. Can you imagine? Guys with automatics. We nearly had a brawl."

"It wasn't me who got upset," Amy put in immediately.

"They stopped us and asked us for our passports. Obviously we didn't have them on us."

The paper lowered, and Jeffrey caught his daughter's eye from the other side of the glass table.

"Has that happened to you, Sam?"

"Never."

"You see, Amy? They stop middle-aged people in broad daylight but not kids on the lam all night. Stupid as they are intrusive."

Sam suggested that it was just the summer drugs season. But Jeffrey insisted on the "lurch to the right" that was all the talk in the *Tribune*. Had they seen what was happening in Hungary and Poland?

She yawned, lying on her side, and resolved not to allow any of his peroration to penetrate her inner calm. She knew why there were armed police on the island because she already knew more than her father in that regard. It was easy enough to piece together. Curiously, she didn't share any of his outrage at the rightward lurch, the demanding of passports, the events in Hungary. She had been listening to the same social justice indignations all her life, and gradually they had lost their effect on her. What did the word "fascist" mean after all these years, after all the repetitions and misuse? She heard it all the time in school, and it was a word that now passed her by in the night. As she reached her twenty-first year she began to realize that she intuited more about the world as it really was than her well-informed father, precisely because everything he knew was pre-known from texts and could not be contradicted by any real lived experience—because he didn't have any. Whereas she had looked into the eyes of Faoud and kept it a secret from him. Her father's indignations seemed naive and bookish. But she listened for a while and agreed with him, then stood and announced that she was going up to sleep. It was a way of not being abrupt or rude. He nodded, however, obviously perplexed. Was there something wrong with her?

She kissed her mother's hot face and said she was tired. The rain was coming. On her bed upstairs she lay with the windows open, listening to it falling quietly over the pines, and her thoughts drifted until a message came from Naomi: *All done with the shipwreck.*

Sam texted back, *Well done. That was gutsy.*

Ten minutes later came another text: *Exhausted, going to sleep for 24 hours.*

Me too, she wrote back, and then the messages fell silent for the night. But although it was true that she was exhausted, she couldn't sleep. She thought about Faoud in the hut at the far end of the island and the faces of the two shepherds, which had seemed, at least to her, to be full of duplicitous resolutions. But maybe that was wrong. My imagination, she thought dismissively. But still, she didn't quite believe herself. She didn't quite believe in her own disinterest in Faoud either. More than that: she wondered if the young man lying on that pallet in the dark was thinking about her in turn, and she was quite sure that, in his way, he was.

SIX

CARISSA WAS ALONE IN THE HOUSE WHEN NAOMI CAME
home after midnight. The maid could tell at once that
Naomi had been drinking heavily, because the girl slammed
doors and threw her boots across the hall floor, crashing her
way upstairs to her room. The Codringtons themselves were
long asleep, dulled by their sleeping pills and booze. Their
snores could be heard throughout the house, even in her little
cell sunk in the basement under thick floors. It was a disgusting
sound, a sound commensurate with her bestial employers, and
usually she wore earplugs to specifically screen it out when she
tried to sleep.

That night they were in full roar, like huge fattened tropi-
cal frogs. Carissa stepped into the corridor outside her room
and crept to the stone stairs leading up to the ground floor. Her
curiosity was aroused. The family's tensions were mysterious,
almost magical to her, and she lost no opportunity to observe
them. Sensing before long that the entire family was unconscious, she went up to the hall and picked up the boots that
had been thrown down so insolently. It sometimes shocked her,
Naomi's disrespect to her own father. But she also felt solidarity
with the tormented girl against her overbearing and arrogant
stepmother. She arranged the boots neatly against the wall and

noticed that they were caked with fresh mud. So Naomi had gone on a long walk somewhere in the rain, and not in the port. She must have wandered up to the hills. It was a curious detail. Carissa went into the salon and sat for a while in the armchairs that were forbidden to her during work hours, then stole a sip of brandy from one of the decanters standing on the drink service trolley. She often did this when her employers were asleep. It was her little revenge.

She stopped by the family photographs on the large table in the salon and looked at the faces of Naomi at twelve, fifteen, and twenty—you could see trouble coming into the eyes. She went up the stairs a little and tried to catch a noise from Naomi's room, but the girl seemed fast asleep too and unlike her elders her sleep was always silent. Carissa went back to her own room half tipsy and determined to wake up at dawn exactly. This she was able to do.

When she started cooking in the kitchen at first light it was still raining, a fine soundless drizzle. She made a potato tart, which Jimmie loved in the morning, and a honey-and-egg concoction baked with filo. They were always up early and they were always hungry. At six-thirty the master came down first in his dressing gown, his hair wet and brushed back. He found her in the kitchen and gave her a playful pat on the behind, to which she had grown accustomed. She led him on a little; it made the tips bigger. As she was pouring his coffee, he said, "Carissa, have you seen my daughter?"

"She came in late last night."

He asked her where Naomi had been and she said she had no idea.

"Bloody nuisance," he muttered, and went into his food with

a pleasureless resolve. It was, after all, the best way to avoid domestic troubles.

Carissa went back to the kitchen and hovered by the door, listening. The master was talking on the phone to one of his henchmen in London. His name was Rockhold, a sort of private investigator. Her English was now good enough to understand most of what they said, and she thought that he was asking this Rockhold to check Naomi's records and bank accounts in England and Italy. The family had a large villa just north of Rome that Naomi also used. Their affairs were complex, and the master could not manage them alone. Soon the mistress came in, the master ended his call abruptly, and Carissa went out to serve her coffee. Phaine, as always, inspected the food casually and made a few sharp criticisms. The toast was a little burned; the eggs were a little dry. Carissa bowed with a "Yes, madame" and apologized. It was a ritual without much substance, a quiet way of humiliating her and keeping her in her place and on her toes. Like the pats on the behind, she had gotten used to it.

"And, Carissa," Phaine said then, "don't ever boil the coffee a second time. I know you do it occasionally because you're lazy. Don't. You think I can't tell the difference, but I certainly can."

"Yes, madame."

The day passed glumly. Naomi came down at midday for her coffee and drank it while Carissa made her pancakes. The girl seemed restless and distracted. When the sun came out she took her coffee onto the terrace and sipped it with her knees drawn up under her chin. The tension in her had increased. The Codringtons had gone out for lunch, and Carissa took the opportunity to talk to her. She was allowed to do it, since Naomi treated her as the only person in the household in whom she could confide.

"They went to Athens yesterday," the maid said now. "I think Phaine wanted to buy summer clothes."

"Did my father say anything to you?"

"No. He was on the phone to London. Something about an investigator. I didn't hear anything else."

Naomi put her face in her hands, and Carissa noticed that her nails were filthy and jagged.

"God, they never let up, do they?"

"No, miss."

"I couldn't sleep last night. I remember you told me once you knew an herbal sleep aid that the islanders use. Do you know how to get some, Carissa?"

"I can find some for you."

"Maybe some hemlock. I know it grows here. My friends used to talk about it all the time. They were convinced the Mialou widow was killed with it."

They chuckled—the Mialou story was a famous one.

"It's certainly true," the maid agreed.

"It's a Greek specialty. Socrates and all that."

"Yes, miss."

"But just some lemon balm would be all right. Just to relax and chill."

"I know a woman who sells everything."

"*Ne pethani o charos!*"

"Yes, miss. I'll go up the mountain this afternoon and find her. I promise."

Naomi went up to her, kissed her cheek.

"You're my savior in this madhouse. If it wasn't for you I'd have gone mad myself."

Maybe you already did, the maid thought. It's possible.

"And, Carissa—I need some antibiotics and some bandages. Can you get me some of those too?"

"I'll get them."

"I scratched myself yesterday on my hike."

Carissa looked at her slyly. "I can get whatever you want—just ask me."

Carissa eventually left the terrace to finish her duties in the kitchen. An hour later the house was empty. The heat had returned, the sun festering on the prickly pear along the walls. She locked the outer door as she always did and went down the long flights of steps into the village. Later in the afternoon she came back with the medications and herbs. The medicine woman had been at home and she had bought a dozen different kinds of plants, leaves, roots, and flowers. She had bought a sachet of hemlock leaves and root as well, because she could use a tiny amount to prepare a sedative useful in the treatment of anxiety and mania. The girl could use it, as far as she could see. It would calm her down and restore her balance. *Konio*—its name meant "whirling" in Greek, but its effect could be the opposite. She made rabbit for dinner and then went to her room and slept for an hour.

When she woke she heard the Codringtons bumbling around in the salon playing records and tinkering with the drinks cabinet. The service bell rang. She dressed hastily in her uniform and ran upstairs to find them seated in deck chairs on the terraces with vodka tonics that they had made themselves. It was a strike against her. But Phaine said nothing. Instead, she asked wearily for some small sandwiches impaled on cocktail sticks. The couple seemed relaxed after their excursion to Athens. Dusk came down with swallows and ships' horns and distant cicada calls. A neighbor stopped by, one of the ancient Americans who lived in the hills like solitary crabs. There were a few rounds of salty laughter, and then he left. By nightfall the Codringtons were merry with drink. At eight dinner was served, and Naomi was there in a white summer dress like a high-society penitent, her hair scooped up around a wooden pin and twisted into a whorl.

"Get a bottle of the Santorini, will you?" Jimmie said to Carissa, barely looking at her.

She went back to the kitchen and waited for further orders. The meal was long, and they were talking heatedly. From time to time a half-shouted word flared up and then she went out, poured some wine, and they behaved themselves in front of her. Phaine at least had a horror of misbehavior in front of the servants. Soon, however, a full-blown argument blew up between Jimmie and Naomi. The English was so fast and confused that Carissa couldn't understand a word. The girl began crying and then hurling insults at both Jimmie and Phaine. She calmed for a while and then it all exploded a second time. This time Naomi threw a glass. It shattered against the wall and the girl stormed off the terrace. Enraged, Jimmie ran after her and bawled something nasty into the hall as Naomi was pulling on her boots. He managed to stop her leaving, but she wouldn't come back to the table. "For God's sake," he kept shouting, pacing up and down until he had exhausted himself and came back to the table where Phaine sat in icy silence.

The girl went up to her room and Carissa brought out the coffee. Phaine addressed her at once.

"You're not to say a word about this to anyone outside of this house. Is that understood?"

"Yes, madame."

"If I find that you did, you'll be fired immediately."

But in fact Carissa didn't feel that the argument was disgraceful. She felt it was long overdue. The following morning, as she made the day's first coffee, Naomi reappeared, refreshed by a long sleep and carrying a beach bag filled with bottled water and cans of tuna. She was going for another long hike in the hills. "I hope you weren't afraid of us last night," she said to Carissa, taking her hands for a moment and pressing them.

"I wasn't."

"It's sweet of you to say. Tell my father I won't be back for dinner. I'm going to eat alone in town. I think I need to be away from them for twenty-four hours, and they probably feel the same way. Just hang in there, sweet Carissa—I'll see you're all right in the end. I really will. We have to stick together."

But Carissa was not sure who the "we" were. It was possible that, in the last resort, it did not include her.

SEVEN

Naomi went down to the port, met Sam there, and hired the same skiff she had taken the previous time. By nine they were at Palamidas, the waters still, the boats piled high with dejected-looking tackle. It took them less than an hour to climb up to Episkopi.

He must have seen them coming, because when the girls reached the first of the houses the shepherd-landlord was there waiting for them, a shotgun slung jauntily across the back of his neck and a dog seething at his feet. But he was cordial to Naomi; he called her *despinis*, miss.

"That friend of yours," he said, looking her in the eye with a fearless condescension that didn't retreat one inch or give any quarter, "he's quite a character, isn't he? You didn't mention anything about single men sleeping up here alone."

But Naomi brushed him off.

"It's a favor I'm doing him. Did he do anything wrong?"

The man shook his head slowly.

"Not that I know of. But I'm sure it isn't legal, him being up here. I'd say the rent I charged you is a steal."

It was obvious what he was getting at, but she had to control her sudden anger.

"All right," she muttered. "How much should it be, then?"

"He's an Arab."

The word he used was *Arapis. Einai Arapis.*

She concealed her slight shock—it was a crude old word.

"It doesn't matter what he is."

"Got nothing against them myself. But it's illegal. If he's an Arab it's different."

And the second time, as if registering her distaste, he had changed the word to the more normal *Aravas.*

"A hundred euros?" she tried.

It was an over-the-top bribe, and he seemed not to believe his luck for a moment. Perhaps he should push for more.

"I have fifty here," she said. "I'll give you fifty tomorrow."

He took the notes and then stepped back a little.

"It should really be fifty a week extra for the risk I'm taking," he said.

"It's no risk."

She wanted to snap at him, but it would get her nowhere and they both knew it. She gave him the fifty; he lowered the shotgun off his shoulders into the crux of his elbow and moved aside.

"If your boy steals anything, it's you who pays," he said as she walked away from him. "I'll know where to find you."

So you know who I am, she thought.

He watched her go up toward the hut.

"Remember that!" he called after her. "Even an egg." Then he added, *"Goustareis Araves?"* Did she like Arabs?

The hut's door was open and Faoud was sitting in the sun on the far side, out of view of her antagonist. He was drying his socks on flat stones and washing his face in a bowl of water. Naomi had brought him razors and shaving cream this time, and a small mirror from the pharmacy. He hadn't asked for them, but it had seemed to her that it was the most expedient way to make him blend in with the Greeks. The shepherd now turned and walked away, the dog following him.

Faoud seemed to understand what had been discussed.

"I think you should shave now," she said. "You look like a cannibal. It's almost depressing." He agreed, and he seemed to find it amusing, saying that the old people in the houses were afraid of him—isn't that what they had said? But he caught Sam's eye as he spoke, and in some way that quieted him.

"Not really. But you'll look better cleaned up."

They had brought scissors as well, and Sam offered to cut his hair. She sat behind him and sheared off the matted excess hair while he shaved, the reflection of his face held still in the mirror. She enjoyed it; she'd never done anything like that before. The slope of his neck was that of a girl's; his skin could have been coated with honey.

When she was finished she brushed the hair from his shoulders and looked at him from the side. It was a remarkable improvement. Naomi asked if he wanted to go for a swim; there was a remote path that went down from Episkopi to the far side which no one used.

"I know it," he said. "But I think it would be better to stay here. Someone will see us."

"It's not the end of the world if they did. You're respectable now. Let's go down there."

He hesitated, then relented. A swim with two girls. "What did you tell the farmers?" he asked.

"I said you were a friend."

"They won't believe it. I don't look like a friend, and they know it."

"Maybe they don't care. I brought you some T-shirts and a sweater. Don't thank me—they were cheap."

He put on one of the T-shirts and suddenly he looked clean-cut, austere, and curiously middle class. What he really needed was a shower, but it would have to wait.

"We'll clean you up, and then I can get you a room in the port."

They had brought a box of eggs, and Sam took them out now so that he could eat them raw, one after the other.

Then he lay down in the grass. The cessation of hunger had relaxed him.

"You're not a very good Greek," he said to Naomi. "You burn like an Irish girl. Are you Irish?"

"How would you know about Irish girls?"

"Well, then," he began:

"I've been around. I went to Paris and London when I was small. My father took me. He told me everyone there was really Irish. He bought me a tie at Old England. Do you know that store?"

Naomi shook her head, and she was incredulous, her heart skipping a beat to find that he was more bourgeois than she was.

"It's near the Opéra in Paris. My father loved it. He bought all his ties there. He still had them when he died. I would have inherited them if I'd stayed."

So, Sam thought slowly, listening to this, you come from money. You know what Old England ties are, and your father was a man of leisure.

"You haven't said where you're from," she said. "We thought it would be rude to ask—so I'm not asking."

"I don't mind if you ask, because I won't tell you."

She took out the strawberries they had brought and the yogurt. Dessert.

"*Mais tu me gâtes!*" he cried, and swore he would buy them

dinner when he was rich again. His fingers, as they darted for the fruit, were suddenly elegant and discriminating.

"We'll see if you do," Sam retorted.

It didn't seem likely. For some reason she disliked his use of a French phrase, though she knew it was irritable on her part, and there was something in his unexpected confidence that struck her as being less innocent than Naomi wanted to believe. When he glanced at her his eyes were clear of all deference or doubt. He seemed to know what he was looking at, and it was not an indulgent knowledge. Her pride flared up in defense of herself, and she thought of a few sharp words she could fling at him later on, when the right occasion presented itself. It was a little more than the usual male insolence.

They ate the yogurt on plastic spoons and threw the strawberries to each other one by one. Maybe, Naomi thought, this silly laughter will reach all the way down to the shepherd with the shotgun. Gossip and islands were natural conspirators, but the time for caring about it was almost gone.

Naomi wondered whether she could bring him down to the port and check him into a hotel without a passport, or using her own. It was one way of bringing him back into civilization. Then she considered buying him a ferry ticket and getting him to the mainland. Yet there was no possibility of continuation in this plan once he got there. She could give him money and send him on his way. Yes—that would work. He would take the money gratefully and move on, or so she imagined. But it was offhand and cruel, and moreover a waste of an opportunity. It seemed to her that there was something magical in this sudden appearance of another human being; it was surely a sign, as she had thought before. She could bribe someone in the port to take him in. But then she would lose her influence over him, and nor did that seem right. She was the savior and she relished the role. It made her vital in a new way. To save another person: it wasn't nothing. It wasn't exactly an achievement, but it was a small shift in the balance of power toward the weak. Such shifts were the substance of one's moral life—they made the intolerable tolerable. She thought back to what Sam had said that day about atonement, and she realized now that the need for atonement was hers. She was righting the wrongs that she herself had committed, even though rationally speaking the two were not connected. Idiotic, but there it was. She had been haunted by the wronged Turk in Dalston for months, and with time it had begun to fester within her. Whether it was a small failure or a large one was immaterial; a chain reaction had been set in motion by her ineptitude and cowardice, and it would carry on creating havoc out of sight and mind for as long as that person lived. Such things did not end when one lost interest in them. Their consequences continued even if one didn't have to live with them oneself. Morality was nothing more than paying attention to the chain reaction while not causing another one. She was feeding an unknown man strawberries on the hill outside Episkopi and she was enjoying it. He seemed to be enjoying it as well. He ought to be, she thought with gratification.

Then, as an entertainment, she brought out another small packet of the weed she had bought from the boat girl, though she wasn't sure how he would respond to it. But he understood what it was at once and didn't push it away. Her gifts were a success.

THEY WENT DOWN the path in the direction of the sea and the beach at Nisiza. Sam was more at ease now. She hung back a little and watched the other two from behind. Naomi had told her to bring her swimsuit, so she must have foreseen this detour all along, and under a brilliant sky there was no room for suspicion or smallness of spirit. In a few minutes of walking in the heat they were soon laughing together, in synchronicity, and there was no ambiguous complexity to ruin the moment. It was there, but it could be left behind for a while. The path was difficult to negotiate and it took a long time to come down to the water. She wondered, and not for the first time, if the old men had followed them down or were watching them from somewhere. The path dipped downward in the shade and delivered them to the small church of Agios Ioannis, with the sea just on the far side of the cliffs.

They sat there against a wall and drank from their water bottles. The beach was by a skerry a few hundred meters away, the promontory uninhabited and encircled by shallow water—a short but prickly hike.

"You know secret places," Faoud said to Naomi. "How did you find a place like this?"

"I used to come here alone as a girl."

"Is there anyone on that little island?"

She shook her head. Sam took off her sunglasses and let the ocean blind her. There were withered olive trees all around them, the earth a pale chocolate color. The wind rushed off the cliffs from the choppy water. She felt now how subtle Naomi had been to bring them down here, away from the world. It normalized things. She felt calm, too, in the shade of the sea-beaten church, lonely on its perch and adrift in the centuries. It must be where the people of Episkopi came. They stood up eventually and scrambled down the rough slopes to the small beach that joined the skerry to the land. They stripped to their swimsuits, Faoud in his shorts, and they waded into the cool water until they were up to their chests. Then they kicked off and swam out around the skerry. Sam, swimming more weakly, trailed behind them a little and the wind whipping off the water deafened her. The other two were talking. On the far side of the skerry they got out and sat on the rocks. By the time she joined them they were halfway through some discussion or other. They seemed to be getting on well, and she felt a shiver of jealousy. "Ridiculous," she corrected herself. She had no right to be jealous of anyone, but it irked her a little that Naomi seemed to have scored a small advantage over her with the stranger. She hauled up beside them and she was gloriously aware of the slight superiority of her body, the way it detained his eye for a moment despite himself. So her power had not ebbed entirely before the magnetism of a rival. Naomi had other advantages, but not that at least. They lay then in silence for a while, soaking up the sun and the saline wind. But Faoud kept his eye warily on the sea. The police have boats and he knows about them, she thought.

"What if we were all alone here?" she said idly. "Just the three of us. It would be kind of nice, wouldn't it?"

"I was thinking that too," Faoud said. "Fine, but impossible."

"Maybe we'd hate each other by the end of the first day," Naomi said.

That's exactly how it would be, Sam thought.

"What about your parents?" he asked both of them at once.

"Mine," Naomi said, "should just go live elsewhere. This island is far too small for them. They overwhelm it. If they left I wouldn't be sorry. I'd be delirious."

He smiled with a timid puzzlement.

"Are they unpleasant?"

"They're who they are. I shouldn't say anything. Sam here, on the other hand, has nice parents. We might let them stay."

Sam decided to say nothing.

"I see," Faoud murmured. "It's always better being alone, isn't it?"

"I dream of that all the time," Naomi said.

The two women both thought about it, unknown to each other.

Sam thought of a Japanese film she had seen over the winter called *Battle Royale*. In the film, children are culled from troublesome schools and sent to an island, where they are forced to play a televised game. They are issued different weapons, and explosive collars are fitted around their necks that control them; they are then forced to kill each other one by one, until only one is left alive. The girls seem to be the more vicious and effective killers. Social bonds, amorous crushes, and platonic loves all fall by the wayside the closer death comes. Even the Japanese island looked like Hydra, lacking merely the sirens, the cannons, the ruined military bunkers in which to hide.

She rolled onto her side and let the stones burn a little into her legs. She wondered if the idea was appealing—an island as a killing zone with nowhere to run. What weapon would she choose—a scythe, a hammer, a recurve bow?

Naomi stood, flexed her arms, and without a word to either of them dropped back into the water and swam away.

Faoud turned mildly to Sam. To her, his eyes had the color of black olive tapenade.

"She could be your older sister. Does she boss you around?"

"Not really. But I wouldn't mind if she did."

He got up as well, and his downward glance was skeptical.

"You coming?"

"I'll wait."

In the end she walked alone over the skerry back to the beach. As she came through the low trees she heard their voices, amused in tone and feckless, the sexual energy unmistakable. For a moment she hung back unseen and watched them lying side by side in the harshness of the sunlight. They seemed unconcerned. They were only a few inches apart and their voices were modulated to complement each other, the ancient dance of words. She crouched and tried to hear what they were saying, but it was carried off by the wind. There was just the beating of her own heart, and the acceleration that betrayed a hatred.

THE GIRLS WALKED back, passing nobody on the way down to Palamidas. Faoud watched them diminish, with the backdrop of the sea behind them. He wondered about Naomi. She didn't seem to have an ulterior motive, apart from the question of attraction. But one had to admit that that last reason was usually sufficient to explain almost everything in the way people behaved. Two people of about the same age, finding themselves in the same place at the same moment, could enter an unexpected charm. He thought she might come back daily and that something might happen between them. As for Sam, it was a different matter. She was ravishingly beautiful but too shy. Yet she also posed a more thorny question, because she seemed to have understood his glances more perfectly than Naomi and with a greater dash of anger. They stopped, turned, and made a sign to him, and in response he raised a hand. It was a little rash on his part, but he couldn't help it.

He then walked back to the hut, poured out the bowl of water surfaced with shaving foam and made his way to the head of the path that plunged down to the wild shore from where he had come. Everything had changed. The shave, the T-shirt and the sweater, the yogurt and the strawberries, the refreshing swim by the skerry—a darkness had lifted. He went down the path a short way and then rolled a joint, lit it, and sat among the stones smoking. It was difficult to grasp how quickly his luck had changed. But didn't Omer in Istanbul always say that it did because it always must? He had a hard time believing that it was because of God. Nevertheless, the events of the previous seventy-two hours were beginning to change his mind. Such things, he now thought, could not happen by themselves—not entirely. There had to be a design behind them.

He shaded his eyes and scanned the sea. Nothing came out of it today, no little dinghies struggling against the currents, no cast-off life jackets washing up on Europa. There was no dread. His traces had been perfectly covered through his own diligence, and the police boat that came around the island once a day would find nothing. Even the vagrant himself had found a new home looking down on them, with God watching over him, and the idea of God had suddenly, to his surprise, been resurrected by the simple act of being given a box of strawberries by a woman he didn't know.

THE FOLLOWING DAY Sam and Naomi met at the Sunset in the evening. They were both in high spirits. The American girl had spent the day hiking with her brother and father, after which she had gone for a swim alone below Kamini, lost in her own moods. Naomi ordered a bottle of white wine for them to split and some souvlaki with bread and oil and a plate of cut lemons. A feast for assassins.

"So we're friends with the refugee," Sam said. "It feels weirdly normal, but I don't know why. My father says—"

But Naomi ignored the evocation of Jeffrey Haldane. In the end, she found him just as Sam had described: boring.

"Friends is a big word," she said. "But since he's from an affluent family over there it doesn't surprise me that we get on. He's educated and secular."

"Over where?"

"From Syria. But his family might be from many places."

"My father says—"

"Let's keep your father out of it, shall we? He doesn't speak a word of Greek. The people here have been talking about this secretly for months. It's an open secret. I think there have been others before Faoud—the locals helped them to get to the mainland illegally before, and maybe they're still doing it. But now the police are here."

It's a shame your father and his wife are so hostile to you. They might have helped, Sam thought to herself.

"But," Naomi went on, "I think we can do it by ourselves. I just don't know how yet."

"Put him on the ferry?" Sam said.

"There has to be more to it than that. Maybe we should go with him?"

"And if they catch him—"

"We'll be criminals too. I don't really care. I could talk my way out of that. But I'm not sure you could. I wish Jimmie and Phaine would just go away—I could invite him to my place and hide him there. It would solve everything."

Sam seemed to bristle at something. A sudden venom came into her voice.

"Why don't you suggest that they go on a trip? They could go to the Peloponnese for a week."

"Phaine would never buy it. She's paranoid about me being in the house alone. She doesn't seem to accept that one day it'll be mine whether she likes it or not. She certainly won't agree to go off for a week knowing that I suggested it. She'd suspect at once."

"Obviously you should just kill them."

Naomi laughed, and the waiters looked over, startled by the sound. Naomi admitted that it was an original idea, the only one that Sam had come up with yet. But it would be hard to explain to the relatives. Sam laughed as well, more because she was surprised at the towering absurdity of the things she was saying. Just as there was automatic writing, there seemed to be automatic speaking as well.

"Depends on who would do it," she added.

"Do you think about killing your parents, Sam?"

They made the "Death to death" toast—a popular one in Greek—and the glasses touched so hard they almost cracked.

"Not regularly, no."

"Me, yes," Naomi said. "I don't know why."

"Really?"

"More when I was younger. Now, I'd just be worried about the lawsuits."

Sam sensed an opening and became more insolent.

"You could do it to Phaine, though, couldn't you?"

86

"What makes you say that?"

Sam sipped at her glass, and her eyes positioned over the rim were filled with havoc and hurly-burly.

"I don't know. You obviously hate her."

"It's not a subtle dislike, I'll grant you that. Did your parents notice as well? I'm sorry if they did. We seem to be incapable of keeping our feuds to ourselves, or at least disguising them. It's wretched."

"I didn't ask them, to be honest."

Naomi said there was something that didn't work between them. Even just between herself and her father. They never did get along—it was something fundamental. Her real mother used to say it was because they were too alike.

"I know you're going to say he spoils me, but he only does that because deep down he hates me. I mean, he hates me in a *certain* way. It's just a visceral dislike. Parents can dislike their children, we're just brainwashed into assuming that they can't. If I was killed in a boating accident, let's say, Jimmie would be distraught but he would get over it surprisingly quickly. Trust me. He really would."

She took out a cigarette and lit it. She felt that the girl was beginning to believe her, and that both of them were beginning to be swayed into entering the orbit of a calamitous idea.

"You think there's unconditional love, but there isn't. The conditions are everything."

THE SEA HAD gone dark; the cannons inset into the plastered wall of the restaurant pointed out toward a void that the fishing boats and their lights didn't humanize. Waves dissolved violently on the rocks below. The Aegean was a dangerous and untrustworthy sea, swept by sudden malevolent moods. It was nothing like the sea of tourist legend. Hundreds of people drowned here every decade, and the sand at its bottom was nothing more than a graveyard of bones and ships. Naomi thought back to nights she had spent here over the years. The bitter lonely nights, but also more tender ones filled with narcotic parties and beautiful faces. Evenings spent sitting in this very spot during holidays when she was still at school in England, troubled and failed in all things academic until she had decided to turn it around and get a degree. The Sunset had been a crucial refuge. But the people she had once hung out with there had all dispersed to the four corners of the world. "There is only sea, there is only weather." A quote from somewhere came back into her mind, lingering there unwanted, and she wondered what it would be like to be alone in the world with all the money she needed, free of the need to work or endure a boss. Since her father had packed her off to an expensive school early on she had grown used to being separated from the rest of the human race and, she might have added, she had grown used to being without him. But being separated from the father was not the same as being fatherless. Yet she could imagine living in the house on the mountainside alone, living in the house in London alone, passing months alone in the villa in Sorano. Who would notice that she was now solitary and not encumbered with a father and a stepmother? People could not disappear from the face of the earth, naturally, but that was a different problem altogether.

"I used to have that fantasy all the time—that I was solitary and I could choose a different name every day. But the down-side—well, your parents would have to die in a nuclear war or the plague. The cons would outweigh the pros."

"Surely they would."

They ordered another bottle, but neither of them felt drunk.

"I wonder if Faoud has any family left," Sam said. "They're probably dead, if things are as bad as they say."

Another two hours, lost in rambling conversations. Above them bats swooped in parabolas above the restaurant lights, maddened by something the women couldn't understand. Yet Naomi talked on. She said she had realized that day what the problem with her life was. A person who has nothing, she said, who is living like an animal surrounded by men with shotguns—she had thought to herself, what does it have to do with me? An observer could say that everything about herself was frivolous, that she was truly born of frivolity. Frivolity had raised her and made her. All of it was worthless, or nearly worthless. You could not at first believe that your whole upbringing, the way that you lived and thought and felt, was worthless from top to bottom. It's impossible to think like that. But suddenly that afternoon she had, and there was no coming back from it. She knew it was true and it came from the way Faoud had looked at her. He saw right through her effortlessly. It was like being stabbed cleanly with a knife. No one ever looks at you like that. No one ever dares. It was as if he was looking at shit and marvelling at its complexity. Marveling that it even existed and was so unaware of itself. So she had been thinking—why was that so, and what made it so? Was it something she could change?

"I wouldn't say you were shit," Sam said.

"Nor would he, but it's not the point. It's a perception—a moment of revelation. No one has an agenda for having it. It just happens and then you can't go back. You're undone."

"Then you go forward," Sam muttered.

"Sure, forward. Whatever that means. Forward to what? If your past is shit, what do you go forward to?"

When they finished the second bottle they looked up to find the restaurant deserted. Naomi picked up the bill. They walked a little unsteadily up to the path and the tower that loomed over it and agreed to part ways for the night. They kissed and hugged, and the helter-skelter laughter of the earlier part of the evening was still inside them. They were now officially a secret society of two, with a third honorable member who didn't yet know that he belonged to it. Naomi ran a hand through the other girl's thick and tangled hair and there was a sensual agreement between them that was too reticent to break the surface of gestures. They felt superior to their surroundings when they were together, no matter who was present.

"Sleep in tomorrow," Naomi said. "Maybe we'll go for a boat ride with the savage in the afternoon."

Naomi walked slowly by herself back down to the port and looked in at the Pirate Cove to see if any pleasant scoundrels were there to buy her a drink. Finding none, she went to the ATM instead and took out three hundred euros. With a foreign card she could surpass the withdrawal limits imposed on Greeks by their own government. She ascended to the villa in the silence of the late night, the cats scattering around her as she crossed the squares. At the villa everyone was asleep, and she let herself in with a feeling of relief. She made herself tea in the kitchen and then sat on the terrace, watching clouds race across a star-rich sky, and in her head she made an inventory of everything that was in the house. There was a considerable haul of jewelry accumulated by her vain and possessive stepmother. There were the credit cards in Jimmie's single, voluminous wallet. There was cash in their bedroom that Carissa had once told her about—they kept it in the wardrobe in an unlocked box, a strikingly fearless gesture on their part. There were the paintings and the artworks, which were difficult to remove but which represented a considerable asset. There were expensive clothes, a few shirts worth thousands of euros, the wine collection, and the cigars. All of it, she thought, belonged to her anyway.

It was her inheritance, but if Jimmie ever had a sudden accident it would be taken away from her by the *salope*. There was a way to prevent that from happening. She did the math and sipped her tea until everything was clearer. It wasn't that complicated when seen from above. She was beginning to form an idea so extreme that it had nowhere to go but forward. But in the larger scheme of human suffering, it was not as extreme as she had first imagined. In the moral sense, it was simple and straightforward.

EIGHT

IN THE MORNING NAOMI WENT ALONE TO VLYCHOS AND took a room at the Four Seasons there, then walked up to Palamidas. There was no one in Episkopi, but she could feel mineral eyes watching her, the old men with their dogs and their silver stubble, which was never shaved or allowed to grow. She went up to the hut in a high sea wind to fetch Faoud, and there she explained everything to him. He was to come down with her to the resort and take the key to the room, which was paid for under her name and with her passport. No one would ask any questions there. Faoud didn't believe her, but she calmed him down. He was to just walk at her side calmly, as if he was her friend. They set off immediately. It was good to get away from the claustrophobic suspicion of the place, to walk down through the summer flowers with the sea burning their senses as they came closer to it. Faoud was lighthearted and playful. He must have slept well. He said that all night he had heard the bells strung around the necks of donkeys and goats and had dreamt of Beirut.

"I went to the American University there," he explained in his soft and careless way. "A few years ago. But I dream about it a lot. Did you go to university?"

"In London. I wasn't very good."

"I don't believe you at all. You have a nice way of speaking."

Before they arrived at the dock and the path that turned toward Molos she had divulged more about her family background. A fuller picture of her father, the houses, the stepmother, the disagreements, the miseries. She rarely spoke frankly to others about these things, but she suddenly felt quite at ease confessing everything to him, if it was even a confession. He took it mildly as she presented herself as the heroine of her family dramas. It was selfish of her, but once she had started she couldn't stop. She wanted him to know how ashamed she was of being rich. That was the important thing, though she forgot that he himself was from a wealthy family.

"I can't thank you enough," he said eventually, but not turning to her. "For everything. The food, the hotel. I don't know why you are doing it. You must be a pure person."

"That's the last thing I am."

"No, I think you are. It makes no sense otherwise. Very few people are like that—"

"I'm the most impure person, actually. But you can think what you want."

"I'd do that anyway," he said.

They came to the resort. In the shade of the hotel restaurant the Russians were at their lunches. No one noticed them making their way up to the room. The corridors were hushed in midday stupor. They went into the room, where the windows had been left open to the sea air and where it was surprisingly fresh. She locked the door behind them and, slightly stunned, they lay on the bed to recover from the hot walk. The two fans blew them dry. Then he slept and she made sandwiches from the groceries she had brought, serving them with pickles on the hotel plates. She lay back down next to him and waited for him to awaken, but he slept on. She couldn't imagine how exhausted he must be. It was a vast fatigue that was integral to persecution, to being hunted and loathed. It was curious that their proximity and their slight physical distance in a hotel room didn't feel awkward. She supposed that, speaking for herself, she had been mentally preparing for it for days and it was, she imagined, the way people evolved: they gravitated toward the most pleasing and dangerous idea.

The afternoon dragged on. She could hear the annoying commotion of people milling around the beach and the growl of motors put at sea. The waves beating on the shore were like small detonations, with a dread-filled lull between each explosion. The light declined and eventually she slept as well. When she woke there were flies circling the overhead lamp. He had moved onto his side and thrown a casual arm around her. If she had wanted to remove it, that was her moment to do so, but she left it in place. He woke in turn and they were entwined. She wanted them to be. They found each other's sleepy eyes, and there was already the certainty and the resignation. So it's just like that, she thought. She took off his shirt and then hers and they lay very peacefully as the walls turned orange from the sunset. Then she turned toward him more fully and began to kiss him. It happened slowly, and while they were sinking into their confusion, her usual train of thought, which never seemed to stop even in her sleep, finally ground to a halt and she was aware only of the onset of night and the resurrected shrilling of the cicadas from the trees nearby.

Later, as he slept on, she woke and took a shower, wrapped herself in a hotel dressing gown, and went onto the balcony. The resort was so remote that an ancient darkness suffocated it. Only the lights from the open-air restaurant and the main house glowed weakly against the cliffs. She recovered her senses and let her hair dry out. Then she stole back into the room, dressed quietly, and went down alone to the restaurant. She took a table by herself and ordered an extravagant amount of food and a glass of retsina. She ate a few skewers of kebab, downed the wine, and then asked the waitress to wrap the rest to take back to her room. While this was being done, she smoked and steadied herself. Her fingers twitched. It was excitement and aggression within herself, not fear or anxiety. She couldn't even say why she had made love to him; it had been an impulsion, and one that would repeat itself. Such acts never disturbed her. But she also liked him. His misfortunes made him charismatic, and therefore arousing. It seemed foolish that she could feel this way when she thought it over.

Meanwhile, the Russian men looked over at her and their mouths were turned up in credulous half-smiles. She avoided their gaze and went back up to the room, tapping softly at the door to let him know that she was entering. He had just woken up and was lying in the dark smoking one of her cigarettes. His face was blank, as incredulous as the Russians had seemed credulous. Without turning on the light she laid out the remnants of her restaurant meal on the bed with the sandwiches and let him eat as he wanted. She put a practical tone in her voice.

"I'm going to give you some money. With it you can leave. You can go to the mainland without a problem."

"Money?"

"It's the one thing I can give you."

"It's a tricky thing, money."

"Not in an emergency. This is life or death."

She sounded melodramatic, but melodrama was built into the moment.

"Who said it was life or death?" he said.

"You're being polite. But you know it is."

"What if it is? It's not your life and your death."

"Yes, it is."

"No, now you are just being polite. I need the money, but I don't want it."

Need, she insisted, always trumped want.

"So you'll go to an ATM?" he protested.

"No. I have another idea. An ATM wouldn't be enough. And my father would notice."

She said she had been thinking about it all night.

Jimmie and Phaine were sitting in that villa, surrounded by all their material possessions that they never used. It was a reprehensible—no, a vile—thing, the way they could do that while people like him were starving five miles away. She had been living with her outrage—at home, through her work—for some time but without being able to resolve it, increasingly tainted by her family's privilege. But now she could do her part to turn the tables on them. It would be the sweetness of a necessary treason. Did he understand? But treason was not an act he could have ever contemplated relative to his own people. Don't trust her, he thought. But she went on: there was nothing to it. He could rob the house while they were asleep.

"Would you do it?" she went on. "Would you do it if you knew no harm would come to them and that everything you took was insured?"

"I can't say."

"Think it over. It's a victimless petty crime. It's nothing, nothing at all. You wouldn't even need to break and enter."

The maid could leave the door open for him and Naomi would tell her to cooperate. He could take whatever he found there, anything he wanted. He could leave within thirty minutes with enough money to take him anywhere in Europe he needed to go. Enough to live on for years if he was careful. It was his escape door, his deliverance.

"Listen to me," she insisted.

"I'm not going to listen to you. I'll get caught. Then I suppose you'll have another plan?"

"You won't get caught. You're invisible—you're not in the records. They could never catch you. You can't catch a person who doesn't exist."

She explained more of her idea. She hurried her own sentences until they began to fall over each other. It was nonsense, but it was not entirely nonsense. Gradually, he listened more tolerantly and her logic began to appeal to him. He could ask for money up front and be on his way, but he was sure it wouldn't be very much. It would be money honestly come by, but it wouldn't be enough to save him. It wouldn't be enough to launch him into a new life. She was right: it had to be more than what she could take out of an ATM machine. She had it all mapped out, down to the last details. He could slip away to Metochi and take her father's car and drive out of the country through the seaports to Italy. On those sea routes there was virtually no passport control, since Italy was a fellow Schengen country. If he went north by himself he would run up against the Macedonian border, the worst of borders to try and breach without papers. Driving an expensive car, on the other hand, no one would ask him questions on the ferries from Patras. He would slip through invisibly. Since Jimmie rarely checked on his car it would be probably forty-eight hours before her father realized that it had been taken, and by then Faoud would be out of the country. He could even sell the car on the other side; all the papers were stored inside it. It was easy to sell cars illegally in southern Italy anyway. The vehicle itself was worth many thousands. Or he could keep it and make his own way to wherever he wanted to go. His options would be numerous. Even the tickets for the car ferry were prepaid and in the glove compartment. Her father erred on the side of carefree trust when it came to such things. It was a free passage with only minor risks, easy when compared to anything else he would have to do.

"In other words," he objected almost at once, "I'd be a thief. A thief dependent on another man's daughter."

But she held her own. "My father has stolen everything he owns. He's a master thief. You would be stealing from a thief, and everything is insured. He'll get a brand-new car out of it and he won't mind at all. You'll just have to change the car number plates. You can do that in Italy for a bribe. That's the easy part."

"You're hiring me as a burglar," he smiled. "But you don't get to keep the profits."

"I don't want any of his filthy money. I'd rather redistribute it. He'll never know it was me either—I'll be the perfect actress."

"No one can be that. Not to your own father."

"I can. I know exactly what to do. He won't think anything that bad of me. It'll just be a burglary like any other. The houses of the rich people here are broken into all the time. It's not unusual. The police will hardly shrug, trust me." She was suddenly vehement. "You'd be smart to accept this, Faoud. I'm giving you a new life. It's as simple as that."

He went over it in his mind. He didn't know the details of these routes as well as she did, but he began to feel that she had worked it out well enough. The easiest ways out of the country were the cruise lines to Italy; that he had heard already. Everything would depend on speed and luck. With those two things he could bring it off and no one would be the worse. It would be a way of escaping peacefully and letting life flow on uninterrupted. When he looked at it this way he felt compelled to accept the premise.

"I'll think about it," he said, to keep her at bay. "I'll think about it tonight."

"There's not a lot to think about."

"I disagree. But I'll know tomorrow."

"Why don't you tell me now? It would be easier if you did. But if you can't, it's all right. I'll call you tomorrow and we can talk about it."

"Don't have any bad dreams," he said as she prepared to leave at last. "I don't want you having any bad dreams because of me."

She walked back alone to Hydra. On the path the shadows under the olive trees cast by the moon were so dark that she lost the threads of her thoughts as she walked through them. The old people drinking ouzo in their gardens, secretive as smugglers. The island gardens with their hum of moths. They always looked up: a stranger walking by. Harmless, but a stranger all the same. She thought about Faoud. She knew that he would accept her proposition and go along with it, and by the time she reached Hydra she felt elated that she had managed to persuade him. She wondered how long it had been since he had been with a woman. Weeks, maybe months. One could never tell, but it was possible that it had been even longer.

At the port she went for a drink alone and she put in her earphones and listened to some *rebetiko* music to seal herself off. She drank Aperol Spritzers with bowls of salted peanuts, since it was her time-honored way of obtaining simple bliss. She thought about Sam asleep in her white room with the icons and the iron bed. What did she want with this appealingly impressionable girl? Naomi wasn't sure herself. It was just an attraction, as her feeling toward Faoud was an attraction. It was a matter of gravity. It was her influence over them that was attractive too, their reluctant malleability. She couldn't understand why people were like that.

When she got home her father was still up smoking his before-bed cigar with a large cup of herbal tea, a soporific that she suspected Carissa knew how to prepare with a dab of numbing hemlock. He was alone on the terrace, listening to Dean Martin with his feet up in his leather slippers. She went out to kiss him goodnight, and he took her hand for a moment as she stood next to him, asked her if she wanted to come to an art party the following night. It would do them both good, would it not?

"I don't think so, Daddy. I can't take any more of those, honestly. Why don't we have dinner at Manolis? Just like old times."

"All right," he said mildly, too weary to disagree about anything now. "I can't stand Manolis, but I'll do it for you. It's time we had a tête-à-tête, you and I. Without Funny, I mean."

"I'd like that too, Daddy. Really I would."

Jimmie then put down his cigar and expelled the last of the smoke. His voice was slightly strained.

"Did you see the Haldanes today?"

She shook her head and let go of his hand.

"I'll see them tomorrow," she said.

"Then where have you been all day? Funny says you're smuggling drugs. I said it seemed improbable—but only mildly so."

"I went for a long swim in a beautiful place."

"I see. But that doesn't really mean anything, does it?"

They smiled, and the long-standing ice suddenly broke between them.

"No, Daddy. It doesn't. But you know what I mean."

"I suppose I do. I'm fond of long swims myself. It's why I have a house here, after all."

She leaned down to plant a kiss on his pugnacious forehead. He was smelling more and more of perfume, she had noticed. Was there something wrong?

"It keeps you fit," she said.

A dry sadness lasted for the rest of the conscious part of the night. She called Sam and told her everything that had happened at the hotel, including the sexual part, though she offered no details. The American girl went quiet for a while. Then Naomi told her what she had told Faoud. She asked if Sam would be willing to help them.

"It's for a good cause," she said several times.

But Sam was surly. "That sounds incredibly stupid."

"It's not stupid at all."

"Stupid and dangerous. Don't do it, don't even think about it."

But Naomi was not at the stage where anything could be discussed, let alone refuted.

"I'm asking you," she said impatiently. "Just don't say no. I know there's nothing in it for you—but it'll be a blow for justice. There's no way you can refuse to do this for him. You'll feel like a criminal if you don't."

"I feel like one now. Is that what you wanted? I think it is."

NINE

EIGHTEEN HOURS LATER JIMMIE DRESSED IN FRONT OF his full-length mirror—cream suit, buttonhole, pink plaid Borelli shirt—and set off alone for the house of Spiro Mistakidis, a wealthy art dealer who also had his summer house on the hillsides above the port. Phaine had gone to dinner with other friends and he was free for a few hours. Not free enough, and not for enough hours, but sufficiently free to flirt a little and talk with his old male friends without reserve. The bare hills rising up into a tender dusk always filled him with a vague yearning and a sadness for times past. He had a well-rehearsed line of Homer at hand to capture it, one that had rolled inside his mind for years, Telemachus pining for Ithaca: "Goat, not stallion land, but it means the world to me."

He picked his way down the steps with his rosewood cane and stopped from time to time to listen to the starlings and take in the twilit white walls. He had never ceased loving this little island and was proud of his loyalty to it. But times were changing. In reality, he was already thinking of selling the house and moving its contents to the Italian one. It was the social life here that was so strenuous. At the Mistakidis house that night there were fifty people and he knew almost all of them. One had to navigate among them, keeping up the banter, and the small amount of freedom he had carved out went nowhere but to hours of such banter. He was introduced to some Turkish collectors and then stood on a terrace in the full moonlight with a silly drink in one hand while torrents of absurd words flowed uncontrollably out of his mouth. Who knew how. Dinner with his daughter proved to be a more attractive proposition, especially as he got to Manolis early and enjoyed a glass of wine by himself, the cane resting against his legs and his shirt unbuttoned. The heat and babble had sapped him, but he revived. Things were rather swell in the larger scheme of things; he had made a few million that year with sales of art pieces to Moscow and Taipei, and with his rainbow of shares. It was the family problems that multiplied and became intractable.

When Naomi arrived she was prim with him, which he liked. They ordered a bottle of white and some *skorpina* fish. How many of their problems, he thought, could have been resolved instantly by just having dinner together at Manolis? He had been a bit of a stubborn fool about it, and now it was almost too late.

"You look tremendous," he said as soon as she sat down, and he meant it. "Those long swims have been doing you good. Your color has come back."

She said she was feeling better the last few days. The heat agreed with her, made her less grumpy.

"Ah," he said, raising his eyebrows and glancing down into the cold wine settled into his glass. "It's always good to feel less grumpy."

"I've been exploring the far side of the island," she went on. "You remember how we used to go there with the Saplamideses? Maybe I'm feeling nostalgic."

"Yes, your mother loved it there."

"I found a life jacket there a few days ago. What do you suppose it means? I know what everyone is saying."

He had the feeling—it teased at him like a draft from a badly closed door—that she was testing him in some way. She wanted to sound out his morality about one of the dark issues of the day. It was childish, but if she wanted to do that he wasn't willing to back down.

"You think they're reaching even here now?" he said. "Let's say they are. I would say one would have to contact the police and let them deal with it. Of course, you can't let people drown—"

"I didn't see anyone," she added slowly. "But I wanted to know what you thought about it. I mean, do you think we have an obligation to take them in—as Christians?"

"I'm not exactly a Christian, Naomi. And you're an atheist. There are no obligations one way or the other."

"So you'd deport them back to Turkey?"

"I was under the impression that they had a safe haven there. They're fed, clothed, housed. No one is threatening their lives. Apparently they have other reasons for throwing themselves into the sea. They seem to like what we have. But what do we have that they like, do you think?"

"I don't think it's that at all. It's just survival."

"No, it's not survival. You don't have to go to Sweden to survive. They are surviving in Turkey, as I just said."

"Barely."

"Well, that's the Turks for you. It's funny how their fellow Muslims are quite happy to treat them like cockroaches or close their borders altogether. That's what they do; but we have to be

Christians, whatever that means. I hear Frau Merkel is a devout Christian too. Personally—"

"There's nothing personal about it," Naomi protested.

"Maybe not, but personally I think we're not being told what is really happening. The whole thing is melodrama. It's a deliberate orchestration, and we're the dumb fall guys on the receiving end of it. You have to wonder whether Europeans are just too stupid to survive now. We don't seem to understand obvious things that are staring us in the face."

"Then what is staring us in the face?"

"They're going under like the *Titanic*. They're going under and they're going to drag us down with them. That's all there is to it. Or else it's something deeper. The traffickers sending them here have their reasons, don't you think?—they don't just arrive, as the media is trying to tell us."

"Then what are the reasons? I want to know what you think."

Jimmie leaned back a little and his whole body shifted in an awkward way as his anger came and went and then returned. So they had to disagree, they had to fight. Was that it?

"I think the issues are obvious," he blustered on. "If we keep them out it destroys them; if we let them in it destroys us. Do we have the stomach for that dilemma?"

"It's not that at all. They're fleeing from horror. You're dehumanizing them by thinking like that. You have no idea what's going through their heads. It's just tabloid boilerplate."

He said it didn't matter what was going through their heads. She didn't know what was going through their heads either. She didn't speak Arabic. Had she lived in an Arab country? He thought not. She knew nothing about them, nothing at all. Less than nothing, she was just romanticizing it. He said that people couldn't run away from themselves. They brought everything with them, whether they knew it or liked it or not. Then you had to deal with that. But she didn't even know what it was—she hadn't thought about it at all. She wanted to be a Samaritan: the easiest job in the world, and perfect for the useless European middle classes.

"I'm not saying you're useless, of course. I'm saying you don't know anything about the Arabs. Nor do I. But my guard is up."

"For God's sake—"

"They're coming from a safe haven," he retorted. "So it's their choice. It's blackmail, and they know it at least. It's a shame you don't."

"They're helpless and you know it—*we* know it."

"Are they?"

Then he poured her another glass and relaxed a little, as if his main point had been made and no other was now necessary.

He said, "Why—have you met any here?"

"Don't be silly."

"Any ten-year-olds wandering the shore?"

Repulsive, she thought.

The sneering certainty coiled around a grain of truth. But she had to give way a little and deflate the animosity between them, because she had only wanted to confirm that he merited his imminent loss of property.

"You'll change your tune," he was saying as a wind-down, "when they start harassing you on the street. What are German women saying now? Confusion. They're hanging from their own gallows."

"Daddy, if you met one I'd like to think you'd give them everything you own, just to prove me wrong. Would you?"

He laughed. "Yes, I likely would. Just to keep you happy. But

I'd probably ask for it back the next day. Reason always gets the better of me for some reason. Reason or neurosis."

"Then I'm just as neurotic as you."

"We live in a culture, Nobbins, where neurosis is all there is. There's no escaping it anywhere."

After dessert they reminisced about her mother. Naomi had long suspected that he had begun to see Phaine while her mother was dying of cancer. He hadn't waited. He had been a bit of a playboy back in the day. There was a streak of Porfirio Rubirosa in him. "Sports, girls, adventures, celebrities, these were the only things that interested me," as that playboy used to say. "In short, life." That was life for Jimmie, too. The Charles Krafft "Disasterware" he used to collect was just a pastime to make money. He had one of Krafft's ceramic delft hand grenades and a pottery handgun with two bluebirds painted on the grip that he kept by his bedside as a joke.

They walked home arm in arm. They dawdled their way through a few late-night bars. At the villa, Carissa opened the door and informed them that Phaine had come back earlier and was already in bed reading. Jimmie asked Carissa if they might have a herbal tea served in their bedroom to send them off to sleep. The maid replied she could make them something Greek her mother used to give her. It usually worked. "That sounds suitably mysterious and potent," Jimmie said, and turned to go up to his wife, leaving the two young women alone in the salon.

They went into the kitchen and Carissa set about making the infusion from the packets of plants and herbs that she had bought from the old woman. It included a tiny pinch of the hemlock as well as some spearmint and valerian. While the water boiled they talked aimlessly. Carissa had spent some of her childhood in the Mani, from where she had retained some curious lore. Her grandmother there used to tell her that the woods of the mountains were still haunted by ex-communicated pagan spirits that the villagers called *daimonia*. When her grandmother was a small girl her own grandmother used to tell her that she saw the god Pan at crossroads in the deep forest. The gods had lived on without anyone knowing. One could become spellbound by these pagan spirits, possessed and enchanted.

The infusion had turned a pale golden green. For a moment Naomi hesitated, but then she abandoned her precautions and began to relate her plan for the robbery. She laid it out calmly and slowly, so that she would appear convincingly ethical and coolheaded, and she was sure that the maid would sympathize. Carissa for her part stood with her arms folded and listened intently until she understood what was being asked of her.

"I can't do it without you," Naomi said. "Nothing will happen to you afterward—things will just go on as before." All Carissa had to do was serve Jimmie and Phaine some herbal tea, then leave the front door unlocked and go to bed. She then had to stay in her room and go to sleep as if nothing had happened. If she heard a few noises she would do nothing, just keep on sleeping. They might ask why the door was unlocked, but Naomi would think of something. She even wondered if Carissa could go up afterward and lock it again. She didn't know yet. For herself, she would sleep at the Haldanes' that night.

"This is all to help some migrant?" the maid said.

"I'd help you too if I could. I think you know that perfectly well. I've never held anything back from you—you know I help you whenever I can."

"Yes, but you know me. You've known me for years. Now you're doing this for a stranger?"

"I can't explain it, but he isn't a stranger to me. I feel like he's my responsibility. I know you probably won't understand that."

Carissa flared up for a moment.

"You're right, I don't. It's the stupidest thing I've ever heard. What if your father finds out? You're done for."

"I know."

"No, you're really done for. He'll disown you."

"Carissa, it's not a rational thing. I don't care that it's not rational. Don't you see? It's an emotional thing. Do I really have to explain it on my hands and knees?"

"Well, it might make it sound less crazy!"

"No, it would still sound crazy. I want to do it *because* it's crazy."

"And to hell with the rest of us?"

"Maybe I could give you something for helping, just in case." She paused, not quite sure if bribery was the way to go. But she realized it was inevitable. "You know what I mean. Don't be embarrassed. I'd be happy to and I think it's only fair. What about five thousand euros?"

"Twenty."

"You've thought it through, haven't you? All right, fifteen."

Carissa hesitated for a moment, then said, "I'll do it if that's all I have to do. Are you sure?"

"Very sure."

"Is he safe, this man?"

"Very safe. He didn't want to do it at all. I think a part of him still doesn't want to do it."

"I suppose that's a good sign."

She prepared the tea tray with some lemon biscuits, and when it was done they embraced. Carissa went up into the gloom of the first-floor landing and set down the tray to knock on the master-bedroom door. Phaine was already asleep on her side, and Jimmie was reading in bed in his silk pajamas. When she set the tray down beside him he gave her a merry eye and told her that she could go to bed now. She went back down to the kitchen and found that Naomi had disappeared.

Alone as she always was at night, she poured herself a brandy shot in the salon and went out onto the terrace to think about Naomi's proposition. Fifteen thousand euros was a lot of money and it was, if she was honest with herself, too much to turn down for something so simple as unlocking a door. She didn't want to harm the Codringtons fatally, but there was undeniably a question of justice in taking some of their wealth and passing it on to a helpless itinerant. Naomi had told her that it would be a few nights from now, because Jimmie and Phaine would be going to a cocktail party earlier in the evening and would in all probability come home semi-drunk and sleepy. A dose of her homemade herbal tea and they would sleep through the whole thing without a whimper. She considered how likely this was. Jimmie often woke up because of his aging bladder, but he stumbled around in the bathroom half asleep and rarely, if ever, came downstairs. She would make the tea strong enough—a little stronger than usual—and make sure of it and then go to her room and lock the door until the following morning. Fifteen thousand euros was enough to buy a whole new wardrobe or pay some of her mother's medical bills, or both. And if Jimmie had paid her fairly from the beginning she would not have had to do it.

She poured herself a second shot of brandy and felt the bitterness of the alcohol reaching down into her stomach. They were filthy Scrooges, the pair of them, except when it came to their social equals, and then, of course, their generosity flowered. But the maid never saw the genuine side of it. All she saw was the hypocrisy and the frugality behind the scenes, a frugality of which she was both executor and victim. You brought it on yourselves, she thought vindictively, and she was certain that she and Naomi had understood the matter simultaneously, without disagreement. Her father in any case had always told her to distrust and hold to account the capitalist class—but how much better it was to rob them on the sly.

THE
NIGHT JOURNEY

TEN

THE THREE DAYS FAOUD SPENT HIDING IN THE HOTEL
room passed in a blur of room service, TV, and thoughts
avoided. But while he waited that last night, the evening felt
long and tedious and the chatter from the hotel restaurant
came and went like music on a radio being turned up and then
turned down. By eleven it was quiet again. He let himself out
of the room, leaving the key in the door, and went unnoticed
up to the coastal path according to Naomi's instructions. A lop-
sided moon lit the first bend where he waited. An hour passed
and still Naomi had not come, though she had promised to
meet him there. He sat on a wall and considered the possibility
that it might be a trap after all. He didn't know what he would
do if it was. Run down to the sea and throw himself into it? It
would be an insalubrious drama with which to end a life that
had once been so promising. In the end he was forced to trust
her, if only because there was no one else to trust. It was said
that a friend with an understanding heart is worth no less than
a sister. At twelve-thirty, however, she appeared. She had told
him to follow her at a fair distance; they were not to talk or greet
each other. She was dressed in black, and as soon as she saw
him, she turned and began to walk back the way she had come.
He followed her, doing as he had been told.

It was a long walk. The world of the Greeks was something

new: domestic and peaceful, self-regulating. It was made fresh, not degraded, by its great age. So there were no cars and motorbikes on this island. Everything was on foot. There were slivers of land in the sea, single lights. After an hour they passed above the Sunset, where a few couples lingered at the tables. The path then curved downward into the port and into the thickets of luxury yachts and cafe terraces, but the people had dispersed. It was a weeknight and the bars had closed.

They went through the village and began to climb up the steps. Naomi turned once and, with a single motion of the hand, encouraged him. He knew that she was leading him to her father's house, and he was curious as to what kind of place it was. He saw that it stood at the very top of the steps, the last house before the wilderness took over, and that around it lay only one other house, a villa almost of the same size and with a similar white wall surrounding it. The girl came to the somber wood door of her own house and rested there for a moment. There were two lamps hung on either side of the door, but above the wall the house was dark. She then came back down the steps, and soon they were face-to-face in the glare of the lamps and she put a finger in front of her lips. She whispered close to his ear a "Good luck" and kissed his cheek, and then looked back up at the door, which was not open. "Move," she said then, "don't look back." As she did this, she slipped something into his hand. It was small change for a ticket to Metochi for the following morning and a set of car keys. He had wanted to say something, but before he could she moved off, skipping down the steps as if she was going back to the port to look for a nightcap. How much better it would be if he could just go with her.

Instead, he loped up to the door and stood before it, not

knowing who would open it. In seconds, Naomi disappeared, the door clicked open, and Carissa peered out. She was young, about twenty-five to his eye. She seemed suddenly taken aback by his own appearance. She stepped away from the door and let him in, then closed it soundlessly behind him.

On the ground floor of the villa there was only one light on. It was in the main room, and it was turned low. She made him take off his sandals and they walked barefoot into the salon, over the rugs and under the static chandelier. There was a large bag open on the floor and she motioned to it; it was for him to fill. She mimed her way through a strange explanation. She had already piled certain things in the bag, he saw. They were things that she must have removed from the bedroom upstairs. Money, documents, and a ring of keys for the house in Italy that Naomi had invited him to use. The money was the most reassuring. It would save him time and it would save him making a blunder upstairs. Then she held up Jimmie Codrington's passport, which she laid inside the bag, and a small slip of paper upon which were written the PIN numbers for Jimmie's credit cards.

It took her a minute to do all this, and then she looked at him cautiously and backed away toward the stairs that led down to her room. When he was alone, he went quickly around the room, scanning it for objects that were small enough to take with him. There were some silver knives and spoons that he pocketed, a ceremonial dagger from the War of Independence that might sell for something. But he felt unclean taking such things. They were better left in their place, talismans he didn't understand and that would bring him bad luck. Theft was bad enough. He closed the bag and listened. The maid had probably gone directly to sleep as promised. He straightened himself and lifted the bag onto his shoulder, even though it didn't contain much.

As he did so he heard a noise at the top of the stairs leading directly down to him. He was only two or three strides from the door, but it was already too late. The voice had boomed down from the stairs, in Greek, words he didn't understand, and the feet were descending, heavily but slowly, the fear in them all too evident. Jimmie had woken up from a drunken sleep when he heard a few noises coming from the ground floor. Because fear came naturally to him, he reached out for the ceramic pistol and hand grenade and went to the stairs in his pajamas. He was not prepared for anything, but confusion and fear and rage had suddenly overwhelmed him, and he held the ceramic pistol as if it might mean something in the world of real burglars and thieves. All he could see without his glasses was a man holding a bag making for the front door.

ELEVEN

AFTER LEAVING FAOUD AT THE DOOR, NAOMI ARRIVED at the Haldanes'. Sam was waiting for her on the porch with an oil lamp and a pot of mint tea. She had grown increasingly anxious as the hours passed, and when she finally saw Naomi she picked up the lamp, scattering little rectangles of light around her, and came to the steps to light them. Here by Vlychos it was more blustery and the darkness of the path was total.

"What happened?" the American girl hissed at her as Naomi came up the steps.

"Nothing. Let's go inside."

"I told my parents you were going to spend the night. I'll tell them you got here an hour ago. They're all asleep anyway."

They went up to the porch and lay down together on the long sofa with its numerous cotton cushions. The tea was still hot and the mint leaves floated on its surface. Naomi related everything that had happened, and she seemed, Sam thought, very pleased with herself. How could it have gone so smoothly? Of course, Sam pointed out, Naomi didn't know that Faoud had done as she'd asked.

"No, but if anything had gone wrong I would've had a call from Jimmie, that's for sure. So nothing went wrong. I'll stay up another hour just in case."

They lay side by side listening to the sea, wondering in different ways if this alibi would hold if it came to a crunch. Naomi thought it would; Sam was doubtful, though she would stick to their story.

"It's incredible to think—" she began.

"That he's in the house," Naomi finished for her.

"You don't want to go find him afterward?"

"How would I find him anyway? He would have to find me, and he won't. If he's got any sense he won't."

"Maybe you should go back to London. It'll be so boring here after it gets out. Everyone'll be talking about it for weeks. I don't think I'll be able to stand it myself."

Naomi turned over and brushed the girl's cheek with the back of her hand.

"I must say, I think you've been incredibly courageous to throw your lot in with me on this thing. Thank you. It was a brave and generous thing to do, to keep a secret."

"Was it?"

"Yes. For once good has been done without anyone being hurt."

Sam let this sophistry penetrate her and then sink as deep as it could go. But in the end she didn't believe in the innate weight of Naomi's sentence. There was a conflation of falsities within it. A robbery was still a harm, people were still damaged by it. Why was Naomi so blithe about it? She talked about it as if it were nothing but a chess game that could be played over and over with no consequences. She seemed to be indifferent to obvious consequences and to equally obvious motives that were not acknowledged.

When Naomi woke it was still dark. No one had called her. She lay awake for a while, mesmerized by the jangling wind chimes, such a crassly Californian sound in that Greek habitat. Afterward she slept longer. She had a dream that she was flying over the desert observing a long and disorganized caravan below her. It was night, but the far horizons were lit up as if by artillery. It was seven when Sam woke her, and she saw at once a coffeepot and Greek pastries and a bowl filled with sugar cubes. The family were still not around.

"They went into town for coffee," Sam said simply, and lay back down next to her. "I told them you were here all night."

"That's good."

"Did you sleep all right?"

"Yes—but I thought I was somewhere else."

"I get that all the time."

Sam poured the coffee and they shared a single cup, taking turns to sip, relishing the intimacy. The sea had turned into a solar mirror. The olive trees around the house burned with their eternal gray sheen. So what world, she thought, had she returned to from the desert? Across that same sea Faoud had sailed an hour earlier and now he was out of sight, vanished forever. She remembered Sam's question from the night before— did she want to go and find him?—and she wondered if she had answered it honestly. She had not. She missed him already, but perhaps it was the certainty that their paths were bound and never to cross a second time. They had better not, she thought grimly. Then they attacked the pastries. Neither had eaten in twelve hours or more. They wondered if they should go swimming or voyaging among the isles. Anything to get away from their families. In the event, however, they abandoned the idea of a boat and walked instead up to the old Ghika house above Kamini. It was where the Athenian artist had entertained Lawrence Durrell and Henry Miller in the 1940s, but the sprawling villa had burned down a few years later. According to island rumor it had been torched by a disgruntled servant. The ruins with their grand archways and solitary pillars had decayed quite a bit since her last visit, when she was twenty. They climbed over the ramshackle fence and wandered through the cavernous rooms. Coolly detached from the world outside, they rolled a joint from the remains of their original stash and smoked in the last fresh hour of the day. It was just after twelve by the time they returned to the house.

The Haldanes were at an early lunch on the porch, and Amy made them sit and eat the moussaka the maid had prepared. It was the very dish Jimmie had urged to have made for them. They must have had a stunned and glowing look on their faces, because Christopher looked at them slyly. Jeffrey took off his glasses, though it was not clear why he was wearing them, and pulled out a chair for Naomi.

"Your phone's been ringing for the last ten minutes," he said, giving it to her. She took it and glanced down at the nine calls from the same number. It was Carissa.

"Oh?"

"We were going to answer, but Amy said it would be rude. If it's urgent, don't mind us—go ahead and call back."

Naomi's face was suddenly hot, and she stood politely and said, "I'll just go down there so I don't bother you."

She strode trembling into the lethally exposing sunlight and made her way about fifty yards from the house so they would not hear. Carissa picked up at once. Her voice was broken and faint, and she seemed to be gasping. It was early in the afternoon, and the maid had surely been up since six or seven. Nothing could have happened during those intervening hours, and when Carissa told her that things had not gone according to plan she was at a loss to believe it. Though stunned, she refused to give in to the emotion. But it was not what she had expected to feel anyway. It was more like nothingness. She went back up to the Haldanes' with an excuse.

"I'm sorry," she said, "the maid has a problem with the house and I have to go up there right away. You know how these things are."

"I'll go with you," Sam said at once.

"I don't think that'll be necessary. I can't see how either of us can really help her. She probably just wants money and Jimmie and Phaine are out somewhere."

It was remarkable how easily her coolness came to her.

But she had to avert her eyes from the panic in Sam's face. The girl grew adamant. If Naomi grew adamant in turn, it would look suspicious; she had to be offhand and relaxed. Unfortunately, Sam had already risen, and her decision to go with Naomi produced a flicker of alarm between the parents, who didn't understand why she needed to do it.

"Is there a problem?" Amy asked.

"No," Naomi said, "really, don't worry. This happens all the time with our maid. Sam, you really don't have to come."

"I'm coming. Mom, don't worry about it, I'll be right back."

"Why don't you call when you get there?" her mother said.

They set off in a bad mood. Naomi explained everything in short, exhausted sentences. It was difficult to believe. Carissa had found the bodies in the morning and that was all. It had gone wrong, she didn't know how or why, and they couldn't change it now.

"What went wrong, then?" Sam kept asking. She was too numb to think of anything else to say.

"Or she's lying," Naomi said in confusion.

At the villa's outer door they stopped for a moment and caught their breath. Naomi stared around her with a wild emptiness, as if she had lost her bearings and her sense. Sweat dripped off her knuckles and made little dark spots around her feet. She opened the door with her own key, turning to give Sam a curious look, and they went inside.

She called softly for the maid. Even in the hall it was clear that the interior was unusually dark and that the blinds of the terrace windows had been drawn down to the floor. There was a vague sense of disorder that their eyes couldn't yet see. The salon was alive with flies, and there the maid was sitting alone on one of Jimmie's British Raj horsehair armchairs with the phone in one hand and her eyes turned silently toward the hall and the two girls. The bodies lay where they had fallen during the night, composed and peaceful, and the flies swarmed around them and around the furniture, which perhaps would never be used again. The most curious thing, however, was that Carissa was not hysterical; she merely appeared surprised to see the American girl, as if that was the more significant calamity.

TWELVE

A FEW YOUNG TOURISTS WERE ALREADY AT THE PORT when Faoud arrived there at five in the morning. One of the cafes was slowly opening for them. He ordered a coffee and sat inconspicuously among the crowd until the darkness began to break up across the sea and the ferry gates opened. It was a wait of an hour. During that time he listened to the chatter of the travelers while watching the quay for police. Most of the former, as far as he could gather, were headed for the airport in Athens. He listened, but his mind was in pieces and the disassembled fragments whirled around according to the laws of disintegration. His father had always warned him to keep to himself and not to talk to people too offhandedly, and now more than ever, it seemed like good advice, which suggested that his father knew the ways of the world better than Faoud had realized. He kept to himself and counted down the minutes while trying to forget the event that had just happened, ten or fifteen seconds of violence that he had never foreseen and which had happened so unexpectedly that when it was finished all he was able to do was close the door and run.

So the crisis had come. But it had left him cold and lethargically calm. The terror will come later, he thought. He recalled a few words from the sura of Al-Isra, though he couldn't say why they mattered to him or why he remembered them now. They were about the journey that the Prophet had taken from the Kaba after he had fallen asleep there—the journey to Jerusalem, where he had prayed with the other prophets and glimpsed the Lotus of the Utmost Boundary. It was the moment when the Prophet had received the tenets of the faith, if he had not misunderstood it. It was the Angel Gabriel who had taken him to Jerusalem and then back to Mecca, after lifting him beyond space and time. And he saw the Garden of Abode as well, encircling the Lotus.

At six-thirty the small boat from Metochi arrived. Only he got on it. When they pulled out from Hydra, he turned once and looked behind him at the other passengers on the quay who were waiting for the larger Athens ferry. But all was normal and no one, apparently, had noticed him. Thus it was both fate and Allah's will, and about those it was absurd to have an opinion.

AT METOCHI INLETS and coves appeared half-lit in the first sun; there were fields of reeds with the water luminous around them. Three people waited at the jetty, lone figures in seemingly open countryside. He came down the gangplank onto the quay and saw at once that there was no security in such a lonely place and that the paid parking lot lay only a short walk from the boat. He went into it without hurrying or drawing attention to himself and went down the rows of cars until he had found the navy-blue Peugeot with a sunscreen drawn across its rear window. The ticket touts for the Hydra boats were not even open yet and the fields echoed with collared doves. A perfect blue sky.

He pressed the button on the key ring to open the doors and the car's lights flashed and the locks slid open with a quiet shuffle. He opened a back door and threw in the bag, then thought better of it and removed it to the trunk, which was almost empty except for a toolkit and the spare tire.

In the confusion his temples burned, his mouth had gone dry and sticky, and yet he had to resist the hysteria and assert the calm that his elders had always admired in him even as a boy. He took a while to compose himself, therefore, and to look through the glove compartment. The car was not yet hot, but even so, his fingers slipped in their own sweat. There were road maps, the Patras ferry ticket for two persons and the car. There was a bound notebook with Jimmie's emergency details printed out on a single sheet inserted into the fly. He would read it later. There was also the parking coupon, which was prepaid.

He opened the map first and looked at the roads flung across Greece. He found Patras and saw that once he got to the isthmus the road from Corinth was more or less direct. He measured it: three or four hours, maybe. He had to go onward, second by second, minute by minute. He pushed his panicked thoughts to the side of his mind and forced himself to think about the distances again: how long would it take? One could never tell from a map, and he intended to drive as slowly as he could. No stops by the highway police, no exuberance. The road from Metochi went up to Ermioni and from there inland up to Epidavros. A road through sleepy villages, and at Nea Epidavros it touched the sea again. It was not a difficult route.

He drove along the sea road to Thermisia. It was very different from Hydra. Few tavernas, only the farmhouses and their quiet orchards. By the road stood red signs for a thing called Silk Oil. He went past the arrows for Ermioni and saw for a moment that marine village's flat-roofed houses scattered across a hill. Soon thereafter the road rose steeply, and the sea was below him when he stopped to recover his senses and to reclaim his calm among fragrant macquis and the tinkling of goat bells in the ravines. It was a terraced land filled with crooked trees and a subtle sense of relation to a sea that was just out of sight. From under the trees came a menacing drone of bees. Farther on the land became drier and more vast. After only an hour the horror which he had been unexpectedly sucked into was no longer fresh. On this ever-curling road it suddenly seemed more distant than it actually was, and a numbing absence of fear had returned.

An hour and a half after leaving Metochi the road swung over another sea, but so high up that he had to look down at it from afar. The signs in English said Nea Epidavros and he could see it below as well, an arc of red tiles and white around a bay. The sun was high enough to enfold the land by the time he reached a mountainside bar called Stork, whose wide terraces overlooked the same town and the forested peninsulas around it. Inside it was sleek and hip; a place for the local well-heeled. He took an outside table and ordered coffee and orange juice, and waited for something inside himself to catch up with the luminosity around him. As he sipped his orange juice, two priests, black as ravens in tall hats, came and sat a table away from him. Groomed and suave men with dandy beards. Faoud glanced away from them, but they noticed him and appeared disdainful. Little birds began to swarm around them.

IMPROBABLE THOUGH IT seemed, he finally felt that he had entered the European bloodstream; along its arteries and veins he could now move like any other corpuscle. Surely, then, his passage had been preordained. It had been made possible by a higher power to whom thanks were owed. As he sucked on his straw, however, the nightmare of the previous night came back to him and he had to keep his hands in place on the table. "It wasn't my fault," he kept repeating to himself under his breath. It had been forced upon him by the mad old man. The man whom Naomi had described several times as a fascist. Well, a fascist then. It mattered less if he was a fascist.

The sophistry didn't work, but it would tide him over until some kind of atonement and shock could take over, and indeed it was the atonement he dreaded, rather than the coming shock.

THE OFFICE OF the ferry company in Patras was empty, and the boats were equally so; it was a matter of minutes to book a berth on the next sailing at 5 p.m. It was a sixteen-hour voyage to Brindisi on the Grimaldi line arriving at nine the following morning, and naturally the Codringtons had booked a first-class private cabin. Was his wife joining him on this leg? No, she was indisposed. No other questions were asked; he was given his tickets for the *Euroferry Olympia*.

It was a long wait and he went back to the car, lay down in the backseat, and slept. When he revived the other cars were boarding. The time had passed easily, God be praised. As he entered the ship a man in uniform asked him for his ticket and then, unexpectedly, his passport. He had not prepared for this, and scrambled to pull out Codrington's passport, which would condemn him as soon as it was opened. But it was not a passport control. As soon as the man saw the cover of the British document he waved him in and the trial was over. He locked the car, took the heavy bag out of the trunk, and went into the slightly run-down interior of the *Olympia*.

He came into a lobby with a circular upholstered sofa and a bronze statue at its center, with slot machines to one side and a depressing restaurant with white plastic tables and nautical themes. It wasn't worth a detour. He went straight up to his cabin, now suddenly exhausted all over again, locked the door behind him, and snapped shut the curtains of its single window. For the first time in days he felt reasonably safe. He stripped off, showered for a long time, filled with dread at the thought of another man's dried blood on his skin. He had to be purified from head to toe, like a man coming home at night from a slaughterhouse.

Then he lay unthinking and passive on one of the two beds with the lights off, waiting for the ship's first shuddering motions at 5 p.m. Only when they were out at sea in the middle of a sparkling ocean dusk did he reopen the curtains and let the dying light into the cabin. He groomed himself in front of the bathroom mirror, shaved using the complimentary razor, and slicked back his wetted hair with the plastic comb. He tried on the different shirts and jackets that he had stolen from the master bedroom at the house—Jimmie's Savile Row finery—until he found a combination that pleased him, then matched them with a pair of white pants that did not fit him, but which would pass. He took two hundred-euro notes from the bag and went up to the restaurant to eat.

Night had fallen and the dining room pitched gently from side to side. He ordered five dishes since hunger gnawed at him; he also ordered a Peroni beer, but when it came he changed his mind and sent it back. It was precisely these small sins that he had overlooked until now, but the moment had finally come to set them right. Water, two halved lemons. He ate lustily, however, and his spirits picked up. He added ice cream and coffee, and then walked around the ship to observe the other travelers.

They were mostly Italian couples, as far as he could understand, with a forlorn child here and there, and the odd single woman wrapped up in herself. It seemed an eccentric cast to be returning from a holiday in Greece. Perhaps the land of the Greeks was no longer as popular as it had once been in his father's time, when all the rich boys from Beirut spent their summers on the islands in their boats. It was safer than Beirut and there were more *roumi* girls. But everyone falls on hard times eventually. Now the Beirut parasites went to Dubai and Bangkok instead. He went out onto the deck and took in the partially moonlit sea. There was no land to be seen, there were no other ships. God had seen to him, plucked him out of misery and set him on his way: it was, if he wanted to see it that way, a call to arms, a rejuvenation. He was sure that his dead father had something to do with it.

But as he stood at the prow, buffeted by the wind, he became aware of someone looking at him. He turned quickly and saw a dark-haired boy of about twelve standing by one of the funnels in a T-shirt and shorts. The boy seemed to have appeared out of nowhere, and his parents were not present. He leaned against the funnel lightly and looked at the stranger in his blue linen jacket intently, as if he knew him. A voice floated up from the far reaches of the deck: "Giorgio!" Faoud was sure that he had seen him before somewhere. The boy smiled and raised a finger to his lips, as if he were hiding from his exasperated mother, and Faoud did the same. Then the boy slipped away.

Where had he seen him before? In Damascus, in Beirut, in Istanbul—his three cities, where thousands of such boys darkened the sidewalks. It was striking how boys of that age all possessed the same gaze. They were like messengers from another world. It was surely another sign that had been sent to him. Thanks be to God, then. But another thought came to him. The boy was the soul of the old Codrington which had appeared in its childhood form. It was her father as a boy, staring at his killer.

The sea calmed, the ship stopped pitching. There is a time for many words, and there is a time for sleep. So he slept for eleven hours with no dreams and the Adriatic gave him solace. How many had sailed across it before him. How many had drowned in it over the centuries. All he heard in his sleep were the bursars clanging their way down the metal corridors, inconsiderate to the last man, and the water pipes laid along his wall. But neither was enough to rouse him out of that sweetness. It was strange, he thought later when he was awake in the dining room having his coffee, because of all the creatures that breathe and move upon the earth, nothing is bred that is weaker than humankind.

IN THE HOUR before he arrived at Brindisi he pored over the road map, on which Jimmie long ago had penciled their yearly route back and forth from Rome. At first he had thought to just drive north as fast as he could and get to the French frontier. But as he perused the Michelin map he began to change his mind. If uproar had ensued in Hydra then the borders would be perilous to cross. Far better to lie low in Italy itself for a while. Then it occurred to him that he had at his disposal the house which Jimmie and Phaine maintained north of Rome, as Naomi had explained to him when she first suggested her plan.

It would be the last place that anyone would think to look for him. For a week, two weeks, or a few days, it would shelter him and make him invisible. He would make his way there slowly, and monitor events from afar as best he could. A new plan every day. Often the best strategy is to play the part and not stick out, to fill the shoes that you happen to be wearing.

HE DROVE INTO Brindisi two hours before lunch. He found an Internet cafe on a despondent street and sat there with a coffee, looking through the news sites for Greece. There was no sign of a drama on Hydra. Perhaps it was too early for such news to have appeared on the wires. He went out into the front of the same cafe and drank two cappuccinos with three spoons of sugar apiece. It was an old Crusader city, down at the heel and filled with an atmosphere of pessimistic expectancy. The men looked like Arabs, the women sly and more Greek, to his eye. The cafes hard and spare, with too much red plastic and too much football paraphernalia. He was dressed too well for it, which was all to the good.

He walked down a few streets afterward and bought a cell phone in a shop that appeared to be run by Indians; they sold him a SIM card that they said he could start up by himself even without an Italian address. He also bought some razors and shaving cream, some bread and cheese, and a pair of fashion sunglasses on sale. He then drove out of the city toward San Vito dei Normanni under a high sun, along a road as straight as an engineer's drawing.

When he got to the crook in the road as it swung around the citadel-like town of Ostuni, he stopped and got out into the sun, sitting behind a low stone wall on the hard shoulder. The land had a very slight gradient, divided by the same low walls, and whitewashed *trulli* stood against the latter's horizontal repetitiveness. It looked fertilely satanic. He sat there a long time watching lizards scatter across the walls and thinking with remorse about the couple he had killed. He still didn't know why it had come to that; panic and pent-up terror and maybe even a little grain of mysterious hatred. It had been unintended, but then who knew what was intended and what was not? His own mind had acted in spite of itself. He was sorry, but there was no use in it. One had to plunge forward, eyes closed if necessary.

He decided he would call the friend of his father's who had given him work when he was living in the neighborhood of Fatih in Istanbul, a businessman who had helped him arrange his flight out of Turkey. He had done some translation work for him in the area of medical supplies. Now Faoud had another favor to ask him. There were underground networks in Rome and Naples that he could use, people who might be able to alter the passport he had now. He opened the phone and called a number in Istanbul. As far as he could tell, the line was active. He tried it three or four times, but no one answered. It now occurred to him that the businessman might well be avoiding his calls. That was the way the Istanbouli were: they were interested in you when you were there, but if you moved abroad you ceased to exist. And yet the man had been reasonably kind to him at the time; had taken him in as if he'd been a stray dog. And he was still a stray dog.

Having no luck with the call, he hung up and drove on.

At dusk, having seen many signs for eateries by the road, he decided to eat in a better sort of restaurant and stopped in a field to change into some of Jimmie's clothes. He placed a pocket square in the jacket he had selected and then continued until he saw a sign for a handsome-looking place called Masseria Marzalossa. It was a large *agriturismo* estate with a hotel and a restaurant, and it seemed as good a place as any to stop. He took a room for the night, paid up front in cash, and ate in the hotel dining room. The elderly couples there hardly noticed him.

On his bed later he went through the credit cards and the clothes and wondered where he could sell the jewelry. It would surely be easier, less inconspicuous, in a big city. Rome or Naples, places he didn't know. He also went through the notebook and the papers that he had found in the glove compartment of the car. There was a map of the region where their house lay with the roads around it clearly marked. There was only the question of whether the vengeful ghost of the white man would be living there.

In the morning he went to the public computer in the lobby and looked again through the news from Greece. There was nothing about Hydra. The murder of wealthy visitors would surely be headline news, but the wires mentioned no such thing. Then he understood what had happened. God had moved Naomi to act in his defense and, naturally, to cover her own culpability.

As for Codrington and his wife, no one could say—maybe they had had an argument and she had gone to Paris to do some shopping. The mysteries and vanities of the rich were inexplicable, and in any case, no one asked them any awkward questions about their movements. They were free to do as they wanted.

THIRTEEN

"THE ARAB WAS VERY CALM WHEN HE CAME," CARISSA said, with no disequilibrium in her voice as she rolled off the incredible words. Her eyes were unfazed, soldiers ready for combat and the impertinent doubts of others. As she spoke she could sense that her confidence alone defended her but that it was more than enough. "I went to bed as you told me. When I was there, I stayed there. I fell asleep."

"I don't understand why Jimmie woke up." Naomi's voice cracked and tears burst into her eyes without falling. "How could he?"

The maid remained calm.

"He must have heard a noise."

"Impossible."

Naomi sat on the carpet and put her head in her hands. The tears rushed out at last, but they were finite. It was just a question of time. She began talking anyway.

"Now we have to sit down and think and not do anything stupid."

"Yes," the maid said.

Sam had sat down as well, and her hand was on her mouth to stop the regurgitation that threatened.

"What time did you come up here?" Naomi went on.

"At seven."

"You didn't call me?"

"I called you, but you didn't answer."

"Yes, that's true. I was negligent, I'm sorry. It must have been terrible for you."

"I've been here alone—"

"Thank God you didn't call anyone else. We have to think."

"I've been thinking," Carissa said.

"Sam?"

"I'm OK."

"We have to stay calm," Naomi insisted.

"I'm calm."

"Carissa, you're the only one—"

"Yes. No one called this morning."

"You definitely didn't call anyone else?"

"No, miss."

They were speaking in Greek and Sam couldn't understand. But she guessed from gestures and intonations that the two other women were not planning to call the police. She protested, but Naomi wouldn't hear of it. She explained to Sam that Jimmie had surely woken up when he heard a noise and came downstairs in his usual belligerent temper. Seeing a man of non-European hue in his house at three in the morning, he must have flown into one of his rages. Faoud would have panicked. The maid said, "It was the poker from the fire. Look." She had laid it on the table, uncleaned.

"Why didn't he just run out?" Sam said. "He didn't have to do this."

Naomi shook her head. "Jimmie would have threatened him. You didn't know him. He must have lost his temper and gone for him."

"We don't know that, Naomi."

"I know it. That's obviously what happened."

"Let the police decide."

Sam said this because she needed to know exactly what had happened. It would be the difference between being guilty or innocent.

"No," Carissa said in Greek to Naomi. "We can't do that. The police will think that we were accomplices. They'll assume it immediately, and they'll find out that I opened the door for him and that you asked me to do it. I'll tell them if they ask me."

Naomi turned to Sam and repeated this to her.

"Then what?" the girl burst out. "We're just going to fucking *leave* them like this? Are you serious?"

"I'm going to talk to Carissa in Greek. She knows how the police work here. I think we should do what she says."

"She's the maid," Sam spat at her. "We're going to do what your maid tells us to? Are you insane?"

"It's the least insane option."

Naomi went back to Greek, speaking as softly and calmly as she could though her whole body was trembling.

"Say we don't call the police," she said. "I don't see what we can do."

"I've been thinking all morning. I've been thinking it through. I know it sounds like the worst idea—but what if we bury them in the garden?"

The sweat was coursing down Carissa's face. She waved away the disgusting flies. Suddenly she got up and rushed into the kitchen, returning with an aerosol fly killer. She sprayed the room for a full minute until they were coughing and then sat back down in the same chair while the flies gradually subsided to their deaths. She went on. The garden was tiny, but it was enough. It was even fitting in its way. How many times had the master talked idly about being buried in his own garden? There was nothing wrong with it. In any case, they couldn't go back to their prior lives, they had to deal with what the present moment had inflicted upon them. Bury them, she said. Just dig the hole and do it. There was nothing to it, and there was nothing else to do. Once it was done they would have time to think again, and—to state the obvious—anything was better than going to prison. She would show them how to do it.

"What a fool Faoud was," Naomi whispered. "He lost his cool and panicked. We put him in a terrible situation."

"Maybe not." The maid's voice was measured and rational. "He didn't leave the money behind, did he? He made a choice. You should have realized he would."

Naomi's tears broke their dam. The realization was beginning to deepen and the first few minutes of shock had given way to emotion. She had never intended to erase her father from the earth and therefore she had not anticipated the sudden grief that came with the annihilation of a lifetime's presence. Everything reversed and upended in moments, destroyed in a whirl of dust and madness. Yet there was no time for either gravity or histrionics; they had to act. She couldn't look at him at first but then she went over and took his head in her hands and rocked it back and forth. She began to lose her breath. "Why did you wake up?" she said to him through gritted teeth. "Why didn't you sleep after the tea? You had to wake up!"

And then it dawned on her that Phaine must have come downstairs, disturbed by the noise, and that Faoud—surprised and panicking—must have killed her there as well. It might have happened in the space of a few insane seconds, unpremeditated and purely accidental.

"I measured the garden," the maid went on, as if this were not happening. Time was short and they had to make a decision. "We can dig it ourselves and bury them there. There are spades in the garden shed and plastic sheets. We can lay them next to the olive tree under the wall. Nobody will find them."

"What is she saying?" Sam said close to Naomi's ear.

"She says we have to bury them in the garden."

Sam stood up and swayed a little.

"Not me. I'm not doing that."

Naomi stood with her and faced her angrily. Her superior will suddenly imposed itself.

"You have to help. I need you, there's no backing out. You're with us."

"I can do whatever I want. I can leave right now."

"No, you can't."

"If you're not with us," the maid said laconically in Greek, "I'm not going to cover for you when the police come. If they ask me, and they will, I'll say you were involved."

Naomi translated: it was mutually assured destruction then. Sam was about to fly into a rage. Her face reddened and she took a step backward, but it was Naomi who gripped her wrist and tried to pull her out of her coming impulsiveness.

"Think a little," she said gently. "Think it through. There's no way out for you. You're already in it with us. It's better just to go through with it."

The girl calmed and the first signs of resignation floated into her face.

"It won't last long," Naomi said, "and then we'll be back to normal."

"Normal?"

"Something like normal. I promise."

"I can't see what you can promise now. You really fucked this one up—why should I believe you of all people?"

"Because you have no choice," Naomi said. "Now pull yourself together."

It was two in the afternoon. In the garden the shade from the old wall reached as far as the center where the olive tree stood. It was tired grass which a gardener mowed twice a month and with the rainless days it had lost its color. The soil was dry and loose underneath it. They found it easy to scoop up with the brand-new spades as they created a large pit.

By four, having excavated the grave, they sat in the shade and tried to recover; they were relieved that no one had called their phones and no one had rung the outer doorbell.

Sam thought about how her future might look now. It had suddenly disintegrated before her. Everything that is solid, she thought, melts into air.

Then she looked down at her arms and saw clusters of ants clinging to the backs of her hands. She uttered a cry of disgust and shook them off. But they swarmed around her feet. She stamped them out, shuddering with a touch of theatricality.

"What is it?" Naomi asked her.

"They're everywhere. Can't you see them?"

But Naomi saw nothing.

Sam said, "They're on my arms."

She threw her hands into the air again to shake off the little vermin.

"Calm down," Naomi said.

She gripped Sam's hands and stopped her flustering. To distract them Carissa made them some mint tea. They went inside and drank it, then laid the two bodies flat and wrapped them in plastic sheeting. They carried Jimmie out first and arranged him gently at the bottom of the cavity. Phaine they positioned alongside him, and then they sat by the edge of the grave and wondered what to do next. "Should I say something?" Naomi said in Greek to Carissa.

"You can say it to yourself, love."

"I can't think of anything," Naomi went on. "I can't think of anything to think, let alone say."

"Then don't say anything."

The quicker the better, the Greek girl was thinking.

Naomi flinched, stood up, and picked up the spade.

"This wasn't my intention," she said, still in Greek, and to Carissa. "You know that."

"It wasn't my intention either," Carissa retorted.

And yet what did intentions matter? No one took them seriously anyway. Naomi threw the first spadeful of soil onto the bodies and then she began the long task mechanically, indifferent to their efforts.

It took them an hour to refill the grave. By the time they had finished, the garden was flooded with sunlight. They patted down the soil and then awkwardly replaced the torn grass, since they had kept the clumps intact and laid them carefully to one side. When they had finished the garden looked almost as it had before, but not quite. They beat down the grass with the backs of their spades and, at the end, they sat together under the olive tree.

In the late afternoon this part of the port enjoyed the silence of the small mountains. Filled with crows, the sky became an echo chamber for their calls, and at the horizon the haze of the sea had turned violet. Carissa went into the kitchen and brought out a pitcher of cold lemonade, and they drank it from the jug, spilling it everywhere. The bobbing ice cubes rubbing their front teeth revived them and soon a form of peace returned. The maid got up and said, with her simple pragmatism, "We have to clean the house. And we have to clean it well."

They worked into the evening, washing down the floors and then the walls. Everything in the bedroom and the salon was put back in its place, the poker assiduously cleaned, the minute displacements caused by a violent moment rectified. There were things missing, but no one who was not family would ever notice them unless they were specifically looking for them. The passports were gone, the personal effects. The simple version of the story they were going to tell was that Jimmie and Phaine had left for a trip. Perhaps they had even decided to drive back to London—no one knew.

But people don't just disappear, Naomi had been thinking all along. The enormity of this problem was as great as the problem of not concealing their bodies. She would have to make it up as she went along.

After all, it wasn't true that people don't disappear. They disappear all the time. Any insurance agent could tell you that, and they often did if you asked them.

AT NINE SAM went back down to the port, leaving Naomi and Carissa in the house. At Kamini she stopped for a beer at Kordylenia's, overlooking the rocks and the moonstone sea, and calmed herself in readiness for the family evening meal. They would ask her where she had been and she would say she had been with Naomi wandering the backstreets of the port. There was nothing more to it than that. She looked down at her hands and the sight of them filled her with revulsion, even though she had scrubbed them so clean that they looked whiter than usual.

Yet she was now so tired that she wouldn't be able to act suspiciously even if her nervousness betrayed her. She would eat quickly and then go to bed and see if it had been a bad dream after all. If her mother started asking questions she would cut her short: Amy was eternally suspicious of the alarming possibility of a Greek boyfriend. Sam would have to disarm her.

She ate a plate of fried sardines and doubled down on the Mythos beers. You couldn't resist a beer called Mythos. She held her tears back and finally they ceased pressurizing her eyes. It would be all right, she told herself. Time would smooth it over like the grass on their shoddy graves. She turned to look at the interior of the small restaurant, and she noticed that the men sitting there playing backgammon were looking her way. It was as if there was something odd about her now, a stigmata that she couldn't see herself. She wanted to yell a "Fuck you" at them, or at least a "*Skatofatsa.*" But instead she raised a hand and called over a waiter.

"May I have some bread? Toasted?"

When it came she ate it with oil, oblivious to the gluten. Somehow she no longer cared about it. She went home afterward, suddenly quickened and emboldened. On the porch the Haldanes were at the table with John Coltrane on the stereo, and in the event she saw at once that they had suspected nothing at all. The faces were open, essentially oblivious.

In fact, her father said as she appeared, "Chris and I spent the whole day fishing. We didn't catch a damned thing."

Her mother was gentle toward her, the maternal eyes curiously empty of their normal anxiety. "How was your day, baby?"

Sam sat wearily and helped herself to some of the feta salad which had been set on the table in a large ceramic bowl.

"It was nice, I guess. Naomi and I explored the port up by the mountain. The Codringtons have all these friends up there."

"Old bohemians, eh?" her father chimed in.

"Yeah, old bohemians. We didn't see any, though."

"They all came because of Leonard Cohen, and now they're stranded."

Sam turned and looked her brother in the eye. He was the only one among them with a devious turn of mind. Now his gaze was mocking and disbelieving.

"The whole day exploring?" he said.

"It's better than fishing."

"Does Mr. Codrington know Leonard Cohen?"

"Probably. He didn't say."

"I bet Dad's jealous," Chris said.

"Did you have lunch with the family up there?" Amy then asked.

"No, her father and stepmother weren't there. I'm not sure they're even on the island right now."

"That's funny," Jeffrey said. "I was sure I saw them last night in the port. I didn't go up and say hello because I had the feeling they don't like me. But I'm sure I saw them."

"Maybe they left this morning, then."

"Maybe they did. But last night, anyway, they were living it up at the Pirate. I'm pretty sure it was them."

Sam went up to her room, lying with the lights off for a long time. She let the tears flow as copiously as they wanted, and eventually they dried up of their own accord as well and she became lucid again. She felt betrayed, but not in a way that she could quite explain.

Of course, it was she herself who had insisted on coming

with Naomi to her house. But Naomi had let Sam be drawn into the events, as she had all along, but without telling her why she needed her. It was because Naomi wanted an accomplice for the times ahead when things might get unpleasant. She needed a foil of some kind—it was not clear for what.

Ahead of them stretched the rest of the summer, now in ruins. As it evolved she would have to play more and more of a game to keep herself above suspicion. The only solution would be to get off the island and go home, or go anywhere away from Greece. But her parents had already paid for the house in advance, and there was no way they would let her leave by herself. She was cornered, and Naomi held the keys to her delectable open-air prison. It was a reason to wonder if she had misjudged her new friend. But she would wait and see what Naomi said to her from then on. It was possible that she was too upset to understand on the first night of a catastrophe.

As soon as Sam had gone, Naomi and Carissa went back out into the nocturnal garden and smoked some cigarettes. They stared at the uneven ground, and horror blossomed inside them silently to which words couldn't be matched.

"What now?" Carissa said in the end.

"I don't know. We'll wait and see what happens. I don't think they had a busy social schedule this month, did they?"

"They told me they were going to have drinks with the Korders tomorrow night. Other than that—"

"Damn. I'll call them tomorrow and say they're indisposed."

"Indisposed? You know how gossip works here."

"I'll say they went to the mainland for a few days. The Korders won't think twice about it."

Carissa nodded, half convinced, because it was lame, but it would have to do.

"We'll have to improvise," Naomi went on. "What else can we do but improvise?"

She went into the house and came back with an envelope with the money she'd promised. She asked Carissa to count it, and when she did she found that it was twenty thousand euros instead of fifteen. Naomi immediately put a hand on her arm.

"Don't say anything. It's for you. I feel terrible for putting you in this situation, so just take it. It's the least I can do."

The maid said nothing and accepted the gift. For her, it was a stupendous amount.

They went inside and made sandwiches and ate them with brandy from Jimmie's stash. They played some jazz and lay on the sofas, smoking in order to banish through a trivial defilement the onset of guilt. The somberness of their mood, however, was soon reflected by the pall of smoke that formed around the dingy old chandelier that Phaine had bought in Kifissia an age ago when Mitsotakis was still prime minister. But Naomi resolved to herself to think only of the future from then on.

FOURTEEN

IN THE FOLLOWING DAYS THE ISLAND WITHERED UNDER a heat sweeping in from Africa. Toward midday the sky had the cold fineness of powdered silver, but at twilight it was still light enough that the mainland could be clearly seen, like a brooding foreign country, magnified by the very water that separated it from the wealthier sojourners on the island. When the wind fell in the suffocating afternoons even the coastal villages were lulled and their paths were baked into a dustless hush that made sleep seem inevitable. People sat inanimately in the shade, their eyes wide open as if waiting for the relief of dark and nothing more, and the American girl had eventually, over a number of idle days, formed the strange idea that all cobwebs in the trees had fallen like herself into a suspended animation.

Along the path to Mandraki, she and Amy made their way shortly after eight, as they had done since the first day of their arrival, mother and daughter locked in a private mental duel of their own, a duel that grew more grueling every day. Amy had come to the conclusion that her daughter was losing her focus and vitality; she was slipping into a special summer depression that she had never seen before. It must have to do with the Codrington girl. One day, as they passed the little restaurant above the cove, she asked Sam about Naomi's father and stepmother. She had not seen them in the port for a while.

"I don't know about their movements," the girl said sullenly. "Naomi told me that they go to parties on other islands. They do their own thing."

"Other islands? I didn't know there were any other islands, socially speaking."

Her thwarted snobbery was roused.

"Maybe we don't understand the whole scene here yet."

"I don't think there's anything to understand, Mom. I've given up trying to understand Europeans anyway. It's exhausting. If you don't understand them it's just the same. They behave just like they did before, and so do we."

"That's a little defeatist, isn't it?"

"I don't think the Codringtons think about us for one second. Not even half of one second."

"I didn't say they did. But still—it's annoying."

"What's annoying?"

"The fact that I don't know about these other islands. I should have done some research."

"Why don't you read Tolstoy instead? It's perfect for that, this place. Just read fucking Tolstoy."

Amy's short laugh reached the boys.

When they were settled, and had drunk their first coffee of the morning, Amy asked her if Naomi was really going to be what she called a long-term investment.

"You mean as a friend?" her daughter asked.

"Even as a summer friend. Maybe you're spending too much time with her. It's worse than a Greek boy. Now I wish you had a Greek boy. A Greek boy wouldn't be so mysterious."

"What's mysterious?"

"I don't know. The two of you. You're not sleeping with her, are you? If you are, you can tell me. I won't tell your father."

"Of course I'm not sleeping with her."

"I've got nothing against this girl, Sam. But you're not yourself lately. Why don't you go to a few parties on your own? It seems to me you could just hang out at Pirate Cove by yourself and make some American friends."

"But I don't want any American friends."

"You know what I mean. Just go out without Naomi. Maybe she's a little too English for you. It makes her too overbearing—"

"Not at all."

But really Sam just wanted to be alone. At midday she left her mother at the hotel and walked around the headland by herself. She passed the rock where Naomi and she had lain that first day and continued on into the wilderness where the thistles grew. She was suddenly sobbing to herself without knowing why, and below her the dark and churning sea offered a tempting annihilation. It would be an act of pure hatred, not self-hatred, and it would destroy everyone she knew because—it was just possible— they deserved to be destroyed. When she was far from Mandraki, in a place where no one passed, she stripped naked and clambered down to the sea. The water there was much colder and she endured it for ten minutes before climbing back up into the rocks. Naomi used to tell her how much she swam there alone. Now she had told her to lie low for a while and avoid contact with her. They had to wait and see what happened.

As Sam lay in the sun and dried off, her rage subsided. When she went back to Mandraki she found that her mother had left and she walked back to Hydra town as slowly as she could, lost in unpleasant thought. She sat morosely at the Pirate, and soon enough, as her mother had predicted, the young Americans materialized all around her and within a few hectic minutes she was swept up in their windup toy momentum. It was not entirely unwelcome. By then she had spent four days alone with her family and she was beginning to feel the mortifying effects. Like her, the boys were on the island for the summer, for the long haul so to speak. Like her they were finding it charmingly claustrophobic. Why didn't she come with them to another party at another house? There was the promise of dope and ouzo and people who spoke the same slang as herself. Most of all, she wouldn't have to spend the whole evening playing Scrabble with her father.

They went up as a group through the angled lanes, a boy with his arm around her. She had knocked back four shots of ouzo, but her legs were still steady. There was a house belonging to one of their fathers. A wide sea-captain terrace with the panorama of Hydra around it and low Turkish tables where the boys cut lines of coke. The boy who had sweet-talked her on the way up told her that they had met before, at the painter's house, and that he knew the English girl she had been with that night. Their parents were friends.

"I kind of thought you two were together. It's cool if you are."

"That's the second time today someone has said that. I'm not *with* her. I'm not with anyone. I don't need to be with anyone. I haven't seen her in days."

"I have. I saw her at a bar three nights ago. She was totally wasted."

"Naomi?"

"She was sitting there alone."

"She's a free woman, isn't she?"

"Didn't say she wasn't. There's a lot of gossip about her on the island."

"I don't want to hear it. If people don't like her, that's their problem, not mine."

"Well, obviously. I didn't say I agreed with it or believed it."

But you want to say it anyway, she thought.

"The old people say she's *daimonizetai*."

"What's that?"

"Possessed. It's because of stuff she did when she was a child."

"They can remember what she did twenty years ago? It's better for us that no one can remember what we did twenty years ago."

"Twenty years ago . . . I was one."

"So was I. But you know what I mean."

"Some of them can remember the children of the 1950s, let alone the 1990s. My parents say she was a little wild but not possessed."

"I don't even know what that's supposed to mean, possessed."

"I guess they mean it in a Greek way."

"What is the Greek way?"

"I think they believe in spirits in a different way."

"Even now," she said, nodding.

"They know what they mean, though. It's very specific."

His name was Toby. Suddenly he had grown more sympathetic. He too was on summer vacation, but from Princeton. He was in his first year there. She asked him if he had grown up on Hydra. His family, he said, had spent their summers there since before he could remember. He didn't speak very good Greek. His father had bought their house at the same time that Jimmie Codrington bought his. They knew each other through the art market.

"Or the local chapter of alcoholics," she said.

"Or that. It's a possibility. They all know each other. They're in London now, though. I have the house to myself."

"Where is it?"

He pointed to the jumble of houses tucked on top of each other. It was there among hundreds of others now forming a maze of lights in the gathering dusk.

"I'll come visit if you invite me," she said.

"You're invited for sure, Miss Haldane. You really ought to change your last name, by the way. It sucks. You could keep your first name and then change the second one. Sam Smith?"

"I like it."

"Samantha Smithereens?"

They each did a line of the coke, but she remembered why she had always disliked this particular drug. It did nothing for her. It left her irritated and overactive. One didn't always want to be too awake. The boys were playing guitars and drinking heavily. She thought that most of them were insidiously boring, tanned but fleshless. Toby was the exception; she had his attention. His eyes were quick and active, there was no toxicity in them. Besides, he knew about the Codringtons, which was useful. It was disconcerting to think how little she herself knew about them. She knew more about their death than about their life, but maybe Toby could fill her in a little. They were growing rapidly closer, and the idea of sex was becoming more likely. It would, in fact, make everything easier.

Her mother would even like Toby. A nice young Princeton man, backed by a good family and a fair amount of willpower. He was a bit more than that, but it was doubtful whether Amy would see his potential. They left shortly after midnight and she called home briefly as they clambered up the opposing hillside to the house he had pointed out two hours earlier. On the way they stopped at a late-night taverna and ate some *souvlaki* and downed a couple of bottles of Mythos. He too was by now addicted to Mythos. In this intervening period the drug sank into her and she felt delirious. They talked about college. Seen from the perspective of Greece and a slow hot summer, however, it seemed disturbingly trivial. He didn't know what he wanted to do with the rest of his time at Princeton; she was already waiting for college to end and something else to begin. He wanted to know what it would be.

"My father says I should go into journalism. He doesn't understand that journalism is over—long over."

"Mine thinks I should be a lawyer. He has a point. But he knows I won't."

"Maybe," she said, "I'll drift for a bit afterward. Maybe I'll come back here and get a job in a hotel." Her voice trailed off, she couldn't help it.

He said, "Are you sure you want to come up? You don't seem sure."

"I have anemia sometimes. That's why I look pale."

"I didn't say you looked pale. I said you looked unsure."

"But I'm sure."

They climbed up to the empty house and let themselves in. It was so hot that it was more comfortable to lie on the terrace, where Toby had dragged his mattress for the previous few nights. It was there they began kissing.

It was a relief. The tension that had been building up inside her suddenly unwound and she let herself go with an anarchic mood. But they had drunk so much that they soon fell asleep. Before slipping into unconsciousness she looked up and saw a half-moon gloating over the port, both a portent and a warning. She slept for four hours without dreams. But she was aware within that sleep of seabirds wheeling above them and crying into the dark. What woke her in the end was the sound of her own voice. She was sitting upright and a loud scream—her own—had shaken Toby awake as well. His arm was extended across her shoulders in order to calm her down. "What is it?" he was saying, as if talking to a child, and as she opened her eyes she saw someone walk away from the terrace and melt into the darkness. Drenched in sweat, she could see that it was almost dawn. The chorus had begun. They decided to get up and go back down to the port. "Did you have a nightmare?" he asked her. She shook her head and said it was the coke. She shouldn't have done it. "Yes, but you did," he said slyly, and he took her hand for the downward return journey. It was an unnecessary thing to say, a slightly cruel thing. Out of character, she thought.

"You don't have any regrets, do you?" he went on when they were at the port and in a cafe waiting for sunlight.

"Not at all," she said. "I just don't remember anything."

His face fell, but he forced himself to smile.

"Well, there's that, I guess."

"I thought there was someone on the terrace."

"Couldn't have been. So you did have a bad dream?"

"I must have. But it seemed real." Her voice sounded empty and disengaged, as if she was not convincing herself.

"No one can break into these houses. They're like fortresses. That's how they were built. All the families were once at war with each other."

An hour later the first ferry came gliding across from the mainland. Its lights were full of swagger, and when it had docked they watched as a sullen crowd of arrivals made their way down the gangplank and onto the quay. They were mostly Greeks, Hydriots probably returning from visits. But after they had all disembarked and fanned out into their hometown, a man who was obviously English in some way came after them, limping and pulling a bag on wheels and dressed in a summer suit that looked forty years out of date. Since he was about seventy himself, however, it was incongruously flattering or at least unremarkable. He wore sunglasses though it was still dark, and he seemed, for a moment, bewildered as he stood alone on the quay, unmet and unknown. His bald head shone under the lamps. He looked around, and for a moment she thought he was going to approach them and ask them for directions. A tremendous dithering tact suggested his provenance.

"He looks lost," Toby said gallantly. "Should I?"

Without waiting for an answer, he got up and went over to the old man. They talked out of her hearing and then Toby came back affably to the cafe.

"Poor guy is booked at the Bratseras. So I gave him directions. It's a three-minute walk."

"Who is he?"

"How should I know? Some old tourist. They're a dime a dozen."

"Alone?"

Toby shrugged it off.

"Most old people are alone these days."

But she wasn't convinced. There was something oblique and wary about him, a lack of tourist cheer.

As soon as he had appeared, he disappeared, and having disappeared he was forgotten. Sam walked home alone as the sun came up and was in her bed long before her family woke. She slept through most of that day. Out in the fields the olives stood fixed by a manic heat and the world around them had gone dead. Their leaves shone bright as steel in the windless glare. The effects of the alcohol and the coke had worn off, leaving her clear enough to feel keenly the disgust that came in their wake. There was a note on the kitchen table that her parents and brother had gone hiking and would be back for dinner. They were so distressingly active when they were on vacation.

As if in rebellion against them, she took a long bath before dressing in a plain white summer dress and going out to read on the porch. Gradually her level common sense returned. She began to think about Naomi again. She called her, and to her surprise Naomi answered. Sam suggested she come down to the house and they could chat alone. Soon, then, Naomi herself walked out of the gloom and came up to the gateposts at the bottom of the path with a quiet but paradoxically purposeful hesitation. It had been five days since they had seen each other.

FIFTEEN

Are your parents here?" Naomi said as soon as Sam had gone down to the gates and they were alone together on the path.

"They'll be back any minute."

"Should I come up and be normal for them?"

"I guess that would be good."

"Otherwise they might wonder . . ."

They went back up to the porch and sprawled on the sofas.

"I went to Mandraki with my mom," Sam said, "and you wouldn't believe how annoying she was being."

"Just be cool with them. We need to be calm right now."

"They don't suspect anything. They never would."

"Have you been all right?"

Naomi was unruffled herself, and anxious to be solicitous.

"I've been sleeping badly," Sam admitted.

"Same."

"What about Carissa?"

"I let her go for three days to see her family. It seemed better to do that."

Sam nodded. "She'll appreciate that."

"I didn't want to be in the house alone with her, frankly. This whole time I've been wondering if she gave them the tea like she said she did. I'm not saying she didn't, but it crossed my mind."

"Are you serious?"

"I can't prove it. But I just can't see how he could have woken up like that."

"Maybe he didn't want the tea. Maybe she gave it to him but he didn't drink it?"

"I checked the cups in their room. They were empty."

"You can't just blame Carissa."

Naomi's pent-up frustration began to reveal itself, but she held it in check.

"I had the strangest day," she began.

She had slept in the salon that night. For four days she had combed through the house looking for signs of violence and derangement, smoothing them all out until the villa was as perfectly organized as it had been during their long absences in the winter. The worst part was the master bedroom. She had to remake the bed, go on her hands and knees and search the floors for stray earrings, and, as it happened, Jimmie's mobile. It had ended up on the floor under the bed. Imagine that. She had taken out the battery and put the phone in the rubbish. Then she had gone through their bathroom and removed the toiletries they used every day. Everything had to disappear. Everything *had* disappeared. She was thorough about these things, "a real lawyer when I want to be." The villa was now restored to order. But still she couldn't sleep well in it. That morning she got up early and went shopping in the town. She took a donkey to haul the bags back to the house, and at midday she made a fish stew and drank half a bottle of wine. It didn't even make her tipsy.

Nevertheless she took a nap in the salon. She was roused from that sleep by the doorbell ringing, the first time since the event that anyone had come to the house.

She composed herself, checked her face in a mirror, and went quietly to the door and peered through the hole. It was someone she didn't recognize. She waited and thought it over, then decided not to answer. The man on the far side of the door rang a second time and eventually gave up and walked away.

An hour passed and she ventured onto the terrace and looked down the narrow stepped path that led up to Belle Air. It must have been one of Jimmie's drinking pals, but she couldn't think who. Sooner or later she would have to face them and give them her story to explain Jimmie's absence. She would have to perfect her lying. Sometime later the doorbell rang again and this time it was someone else—the American her father and Phaine called the Ancient Beatnik. She braced herself and opened. She didn't know the man's name, but he had been in the house before as their guest, and so she feared him less.

He uttered a little "Ah!" as she opened the door and peered up at her through blue-tinted specs. The conversation was brief. He had come up to remind Jimmie that he was expected at the annual arts festival ceremony on the mountaintop the following week. The Codringtons attended every year, but since Jimmie had not been around for a few days the Ancient Beatnik had thought to come up and remind him.

"Is he here now?"

"They left Hydra, I'm sorry to say. I think they drove somewhere for a few days."

"That's weird, man. Are they coming back soon?"

She said she didn't know, she rarely consulted with them about these things. Did they have his number? Of course they did. He looked confused for a moment, then thought it over and gave her what she supposed was a beatnik smile. She offered a few extra thoughts: maybe they had gone to see Phaine's family in Athens? Or maybe they had gone to the Mani. Jimmie loved the Mani.

With these ruminations she got rid of him. She went back to the terrace and watched him totter down the path, steadying himself with outstretched hands against the walls. That might have been the end of it for the day, but two hours later the first old man reappeared at the door and this time he rang the bell more insistently. Once again, she considered not opening. But somehow the visit of the Ancient Beatnik had changed the odds and this time she felt compelled to do so. It was a dapper-scruffy English gent by the looks of him, in sunglasses and wearing a ridiculous foulard with a wilted pocket square with a pattern of rose and yellow butterflies.

The linen suit, in the way of linen suits in the heat, had gone a little to hell. Despite the dandy touches, the man looked like he had spent the night in a comfortable dumpster. He took off his shades as soon as the door opened and his eyes were the pale oysters of old men on the slide, and the freckles on his forehead looked as if they had appeared within the last few hours at first contact with a Greek sun. He looked mildly surprised to see her. But she was pretty sure that she had never seen him before, either in Greece or elsewhere. Nevertheless, he didn't greet her with any sense of unfamiliarity. On the contrary, he shook her hand and said, in a voice from another age, "You must be Naomi!"

As soon as her name was mentioned, so casually and yet so irrevocably, she was obliged to open the door wider and suggest—by body language alone—that he come inside.

"My name's Rockhold. I'm a good friend of your father's."

"I'm afraid they're not here right now. But would you like to come in? I can make some tea."

"I'd be delighted to. Nothing better than a spot of tea when it's hot."

She could see that he was perspiring. He had refused to dress down for the heat, which was a charming and anachronistic mistake. She also now saw that he held a straw panama in one hand—he had removed it before she had opened the door. As he stepped into the hall's cool there was a look of relief on his face. He left the panama on one of the coat hooks by the door and they went into the salon. Rockhold looked it over as if for the first time. He admitted at once, in effect, that he had never been to Hydra before.

"My father didn't invite you?"

"No, I'm not the inviting kind. People hesitate before inviting me."

He smiled broadly, as if this statement made perfect sense, and sat down, clearly a little tired by the long climb up the Hydriot steps.

"I'll make some tea," Naomi said, and she went to the kitchen.

Her hands were shaking. Yet he was mild enough. Just maybe not the friend she had assumed him to be: something else.

She came back with the tray and set it on the glass coffee table. As she did so, he said, without fuss, "I see your table here has a nasty crack. Someone drop something on the glass?"

She hadn't even noticed it. But there it was, a spidery crack at the table's corner. She tried to smile.

"Yes, the maid broke it last week. She drops things."

"Does she, now? That's not much of a maid, then, is it?"

"She's wonderful otherwise."

"I believe her name is Carissa?"

She was pouring for him, but her hand froze and she had to steady it and continue pouring.

"That's right. That seems like a funny thing to know, Mr. Rockhold."

"You can call me Samuel. Your father and I are old friends. In fact, we were in the army together. Perhaps he didn't mention it. One rarely mentions the men one was in the army with." The eyes were suddenly merry and all-forgiving.

"Not to me, Mr. Rockhold."

"Well, your father likes to keep a few of us back, as it were. Cards up one's sleeve and so forth. There'd be no need to mention poor old Samuel to one's daughter. Old acquaintance half forgot and all that."

And yet, she thought, you're here and indeed right in front of me. A stranger with a glass eye. She had noticed it about him as soon as he had sat down. It was like a marble, its blue not quite matching the live one.

"Where were you stationed with my father, Mr. Rockhold?"

"Gibraltar. Days of our life. Thought they'd never end, as the song goes."

"Jimmie says he had a miserable time there."

"Well, you know how it is. Can't have everything your own way, can you? No one ever has it all their own way. Jimmie was a bad fit for the old discipline part."

"But now you're in Hydra."

"So it seems."

"Are you just passing by?"

"Well, now we've come to it, haven't we?"

He put a hand on each knee and she saw that the sweat on his face had finally dried. She looked down at the previously unnoticed crack in the glass top of the table and cursed herself for having missed it. It was a sign that not everything was as it appeared. Because it was not in Jimmie's character to let a cracked table go unnoticed for more than twenty-four hours. The visitor said that he was, if one could put it this way, a confidant of Jimmie, rather than merely a friend, and that— since she had asked—he was here on a bit of business for the Codringtons.

"But, my dear," he said, "you haven't told me where they are. It's rather unfortunate if I've missed them."

"They left for the mainland last week. I'm afraid they didn't tell me where they were going—they never do. They up and leave on a whim all the time. I think my stepmother feels a little claustrophobic on the island."

"So they might have gone to Athens for a few days?"

"It's possible. They haven't called yet—but we're not always on the best terms anyway. It's not usual for them to call me."

"How vexing. For both of us!"

"It's not vexing, Mr. Rockhold. It's always been like this. We don't have the ideal father–daughter relationship, I'm afraid."

"So I gathered."

"I'm sorry for the inconvenience."

Rockhold waved a hand. "Not at all. The sun is shining, is it not?"

"Where are you staying?"

"At a very nice hotel in town. I'm quite happy there. A young man recommended it to me and so far it hasn't disappointed. I'm used to improvising, you know. Maybe, if you are free, we might have dinner sometime. What do you say?"

Suddenly trapped by an affable invitation, she stammered that she would be glad to. Before she could come up with an excuse he had locked her into the following night at the Sunset.

"Unless something comes up," she tried desperately.

"Do things often come up on Hydra? By the way," he went on, "you should get that table fixed. It might break completely the next time you put something down on it."

The tea finished, they stood and Rockhold went back into the hall and put on his straw hat. A thermometer hung on the wall there and the mercury showed a temperature of 72, and that was in the cool part of the house. She let him out and they were pleasant to each other, though her heart was beating wildly with resentment and fear. Who was he and why was he there? He stepped out into the hurtful sunlight and winced, but with a certain amount of humor.

"Furnace, isn't it?" He laughed.

"You should eat at the Bratseras," she said. "The food is really quite good."

"Is it? Funnily enough, that's where I'm staying."

"If my father calls, I'll let you know."

"You do that, my dear Naomi. I'll be anxious otherwise."

"He won't call, though."

Rockhold looked at her from under the hat's brim, and his eyes were cool and unassuming. "You never know with him. He's an unpredictable creature of the deep."

SAM WAS ABOUT to tell Naomi that this was almost certainly the man she and Toby had seen in the port that morning, but she held back and thought better of it. Naomi would start asking questions about Toby, and she wanted to keep him out of it. But they were both thinking the same thing. Something had gone wrong and the thing they had feared had come to pass. I need to get out of this as soon as possible, Sam thought to herself. For in any case how did I get into this in the first place? I'm such a *skatofatsa* idiot. But she knew it was too late. Naomi gave her a reassuring smile and said, "It'll be all right. I'll play along with him."

"What does he want?"

"No way of knowing. But he's not just a friend. He's something more."

Sam pursed her lips and her fury was contained behind them. She said, "I knew an investigator would get involved."

"If that's what he is."

"Of course it's what he is. What about the Greek police?"

"If he's an investigator," Naomi said slowly, "I have a feeling he'll keep the Greek police at bay for a while."

"You hope."

"He came and he'll go," Naomi said. "I'll handle him if that's what he is."

"You'll handle him?"

"He's a canny old codger, that's all. He was with my father in the army. He's harmless. Just nosing around."

"But why?"

"Maybe he was expecting a call from Jimmie and it never came. We have to expect this sort of thing. We just have to play it cool."

Sam flared up for a moment.

"I knew we should have just gone to the police. Now we have to play cat and mouse with one of your dad's army buddies? How do you know he's just an army buddy?"

"Well, as I said, he's not the police, is he? That's the good part."

The hysteria rose in both their voices, and yet they were not shouting, they were barely whispering. "You better think fast,"

Sam said. "Or we're fucked." Naomi reminded her that they were doing this for Faoud, not for themselves, and after it had all blown over it would be different.

Sam lowered her voice, which had been rising, on the off chance that her family were close by, making their way back across the fields.

"Did it occur to you that he might've been using you?"

Naomi was so astonished that she merely blinked.

"Using me?"

"Maybe he didn't care if he had to kill them or not, he just wanted the cash."

"But I gave it to him."

"Because you're a white girl. Of course you gave it to him. He knew you felt guilty, and he took advantage."

"That's absurd, and you know it."

"No, I don't know it. I don't know anything. All I know is that you and I are stuck on this tiny island with an old man who likes to ask questions. It's starting to freak me out."

The returning family suddenly came into view. They were sunburned and brimming with energy, carrying bundles of wild flowers and knapsacks, the Swiss Family Robinson crackling with chatter and unconscious satisfactions. When they saw that Naomi would be joining them for dinner Amy appeared a little cool at the idea, but Jeffrey took the lead in stirring up some enthusiasm. The maid had already made her famous moussaka and the wine had been opened. They were, in reality, too hungry and too happy to care either way.

They showered with extraordinary efficiency and were seated at table within fifteen minutes. Night had fallen now and donkeys in heat brayed in the darkness, aroused by something new. Sam ate in silence while the others bantered, a fact that did not escape the notice of her mother. Amy, in fact, had become vaguely and almost unconsciously suspicious—but of what she wasn't yet sure. Something in Naomi's body language, something in the taciturn silence of her daughter. But there was nothing to be said. Before desserts were served, she caught Sam alone for a moment in the kitchen as they made coffee. Amy touched her arm for a moment and said, "Everything all right, sweetheart?" The girl shuddered away from the touch and then collected herself.

"I'm fine," she said tersely. "I just have a headache."

"Where did you go last night?"

"I did what you told me to. I went to a party and met some Americans."

"That's great, sweetheart. I hope you had fun." Amy was hugely relieved.

"It was cool," the girl replied.

At the table, Naomi told stories about Hydra life—from days gone by, as she said—and the Haldanes listened until Jeffrey took out his pompous pipe and lit up, signaling a change in the conversation. He and Christopher had been reading *The Odyssey* every night before bed. They had come to Book 5, and Christopher kept asking him if the island of Ogygia, home of Calypso, was Hydra.

Of course it was not. But when Homer described the island rising up "like a shield," well, it was suggestive of this island too. Jeffrey puffed on his pipe and turned a vacant tobacco eye on his guest.

"Then Christopher said the most beautiful thing to me. He said, isn't Odysseus just like the refugees today? How does he put it?—tossed on the stormy waves, destroying himself on the barren sea. The foiled journey home, the current bore him there, or something like that? Scudding across the—scudding across the sea's broad back—scudding somewhere—how did it go with the scudding, Chris?"

The boy looked up sheepishly. "Left to pine on an island in the nymph's house?"

"Yes, that too. That's how he ended up. Pining and weeping for home, nowhere to go. It makes you think, doesn't it?"

"About what?" Naomi said.

"About how it's all the same. Nothing ever changes."

"That's a stretch, to put it mildly."

But the look of self-satisfaction on his face was disarming, and she left it at that. After all, she should be the last person to disagree when she thought about it. But even if she did disagree, what difference would it make to either herself or the bore?

"Everyone knows the island was Gozo," Christopher then said. "Not here."

"That's right," his father said. "But who knows if it even existed?"

"It didn't exist," the boy said.

"Did you know that Calypso means 'she who hides herself'?"

He turned to Naomi, but without knowledge of the ironies he was unconsciously manipulating.

"Forgive us, Naomi, my son and I are the most tremendous pedants when the mood takes us. Once we get going only wild horses can stop us, and there usually aren't any wild horses around—are there, Sam?"

"Only goats, if you're lucky," she said.

SIXTEEN

Faoud stopped in Fasano. The town was dominated by a long rectangular piazza filled with old men taking in the sun in their shirtsleeves and with crowds of tired pigeons. He went through both men and birds anonymously, aware that now he could pass for Italian without much difficulty. He came upon a shoe store in a street nearby and tried on a few pairs of fine Italian shoes until he found two that fit.

Five hundred euros seemed obscenely steep to him, but shabby shoes could give a man away, even to an idle eye. It was a question of the economics of appearances. There was no price to be put on the vital element of concealment and the ability to blend in. He was also, he admitted to himself, desperate to step away from the persona of a refugee and step into a different one altogether. Shoes: so banal and yet so magnificently significant. He paid with one of the credit cards, and there was no incident. He wore one pair out of the shop and back into the sunlight, where the tan leather shone handsomely and gave a lift to his self-confidence. Whatever happened now, life or death or prison, he would go into it finely shod. There was an enchantment in the metamorphosis.

From Fasano a road swung south toward Marina Franca. He decided to follow it, because the Codringtons had marked it on their map and he didn't want to go onto the autostrada. The

smaller roads were safer, less policed. He drove until midafter-
noon, when he came to Marina di Ginosa, the whole length of
it a shambolic and hideous carnival of seaside campsites, pizze-
rias, clubs, sugarcane fields, and roadside bars filled with people
in swimwear. In a quiet way, he was shocked. Where were the
superbly dressed and imperious Italians he had seen so many
times in films, the Sophia Lorens his father had so admired
once upon a time? He went into a cafe and got a *spremuta* at
the bar, and soon he heard a few tones of Arabic coming from
the men huddled with him around the zinc bar. They had not
fingered him as one of their own, and he was content not to be
counted among their ranks.

By the road the wind swept through the high cane, and
along the verges men walked in single file, men from the south
in nylon jackets and cheap scarves even in the rising heat. He
drove on in the direction of Matera. On the way he passed a
roadblock that had just been dismantled. The *carabinieri* were
taking away the cones and loading them into two police vans,
some of them standing now by the verge with their weapons
cocked. There, in the sour dust, two men sat in handcuffs, their
heads drooped and despondent. Ten minutes earlier and he,
too, would have been stopped.

God, once again, had watched over him and saved him
among the Unbelievers. But next time he would have to be
more prudent. He drove past the policemen slowly, and for a
moment their eyes locked and disengaged without incident. It
was a shame that he was alone; a couple had a far better chance
of not calling attention to themselves. Soon, however, he was
in Matera, the modern part of which was like any other Italian
provincial town, defiantly morose. He parked the Peugeot on
a wide street, took a shoulder bag, and walked down into the

ancient labyrinth that lay below it. It seemed to him that there, where few cars ventured, would be a safer place to lie low for a night.

On the far side of the little town were only rocky cliff faces pocked with caves and slopes of heather and prickly pear. There were signs for hotels everywhere, places built into the long-abandoned caves where peasants had once lived with their animals, like animals themselves. He found a modest one just above a belvedere with views of the ravine and threw his bag onto the bed, then washed and shaved and drank the mineral water that was on the bedside table.

It was about six o'clock now and the bells were ringing, the echoes thrown back and forth across the ravine, whose far side looked like a place where saints and eremites had once lived.

He was alone in the hotel and the owners seemed indifferent to his existence, a fact that after all was to his advantage. He slipped out unnoticed and walked along the cool expanse of the belvedere. Soon he was climbing steps at its far end and ascending through tunnels and arched passageways toward an unknown destination.

Eventually, he came out into a wide square right on the edge of the precipice, with a church clinging to its far corner and occupying one side of the piazza. It was open and so was a cafe; a Japanese man sat alone at one of the tables smoking a cigarette. Faoud looked around, saw nothing threatening, and walked slowly up to the wall and looked down into the darkening ravine. The noise of birds massed in the twilight was so great that it unnerved him. He wondered if long ago the Muslims had come this far in their conquests of southern Italy and whether it was they who had marked it out as a sanctuary that reminded them of their native lands. The fragrantly dry heat of the late day wafting up from the grass slopes would have pleased them just as it pleased him now.

The bells had fallen silent. He went into the church, where there was a small gathering of old people, and he wandered down the nave feeling things that had never occurred to him before. He had thought to offer something to the souls of the two people he had destroyed, but there was no way to do this within the unfamiliar parameters of Unbelief. Nevertheless, he sat in the pews and formed the internal words of an apology and a penance. God, all-comprehending, would understand his reasons and even the accursed place in which it had to be performed, since there was no choice but to enter into the church of Pietro e Paulo and pray for the Codringtons, who were even more innocent than he was. More innocent, but clearly less favored by God.

His penance inside the church had suddenly lifted a certain weight from his mind and he felt freer to enjoy an hour at the cafe where the Japanese man was sitting. So he stopped suddenly and veered to a free table, catching a waiter's eye. Almost immediately a girl, an Italian he would have guessed, had noticed him in his new shoes and his odd-fitting ivory pants, and while waiting for him to settle down she lit a cigarette. The Japanese man slowly got up and walked off into the night. He and the Italian were alone.

"Excuse me," he began in English.

He had guessed correctly. She was Italian, but her English was good. It was always the way these days among reasonably educated people. Her name was Benedetta. She was twenty-two and an art student; her father owned a furniture-restoring factory in Brescia specializing in the eighteenth century.

"I saw you go into the church," she said. "But you're not a Christian."

This was the way that flirtations sometimes began, with subjects one didn't really want to broach.

"I was a Christian for five minutes in there."

Smile to her, then; it was not true, but it didn't matter.

"Five minutes is a long time to be one," she said.

They talked for an hour. He lied with a considerable fluency and before long he began to think that she was believing him. Soon they were walking together through the silent old town. He said he was driving to Rome the next day, he could give her a ride if she needed one.

"I was thinking of staying here for a while," she replied. "But maybe I'll change my mind."

"Do whatever you want, Miss Benedetta."

"*Allora ci vediamo domani.*"

"Means?"

"We'll see tomorrow."

She reached out and touched his hand, but he shook his head, immediately understanding the invitation, and said, "I have to sleep tonight. I slept badly last night."

Then, making up for his prurient refusal, he repeated his previous offer to drive her to Rome the next day if she liked.

With the same coolness with which she had registered the rejection, she affirmed her acceptance of this offer. She then went back to her hostel, while he lay awake in his own unassuming hotel smoking for a long time and thinking things over. This was improvisation from day to day; there was something exhilarating about it. Slowly but surely, it was purifying him. He didn't need to have a plan or a destination: God had already decided for him.

He didn't sleep, and so when she showed up at his hotel at seven the next morning he was already awake, perfectly dressed as a more handsome Jimmie and ready to leave. They took coffee together outside, in front of his room, and he saw that she had a small rucksack with her, though nothing else. He gave her the bread basket. Clouds had massed overnight, and now, spitefully, a few drops of rain fell. There were silent flashes of lightning in the far distance, and under the hostile clouds the slopes looked more intensely green and yet ravaged by neglect.

They walked up to the new town with their bags and found the car. It began to rain more consistently as they drove to Potenza, passing the villages perched on their towering hilltops, the campaniles watching over the futile centuries and the invaders that came with them.

By the road, under the shade of spreading trees, African prostitutes sat stoically waiting for clients. On the far side of Potenza town they saw the first signs for Eboli and then Salerno. Before Eboli there was, as he had expected, the first police roadblock. A stab of fear and he slowed, as he had to, and the girl glanced over at him for a moment as if something had suddenly occurred to her. But he was glacial in his calm. The *carabinieri* here were not stopping the cars, merely looking them over. When they saw the handsome young couple in the Peugeot they waved them past.

Five miles on the sun returned and they ventured down a side road and got out. They stretched their legs and lay for a while in long grass and a multitude of poppies. She seemed a little shaken by the roadblock, but was hesitant to ask him directly if she had cause to be shaken, though she did summon up the nerve to ask him if he was running away from someone.

"What an idea," he said.

The Africans. They were everywhere now, laboring up the peninsula from the detention centers in Sicily. They had heard all about them in Istanbul. But even with them there was peace in the land of the *roumi*, when you lay on your back among the poppies staring up at blue space; it was outside of time. There was no gunfire, no chaos, and the quietude of the land was the most striking thing about it, the most salient characteristic of its oddness.

At noon they came to the sea at a place called Castellabate and saw a village perched far above the sea with a sign for a restaurant and hotel called Il Frantoio. Since it seemed remote and pleasant at the same time, he suggested going up and having a look.

The former olive mill converted into a hotel clung to the edge of the cliff and looked out at a shadowless sea upon which the ferries from Salerno moved with a lovely indolence. They rang a bell. To the door came a massive man with an eye patch, the owner, and after a cursory up-and-down glance at their clothes (Faoud made up for Benedetta) they were invited into a large dining room and a shot of limoncello in glasses shaped like tulips. The owner spoke to Benedetta, and her ID card was enough to satisfy him. Then Faoud handed over Jimmie's credit card. Blind in one eye, the owner's active eye had an exaggerated keenness that cut into others with intensified precision.

They went outside to a panoramic terrace. The owner served them from a bottle of cold Falanghina, but Faoud held his hand over his glass.

"I'm having a day off," he said with a smile.

"*Bene fatto*," the man said. He went on: "One night or two, Mr. Codrington? We have a set menu in the evening which you will love."

Faoud turned to Benedetta as if she were his wife and therefore needed to be consulted on the matter.

"We'll try one," she said. "And then see."

They went up to their room drowsily. The windows opened also to the sea; the sun's glare made the walls mustily luminous. She lay on the bed as if expectantly, but without any nervousness. He went to the window and bathed in the marine light for a while. It was one of those days when the convergence of sea and sky at the horizon was imperceptible to the naked eye. The girl turned on her side and watched him. The fact that he didn't want anything from her did not seem to have any effect other than amusing her, but there was a soft, baffled contempt all the same, expertly concealed for a while. Her body language spread on the bed was a clear invitation. But he was not sure if he would accept it. It was, after all, a gift from an alien world that he was not entitled to accept. Taking it by force would be more appropriate, but that was not in the code of a gentleman. Eventually, he tired of the struggle with himself and took off his jacket, unbuttoned the Abbarchi shirt, and turned from the windows to the girl, who had now rotated onto her back and was staring up at a small, dusty glass chandelier. The owner had solidly bourgeois and ponderous tastes, but his rooms were cozy and conducive to disarmament. He went to the bed and ran his fingers through her hair and she said nothing, but she didn't brush the fingers away either.

During the night he left the windows open and mosquitoes poured in from the forest and ate him alive. He only realized it when it was too late and his body was covered with venomous little lumps. Even the mosquitoes, then, in this sinister and inviting land sensed his hostile blood and went on the attack. He closed the windows—she was still asleep—and the room became suffocating. Cursing, he got up and opened them again. The tiny demons were still there, hovering just out of reach.

Suffocate or be eaten alive: such was the choice with which God had tested him.

It was for His reasons. He thought of creeping out of the room with all his belongings, letting himself out of the hotel, and driving away quietly. But he had suddenly found himself attracted to the Nazarene woman's attentiveness as they were kissing, but not making love. He considered that since God had thrown this woman in his path he should not be so hasty in discarding the gift. Another two days, perhaps, and then he would go back to being alone. But who could say? Life was undeniably more agreeable with her at his side. And so far she had not shown any inclination to expose him. She wanted something from him as much as he wanted something from her. *Jayid jiddaan thumm.* One didn't have to be a fool about it.

Satisfied without sex, he slept much better. But when he woke, he found that it was he who was alone, and that it was Benedetta who had slipped unnoticed out of the room. Nor was she at breakfast. The owner, bringing his coffee, simply said, "No one saw her. Did she go out for a swim?"

"A swim?" Faoud said.

Slowly, it dawned on him.

He went to the car and found that the money was gone. To his own surprise, he didn't fly into a rage; he was merely glad that she hadn't taken the car as well. It was the way of these thieving Europeans. One had to face them down with a calm resolve and a capacity for revenge. He went back inside the hotel as if nothing had happened, for after all the last thing he could afford was a scene and a brush with the police. She must have guessed as much.

Therefore, he sat instead on the terrace in view of the azurite sea of the Romans and drank his coffee with the owner's homemade croissants. Afterward he walked calmly around the compact village of Castellabate and dried the sweat at his temples. Heat blew in from the olive fields. He forced himself to forget about the affront and to contemplate only the future: that, and the cool stone arches of the dead Christians and the smell of their pasta boiling in pots nearby. Their world didn't matter anyway—it was nearly a ruin.

DAIMONIA

SEVENTEEN

ROCKHOLD WOKE PUNCTUALLY AT THE BRATSERAS IN A room full of dried sponges. Hours of nightmares flooded his mind still as he groped for the glass of water by the bed and tried to see the sun glimmering behind the slats of the shutters. He called his wife in England at once.

"Minnie? Don't forget to water the sunflowers."

"Did you have a nightmare?" the little voice at the other end asked, by way of brushing his injunction aside.

"I was being eaten by dolphins."

"How horrible. Poppy, make sure you eat your grapefruit."

Obediently, he ate a grapefruit alone by the hotel pool. He dressed up even for this humble occasion, because military habits die hard, especially when they have been acquired over many years and at considerable psychological expense. In this respect he was unlike Jimmie. The panama laid to one side, the plump linens, the suede drivers easy on his feet. I shall grow old, I shall grow old, went his mantra, I shall smoke my cigarettes rolled. All the worst expectations had come brilliantly true, as they always must.

The wealthy foreigners staying at the Bratseras got up later than he did and so he had an hour by himself next to the ripening lemon trees with only the Russian waitress to talk to. He read his e-mails, emptied his mind of the night's unpleasant dreams, and went over the notes he had made the evening before over a lonely dinner. Days had gone by with no word from Jimmie. It was an unprecedented aberration. He had explained it to Minnie, because he was showing signs of insomnia and anxiety about Jimmie's disappearance and she had noticed. Finally, she had suggested that he take a plane down to Athens and sort it out on the ground. It was the only way to resolve something difficult, and with that he had wholeheartedly agreed. His old friend paid him, and paid him handsomely, to look over his shoulder and ward off the dangers, the inconveniences and the sudden disasters that are always waiting to happen to a man like Jimmie Codrington. He was "the sword," as Jimmie had called him, the old man who sorted out the young ones. There was a great and secretive bond between them, formed by a long friendship, that had ended by being a form of patronage when Rockhold had fallen on hard times. Jimmie's business dealings were far-flung and lacking in all transparence; he dabbled in things that attracted him because they were dangerous. Rockhold was like the bodyguard one never sees or hears, though his function was not a physical one most of the time. He was too old for that. "You're my eyes and ears," Jimmie often said to him to reassure him that he was always needed, and he would add, "My intuitions and hunches, too." They talked every day, or almost. When his friend didn't answer his phones for days, Rockhold knew that it was time to move and search and resolve.

He had only been to Greece once before, many years earlier. It was an unfamiliar theater of operations. He decided not to jump to any conclusions nor to panic, and so he took it one day at a time, with an open mind. But the situation was baffling. It was eccentric, for one thing, for Jimmie and Funny to not even be on the island; the girl was as distant and remote as her father

184

had often portrayed her. Though a "quisling"? That was a little too sharp. She was just a smooth actor, though a smooth actor is certainly not to be underrated. He went down to the port after his breakfast and ambled slowly among the idle yachts to see if he could "pocket" any early risers on the decks or the quays, mariners manning small boats who might recognize the photograph he carried of Naomi. Day after day he did this, until he found the old Greek who had rented her the boat in which she had gone to Palamidas.

It was understood that Naomi had paid for his silence, but he gave this precious silence up for a slightly greater sum. His English was fragmentary, but it was enough. Rockhold got the word "Palamidas" out of him.

He went back to the hotel and asked the two middle-aged ladies manning the desk if he could hire a translator for the week. One of them had a nephew who would be glad to make a few euros, and he was at the hotel within an hour. It was a boy of about sixteen whose English was good enough, and they went together back to the port and rented the boat. Since neither of them knew how to use it, they rented the owner as well.

Through the boy, Rockhold asked him to take them to where he had taken Naomi. It was an easy request to fulfill. The sail to Palamidas passed along the coastline that Rockhold had heard about many times from Jimmie. The villas, the steps, the burned-dry hills. But it didn't impress him as much as he had expected. The odor of foreign wealth lay upon it. At Palamidas they left the boatman at the shore, and Rockhold and the boy climbed up the hillside where the boatman said the girl had gone many times. Surely, he added, to Episkopi. They reached it at about ten o'clock.

To Rockhold's eye it looked to be a different world from the villas of the coast. It was abandoned and windswept, and he liked it better. A thoroughly miserable place, but miserable precisely because it was beautiful—and vice versa. The south, he thought. They knocked at some houses.

Before long they saw two men smoking pipes and reclining at their ease on a grass slope. The old shepherds had turned intransigent gazes upon the newcomers, but they made no motion of acknowledgment or welcome. Rockhold and the boy struggled up to them and the boy made the first greeting.

"This gentleman is looking for a girl," he said to them. They glanced up at the strangers with a cool, even flagrant, disregard. "Here is her photograph."

The picture of Naomi brought a quick snort to one of the men.

"Ah, that one!"

The boy translated, but Rockhold betrayed no feeling.

"He recognizes her?"

After the translation the man said, "She was up here to see her lover. I rented him the shack."

"Which shack?"

"Up there." The man flicked a hand toward a run-down hovel higher up.

"Lover?" Rockhold said.

"Eh, she had an Arab in there. He was there a few nights. It's against the law, but I didn't say anything."

"What was his name?" Rockhold asked.

"How should I know? I didn't invite him round to tea."

"How do you know he was an Arab?"

"I can tell them a mile off. I saw his boat arrive. They dropped him off, then left. That was unusual."

"You didn't tell the police?"

186

The men looked away finally, and the pipes absorbed them.

"She must have paid them," the boy said quietly to Rockhold in English.

So that's how it works here, the Englishman thought.

You paid a man off, he held his tongue, and secrets went to ground.

"Can you ask him if she did?" he persisted.

But the boy shook his head. Such questions were extremely impolite.

Rockhold asked if he could go up and have a look at the hut, and the man agreed without visible reluctance.

"I haven't touched it since he left," he said to the boy.

Rockhold went up there alone. The hut was a shambles, but there was nothing in it that betrayed the presence of a stranger. He went through it quickly and then came back out into the sun. So Naomi had had a lover up here. Had she told Jimmie and Phaine?

When he went back down, the Greeks were laughing all together. He had the feeling, unconfirmed, that they were laughing at him. Undeniably, he was no longer a dashing figure, but he was annoyed that the boy had apparently joined them in their mockery. He took out his notebook by way of retaliation.

"When did Naomi last come up here?"

Predictably, the man was vague.

"A few weeks ago. I can't remember. They left together."

"She and the lover?"

"They went down to the resort. My cousin says they checked in there together."

"And she never came back?"

"Why would she? She wasn't coming to see us."

"Well, then we'll go to the resort," Rockhold said to the boy.

When they got there the receptionist wanted to know who he was and why he was asking questions. Rockhold said that he was trying to find a young friend, a man who had stayed there with an English girl.

"The man in room 34?"

"I don't know what room it was."

He showed them Naomi's face and it was agreed: room 34.

"When did he leave?"

The girl looked through the book and saw that it had been only ten days earlier.

Rockhold wrote everything down in his notebook. He wanted to go and look at the room. He asked her if the young man had left his ID with them to photocopy. But it had been Naomi who had done so.

"And the young man," he kept trying, "do you know where he went from here?"

The girl shook her head slowly. "Guests don't tell us where they are going."

When he had finished his interview, he gave the boy forty euros and told him to take the boat back to Hydra with the boatman. He wanted to return on foot himself. There was only one path winding its way to the port and it was impossible to get lost on it. In truth, he was relieved to be alone again. Being a great hiker, he was always inclined to hit the road alone.

When he had climbed out of sight of Palamidas he felt more contemplative. He walked slowly, never letting himself get out of breath, and he took the inclines with care. An hour later he was at Kamini. He sat in Kodylenia's and watched the sea. Something told him that the sea was the key to the mystery with which he was confronted, because the lover had emerged from it and it was likely that he now had to track the lover. Jimmie had left a last message on his phone and it had not been quite "right." *Call me back.* It was the kind of message that the irascible and confident millionaire might well leave, but there was something wrong about its timing. The early hours of the morning, Greek time.

Farther along the path he passed a few of the villas with their blue shutters and their porches filled with amphorae. Donkeys in the surrounding fields stood untethered in their own pools of midday shadow, the verges conquered by dark blue flowers. A family sat eating lunch with wind chimes tinkling around them. They looked up; he doffed his hat in his courtly way and one could see why the Codringtons lived here, because despite the new wealth and its trash it was, just under its shiny skin, the old Europe still. A few shreds of manners survived from the old days. He had learned to say *"Kalo apogevma"* and smile, and at the Bratseras he took a siesta and then swam in the hotel pool with a feeling of detachment from which the traces of religion had not been entirely withdrawn. That feeling was imposed on all living things by a Mycenaean sky and a scent of lemons.

AT THE VILLA, Naomi had spent several days by herself. She slept in the salon because she couldn't bear to go upstairs to the bedrooms, and there, like a squatter, she lived on bread, feta, and the robust tomatoes that she bought every morning in the port market. Rudderless, day by day she sunbathed on the terrace and her nightmares came by noon's terrible light. This left her nights unusually empty and free of worry. She ate at the same table where she used to eat with Jimmie and Phaine. She served herself wine and afterward mixed a cocktail while listening to Jimmie's jazz. Above the record player there was an old photograph of him sitting inside Ronnie Scott's in London with a Castro-size cigar, staring out at the unfriendly future that would eventually erase him. She rolled a joint after a few squares of chocolate, and all in all it was not what she had wanted or planned; it was just what had happened.

In the afternoons she sometimes walked down to Mandraki and beyond, taking care not to cross paths with the Haldanes. She lay alone on the hot slopes and waited for the girl in the rowing boat to appear. She was glad to talk to someone in Greek and exchange a few euros for the precious weed. Someone who didn't know her or Jimmie and Phaine. Dorinda was surely not the girl's real name, but she was not in any way duplicitous. The girl tethered the boat and they sat together among the burning rocks.

"I see the Turk left and went to the mainland," Dorinda said.

"He's not Turkish."

"He came from there. My boyfriend told me about it."

"They all come from there."

"Maybe they do, by God."

"By God" was lovelier in Greek: *apo ton theo.*

"I thought it was a shipwreck."

"Maybe it was, *apo ton theo.* What do you think?"

"Me?" Naomi said. "I don't care about anything anymore."

"It's a good attitude. Are you staying for the summer?"

"For a while. I always stay for the summer."

"I have some new clients here—from Athens. If you come this way I'll be here every day. I'll be a millionaire by September!"

The weed that Naomi smoked on her terrace was earthy and hard-hitting, and it laid her low for the nights when she couldn't sleep. On rare occasions, Sam joined her and they played checkers and danced together to Jimmie's records. The American girl was becoming leaner and more tanned. Her hair had begun to show sun-dried streaks, and Naomi knew that she was hanging out with a boy about whom she never spoke.

"But where is Carissa?" Sam asked. "Isn't she supposed to be back by now?"

"She comes back tomorrow morning. But I've decided to let her go. There's nothing for her to do now. She'll be upset, though."

"She won't turn on you?"

Naomi had been considering exactly this.

"Anyone can turn on anyone. But she won't."

"She's loyal to the family?"

"Something like that."

Sam snorted scornfully. "That's a good one!"

"It's the way we are here, little Sam."

They got drunk together on mastika, and in the night's heat their skin became lustrous. Sam told her that her father had become curious about the whereabouts of the Codringtons, and had asked whether they had left the island for good. She'd told him that for all she knew they had. There was some time yet before they returned to New York, and the nightmare was going to consist in keeping up the lie.

"I know, Sam. But we just have to go on as we are. Everyone leaves the island in September. The place is deserted. At that point we're home safe. You just have to believe."

AT SEVEN NAOMI went down to the port to meet Carissa on the ferry. She dressed in black like a young widow, with sunglasses and red lipstick, and sat at the cafe closest to the dock where the boat would arrive. Carissa saw her at once as she came down the gangplank: healthy-looking, slightly plumper, having gorged on mama's cooking for a few days. She wore a new dress and looked, to Naomi's eyes, completely different—suaver and less demoralized. It was the effect, too, of not having to endure Phaine's bullying and Jimmie's priapic antics. She had gone back to her people and she had thrived. Perhaps it would make her more difficult to deal with.

It was the first thing that occurred to Naomi, and it turned out to be true. They rented a donkey to carry Carissa's lone bag up to the villa, and on the way they stopped in leisurely fashion at a bar. The employer-employee relation had disappeared completely. They had always liked each other and had always been complicit. But now that the Codringtons were dead the pivot had shifted and Carissa had lost her mild subservience.

Her Greek was rough and obscene now, and she bawled with laughter when the barmen made jokes that were directed at the two single girls. Naomi was ruffled, but she held her own. She thought she might as well broach the difficult subject at once, and she asked Carissa if she really wanted to carry on working at the house now that it served no purpose.

"I've been thinking about it," the girl said without even blinking. "You know I've been with your family for seven years. But I saved up some money."

"I'm glad to hear that."

"Now that the master and madame are gone, it would feel awkward carrying on there. You don't need a maid."

"No, I don't," Naomi said.

"So I don't know about staying on with you. But I have the feeling you've made that decision already."

"I have?"

"I think you have, Naomi. What do you want me to do?"

"I hadn't thought about it as me wanting you to do something."

"You want me to disappear, though. It would be better for you."

"I'm grateful that you did what you did."

"I'm grateful for the money. But it won't be enough, I'm afraid. I can go away tomorrow if you like. You see, I want to buy a shop in my home village. I found the place. I figure the master must have been worth several million."

They were in a narrow alley, the cafe tables pressed hard against the walls. The air was thick with stupefied wasps attracted to the unremoved alcoholic glasses standing on the tables. Naomi lowered her voice and leaned in a little so that absolutely nothing she said would be heard.

"Maybe we should discuss this up at the villa?"

"As you like. I really don't mind where we discuss it."

"But you know, Carissa—I didn't do anything for money. It was all an accident."

"Yeah, whatever it was. But it came in handy anyway."

"It's not really as simple as that, is it?"

"I don't know how simple it is," Carissa said. "Why don't you tell me? For all I know, you wanted them dead."

They were silent as they climbed up to the house. Once there, Carissa made them tea and they sat on the terrace in the shade.

"If you can pay me tomorrow," the maid said, "I can just leave right away and go back to my mother. My mother won't ask any questions. What do you think?"

"It depends how much you want."

"I've been thinking about it. I know the estate won't be settled for a long time and until your family decides what happened to your father. Maybe they won't settle it at all. But I'm sure you can access the money."

"How would I do that?"

"You can do it, Naomi. I know you."

Naomi held her tongue, because maids always knew more than they let on. They knew everything, in fact.

"It would be pretty dangerous to take out any large sums," she said. "Don't you think?"

"You can pay in installments, I don't mind. There's no hurry. I was thinking—you could do fifty thousand euros. It's not too much to ask. I know what the bank balances are and it's not too much. It wouldn't be a burden on you."

"You have it all worked out, don't you?"

"I didn't sign up for being an accessory to murder, you know. It's not fair to me. Not at all. It's your fault it happened that way."

"Yes," Naomi said bitterly, "you're right. It is. In a way, it is."

"I know you couldn't have foreseen it. But it was a stupid plan that was bound to go wrong. Now I'm ruined by it."

"You're not ruined."

"If the police show up, I have to disappear. And I want that shop when I disappear. But I need money to do it."

"All right, I understand. I'm not an idiot."

"You're just selfish. You always were selfish, Naomi. It wasn't about helping the migrant, it was about you and your father and

Phaine. I know, they were cruel to you. It's not entirely your fault."

"But I can't give you fifty grand just like that. If I get you five, will you go back to the mainland? You'll have to trust me for the rest."

"No, Naomi, you'll have to trust *me*. But I know you'll send it, because it would be pretty bad if you didn't."

Naomi sipped her tea and decided to be as cordial as she could.

"You're a very good blackmailer," she said. "I wouldn't have guessed you had it in you. But I understand. It's nothing personal, is it?"

"On the contrary. It's very personal. I wasted seven years of my life here slaving for you. I'm not letting it go to waste. Five thousand and I'll leave tomorrow."

"Is that a promise?"

"Of course it's a promise. Don't be silly. I don't want to be here anyway."

"You'll go back to your mother's village?"

"I'd be happier that way. I told you I found the perfect shop to buy."

Naomi got up and went to the kitchen to look for some honey to spoon into her tea. She found the honey, took out the spool, and dripped a small amount into the center of a saucer. She then opened the rackety utensils drawer and saw her father's cooking knives laid out in their rows, some of them large and serrated. She picked one out, turned it against the opposing palm. The girl had half turned in her chair on the terrace, gazing out from the shade at the mountains, but her ears twitched with feral intuitions. Naomi replaced the knife and closed the drawer. When she returned to the coffee table she scooped the honey into her cup and her unstable hand immediately caught Carissa's attention.

"Are you upset?" she asked Naomi.

"No. I'm just trying to think everything out. I can't sleep at night, too—you should give me some of your hemlock tea."

"But I left it here for you."

Naomi blinked, and a faint redness appeared at the tops of her cheeks.

"I didn't notice. But speaking of that, I did want to ask you something. I can't understand how he could have woken up like he did. After you gave him the tea—"

"It can happen."

"Maybe it can. But did you give them the full dose?"

"What are you saying?"

"I mean, did you give them the full dose, Carissa?"

"I told you I did."

"Then he couldn't have woken up."

Carissa's fingers had dug into the arms of her chair and her teeth had set. There was a short tussle of words, the mutual anger rose, and then Naomi gave up on it and said that in the end it didn't matter. What was done was done. But now, regardless, she didn't believe that Carissa had given them a full dose. The girl had employed a considerable cunning to get her way.

"He could have woken up," the girl said quietly, "believe me. They had been drinking all night. The alcohol interfered."

During the afternoon Carissa slept in her old room and Naomi went down to the port to shop for her. The old friend of her father's, meanwhile, was leaving messages every hour, asking for dinner, and sooner or later she would have to accommodate him. It was better to do it once and get it over and done with, since avoidance on her part would merely serve to make her look suspicious.

When she had returned to the house she answered the last message from Rockhold and told him that she would meet him at the Sunset for dinner at eight. She had prepared her story meticulously over the previous days, and she felt confident she could pull off a credible performance for a seventy-year-old still open, she thought, to the charm of women.

EIGHTEEN

I N THOSE DAYS WE WERE QUITE DIFFERENT, YOUR FA-
ther and I. Jimmie was all for jaunts to Malaga and even
Tangiers. He had energy. He was friends with David Beaufort,
even then. He went all over the Med in his Spanish beret and
this wonderful red necktie he had. We used to call him Tally-
ho. It was the Hemingway thing. You wouldn't understand. I
was rather in awe of him then. He was a splendid pilot too—it
takes something special to be a pilot that good."

"He never talked about being a pilot."

Rockhold held up a shrimp by its tail and shook it slightly as
if it was still alive and something could be shaken out of it.

"The thing is, one gets tired of one's own stories. It happens
by the time you turn fifty. You've heard them all a thousand
times, and they get worse with each retelling. Finally, they become nauseating."

"Maybe he was ashamed of something."

"Shame? That would be a big emotion for Jimmie. I think
not. Fatigue, more likely. He was a terrible gambler too."

Naomi didn't even raise her carefully tended eyebrows.

"Did he break the bank at Monte Carlo too?"

"I'm sure it was on his CV somewhere. I always wondered
about him being a father, though. Did he ever take you on holiday aside from coming here?"

"Never. He was a terrible dad."

Neither of them was quite serious: summers on Hydra were hardly negligible as holidays.

"I'm sorry to hear it. I rather gathered—"

"Terrible dads always lie about being terrible dads. It's the icing on the cake of being a terrible dad."

"You mean, he *is* a terrible dad."

"Childhood's always in the past tense, Mr. Rockhold."

Rockhold's head slipped to one side and his smile was off-center, too. The daughter was prickly. It was better to tread carefully.

"Do you think they've driven back to Italy?" she asked.

"Well, it looks like it, doesn't it?"

"Do you *know* they did?"

"I do have to come clean a bit, Naomi. I look after some of your father's business interests. Not all of them all the time. But some of his financial and security concerns. We are normally in close contact. While he does sometimes go off on a spree with Funny, it's unusual for him to be gone more than a few days. On the way over I took the trouble to stop in at the car park at Metochi where they keep their car. It's not there."

"You know about Metochi?"

"Jimmie thought of it as a secretive little place."

"So they did take the car?"

"I don't know. As I say, it rather looks that way."

"That was very sly of them."

She felt that she was holding him at bay quite well, and she began to feel more confident.

He said, "May I ask, were they having rows lately?"

Seeing an opening, Naomi took some trouble to appear surprised.

"Come to think of it," she said, "they had been fighting more than usual. Not that that's any of my business. I don't know what goes on between them."

"It had occurred to me that they went off to solve some romantic problem. Couples do that, I hear."

"Do they?"

"Seems rather exaggerated to me."

"So the car is gone." She sighed.

"A bit rum, that." Rockhold poured wine into her glass. "Maybe they went on a tour of classical sites."

"Extraordinarily unlikely."

"I always thought he was an Ancient Greece buff. Maybe I misunderstood."

"They had a few arguments about the houses," Naomi went on, not wanting to get onto the subject of Ancient Greece. "But I never listened in on them. I think Phaine wanted to sell the place in Italy. But Daddy is very fond of that house."

"So they might have gone there?"

"I really can't say. It's possible."

They talked on for a while, Rockhold ordering one bottle after another. He did most of the drinking, and it seemed to have no effect on him whatsoever. It was a different generation, and they drank in a way that was now incomprehensible to younger people. For them it was like showering or taking out the dog.

"About that maid," he said eventually. "Is she here or did she leave as well? Maybe Jimmie gave her some time off since they would be gone."

"Carissa?"

"That's her name, isn't it?"

"She's not at the house. So she must have gone home for a while."

He asked her what she looked like, and for the first time Naomi stumbled over her words as she tried to think them out. She tried to be vague, to mislead a little.

"Either way, I think she might be of help," Rockhold said affably.

"I doubt it, Mr. Rockhold. She's a bit dim and she doesn't know anything about Jimmie and Phaine. My father keeps her on out of loyalty."

"That's very decent of him."

"It's very stingy of him, actually."

"Do you have a number for her?"

"I'm sorry, I don't. It's my stepmother who deals with that sort of thing."

He accepted this and let it go. Should they move on to whiskey? She declined, and he ordered for himself. He remarked that it was a special spot, this Sunset, and that the toy cannons put him at ease. He asked about her childhood on the island. Did she have many Greek friends from those days? The ex-pats seemed to be a tightly knit group, as such people always were. The island English were bookish, socially privileged, keenly interested in the culture around them. But lately, the Russians and the Emirati seemed to be displacing them. He had met quite a few of the English in the few days he'd been there. They were uniformly delightful. They all had good things to say about Jimmie and Phaine.

At that moment his phone began ringing and, glancing down at the incoming number, he told Naomi that this was a call he could not ignore. He got up and walked to the path above the restaurant. The call was from his assistant in London, a woman called Susan who was also on the Codrington payroll, though Jimmie barely knew of her existence. His own wife barely knew of her existence. Susan tracked credit-card transactions and the various movements of Jimmie's operatives. She was calling him about some new transactions in Italy.

"Mr. Codrington used his card a short while ago in a town called Fasano. It's in southern Italy."

"Fasano?"

"At a shoe shop."

"He bought some shoes?"

"Apparently."

"Where is this Fasano?"

"I'll send you a map."

"What kind of shoes?"

"Expensive shoes."

Well, I'll be damned, he thought.

"He wouldn't buy cheap ones," he said.

He went back to the table, and instead of dissimulating he told Naomi exactly what he had just heard.

"Italy?" she blurted out.

"So it seems. He bought a pair of shoes in a place called Fasano."

She thought for a moment. Would Faoud buy a pair of shoes with Jimmie's credit card? He must have. He didn't have any shoes, but he could have used cash: it was a mistake.

"I'm rather surprised," she lied. "They left without saying anything to me. It's quite rude."

"Maybe something came up?"

"Came up? I doubt it."

She was put out, and he took note. But there was no way of saying what it meant. He treated her with care from then on, steering the conversation away from her father and stepmother so that she would be put at ease. He let it be known that he was satisfied that they were on the road in Italy and that he would, perhaps, leave the island soon and go to Italy to find them himself. There was now no reason to persist with his inquiries on Hydra.

"I've called them at the house in Sorano," Naomi said, "but they never pick up. Do you think something could have happened to them?"

"Not if Jimmie is buying fancy shoes."

"What will you do in Italy, then?"

Rockhold wasn't sure himself.

"Find them, I suppose. I can't imagine why they're hiding from us. It's extraordinarily childish."

"I couldn't agree more."

"By the way, are you staying here all summer? Or going back to London?"

She looked at him steadily, and she held her whole body erect and poised. He was a man, she now realized, who had to be fended off with a light touch. She didn't feel that he was entirely suspicious of her, but his half-suspicion, his invisibly alert animal antennae, were attuned to the slightest muscular reaction on her part. He was a bloodhound, and his nose was refined. It didn't matter that he called her "dear" and paid the bill.

"I'm not going anywhere, Mr. Rockhold. In fact, I'm thinking about moving here. It's my summer home, after all."

"What a delightful idea."

"Of course, I have to ask Jimmie and Phaine first."

He looked at her and his eyes seemed to separate; she reconsidered what she had thought before, that one of them was glass. But there was no way of asking.

He walked back to the Bratseras alone. In the little area by the port there was a jazz concert without a stage, the musicians playing with their backs to the water and the lit-up yachts. He sat at one of the cafes and got himself a Pernod. He called Susan back and asked her to book a ticket to Bari on a flight out of Athens, and then lost himself in reverie. His eye was itching and he couldn't wait to get it out for the night, but the evening was too enjoyable to abandon. He thought about Naomi instead. Her father had always said she was a tremendously gifted liar, and he wondered if he had just been treated to a perfect demonstration of this talent? He had noticed her heels, the earrings and the lipstick. It was too much for an hour or two at the Sunset with an old man. She had gone a little too far. There was a fracture just below her surface which made her seem decentered, and yet she herself was not aware of it. She was lying, but he could only detect this falsity with the part of his consciousness that was unconscious.

LEFT AT THE table, Naomi called Sam and made a suggestion. Why didn't they go to Athens the following day and escape the claustrophobia of the island? She had to go into the city to take out the money for Carissa, but it was a boring trip if she did it alone. Sam not only agreed, but jumped at the idea. She said she had spent a painfully dull day swimming by herself and she asked if they could do something different in Athens.

"Different in what way?"

"Can we go to a fancy restaurant? Can we get drunk? Blow off some steam?"

"It's about time," Naomi said. "And it's my treat."

She returned to the villa and found Carissa awake and enjoying Jimmie's brandy. It was shameless now, and her expression was openly insolent, but Naomi let it slide in the interest of peace. Instead, she went to her room and waited for the maid to do the same.

It took a long time. Carissa sang to herself in the salon and played the radio; it was close to midnight before she went down to the basement and closed her door. When quiet had returned Naomi went back down to the salon and saw that the maid had left everything on the table where she had eaten. Her soiled wineglass, plates with cheese rinds, serviettes. She had left everything on purpose. Naomi went around the room making sure she hadn't stolen anything, then scooped out Phaine's heritage silver spoons from the service drawers and took the two silver candlesticks that stood on the mantelpiece, bracketing pictures of Jimmie and Phaine caught as if unawares in various corners of the world. She rolled them all into a tablecloth and took them upstairs to pack into a sports bag. Then she returned to the salon, turned off the lights, and locked the doors. Perhaps it was the final night of being with another human being in the Villa Belle Air. She wrote a note for Carissa explaining that she was going to Athens in the morning and would be back in the evening the following day with the money. She wanted to spend a night in Athens just to be sure. She hadn't wanted to tell her to her face; Carissa would have grown suspicious and she would probably have objected. She left it on the dining table and went out into the garden, where the tree's upper branches were bathed in silver light and long-domiciled cicadas sang in the walls around it. It was not a cemetery, but a hushed sanctuary filled with bones, and this simplicity made it more beautiful than it had been before.

THE EARLY FERRY to Piraeus passed through a narrow strait separating the mainland from the island of Poros. By Galatas the waters were little more than a canal, and every time she went through it Naomi felt the dread that came from being squeezed into that arid defile. They observed the scene from the deck eating souvlaki sandwiches with mayonnaise, their noses painted with sun cream, and this time she felt no dread whatsoever. They passed Aegina, its calcimine houses shining under a cloudless sky, tidy as shrines. They were happier as soon as Hydra and Poros had disappeared below the horizon and the luminosity was ahead of them and not behind.

Separately, it occurred to both of them that they could make a run for the airport and take their chances. They had their passports with them. But the enticing thought came and went, and once it had gone it would never return. At the port they half ran into the street and stopped a taxi to take them into the city; to the neighborhood of Caravel and a cafe called Oroscopo where Naomi had been going for years. It was a Sunday, and the streets were subdued, though not far away from Oroscopo a clown in dreadlocks performed fire tricks at a traffic light. They had the first drink of the day, two beers, and ordered omelettes. They suddenly felt exultant. Naomi finally opened the bag she had brought with her and showed Sam the silverware. She was going to take it to a shop she knew near the Plaka and sell it off.

"That's wild," Sam cried. "So now you're going full gangsta?"

"I may as well. I don't want this crap in my house."

"Won't they ask where it came from?"

"You forget, I was a foul teenager here. I know all the places. You don't think it's my first time selling Phaine's silver on the sly, do you? She never noticed. She certainly won't notice now."

"Her ghost will."

"Well, her ghost can't stop me. I don't believe in ghosts anyway. I've already decided I'm going to make some changes in her arrangements."

"So you're going to renovate the house?"

"I'll wait till everything dies down—then yes. I'm going to clear it out and start again. I'm going to paint it all blue inside. It'll be so much more beautiful. I'll make it like my mother wanted it to be. She had taste, unlike that bitch. Jimmie had taste, only it was bad taste. I suppose it's better than having no taste at all."

At high noon, with the shadows at their most diminished and the streets lit as if by neon, they took a taxi to the Plaka and climbed up to the Acropolis through the slopes of pines, which broke up the heat. At the Propylaea they took some selfies against the steep steps leading up to the Parthenon and suddenly the secret society of two had begun to blossom once more without anyone to inhibit it.

When they got to the Parthenon and into the full sunlight, the view of the islands far off in their haze took their thoughts away, and in response they sat on one of the walls and looked down at the Theatre of Dionysus below it. The walls, more ancient than the temples, with their darker color and weeds, always filled Naomi with memories of her father. Childhood summers, when Jimmie took her here with her mother and they had picnics on the walls. It was her father's one noble idea: the transmission of the idea of Eternal Greece. But it was a mystery why he had this idea in the first place and why he didn't act on it in any other part of his life, let alone his insalubrious business dealings. The two elements existed side by side in his character without anyone's knowing how or why. Perhaps it came from his own childhood, since he had always been an avid reader. And because it came from his own childhood, it had entered hers and had remained with her. Sitting on the wall with Sam and saying nothing was her last farewell to him.

After an hour they went back down to the Areopagus and a fiery view of the city. The rock, unchanged for millennia, the place where Solon and Pericles stood; and the twenty-first-century city, battered almost to death. Tourists streamed back down to main paths, Koreans and Taiwanese, and as dusk fell the site's solitude reimposed itself. They sat close together without talking as thousands of lights came on, and Sam thought, we could stay here all night, I wouldn't mind. She was admiring Naomi more, and was almost in awe of her decisiveness, her ability to turn on a dime and improvise for her own benefit. She had not been fazed for more than a few moments, although Sam admitted to herself that there was also something unsettling about this same quality. Quiet and dogged, Naomi had swept onwards like the beautiful criminal she was at heart, unaware of the complexities of conscience.

"We'll spend the night at the Grande Bretagne," Naomi said at length, taking her hand for a moment. As if, knowing this city better than anyone who spoke their language, she had the credentials to decide everything two girls might do during a free evening in it. "It's where we Codringtons always stay. There'll only be one of us now, but I'll have a Haldane with me—and that's far better all round. I think I can pay for it with a candlestick. Maybe two."

They walked down into the Plaka. Its once-maddening tourist crush had diminished, which was precisely why it had become more quietly desperate. Just beyond it were old boutiques on the verge of extinction and, conversely, pawnshops doing brisk business. Naomi sat Sam in a cafe and made her wait while she sold the silver. It was pointless to involve her in a transaction that might be witnessed. Agreeing this time, Sam waited with her *metrios*. A half hour later Naomi came back without the bag and with an impressive amount of cash.

"We could fly to Bali with this. Shall we?"

"Let's!"

Instead they took another taxi to the Grande Bretagne on one side of Syntagma Square and checked in with Naomi's Greek ID card. The staff knew her well, however, and they asked immediately after Mr. and Mrs. Codrington.

"They're in Rome," she said coolly. "Can we have Daddy's suite? This is my cousin, Samantha."

"Certainly, Miss Codrington."

"And bring up a bottle of gin with some Canada Dry."

They bowed by just moving their heads.

Naomi and Sam went up to the suite and closed the tall windows against the sun. In fifteen minutes the room had cooled down. There were sets of games in the room, and they played Scrabble on the bed all afternoon while drinking the gin and Canada Dry. Sam was the winner.

"I'm going to take you to an amazing restaurant tonight," Naomi said. "A known Codrington nightspot. But I think, *apo ton theo*, that you've earned an evening there. And so have I."

"By God, eh?"

They slept for two hours, then dressed. Descending to the haughty lobby, they asked for a taxi to go to Kolonaki, where they were let off at a quiet corner with no crowds and from where they sauntered up a small street to a place called Spondi. Jimmie and Phaine knew the owners well, and there were unassuming outer walls to protect them. They came in and the waiters looked happier than usual to see them. They were accustomed to uttering cries of "Mister Jimmie!" and displaying a dramatic courtesy toward the Greek woman, Phaine, whose father they had known in the days of Costas Simitis. For it was Phaine's Athenian family who enjoyed gravity here.

They were shown to Mister Jimmie's usual table.

"Just bring us something delicious," Naomi said to them in Greek. "My cousin has never eaten here before. I want you to show her what you can do."

They were still tipsy from the afternoon's gin, and Sam was the tipsier of the two.

"My parents never take me anywhere like this," she said. "Is this for real?" She examined the gold rims on the plates.

It was clear that the waiters had known Naomi since she was a little girl. They brought out a Ktima Chardonnay from Pendeli, Mister Jimmie's favorite juice. The food came when they were halfway through the bottle: "Parmesan" with girolles, puff pastry with Brillat-Savarin, and then a plate of olive oil from Hania. The waiter at their table told them that there was once a cult of Dionysus at Pendeli. The waiters always told the same story when they ordered the Ktima. Ancient wine, then, ancient apart from the Chardonnay, that is. They took a second bottle of it.

"Did you really come here when you were a kid?" Sam asked.

"My parents used to bring me here to civilize me, I think.

It was much nicer back then—the city, I mean. Everything. We can come here every week if you like."

"I wish we could live at the Grande Bretagne for the rest of the summer. I'm sick of the island."

"It'll be all right. I have some news. The English guy is leaving for Italy. He got a call from his office—"

"He's leaving?"

Naomi lowered her voice and leaned in.

"The credit card was used over there. It means Jimmie and Phaine are still alive and kicking. Isn't that wild?"

"So there are ghosts after all."

"There are. And they like buying expensive things. Apparently, it was a pair of shoes."

"Sick."

"He's leaving today, I think."

"But what will he find over there?"

"I don't have the faintest idea. I guess he'll hunt down Faoud and not find him. I hope Faoud has the sense to ditch the car and disappear. They'll put out a search on the number plates."

"But what if they catch him?"

"Then we're in the chocolate, as the French say. *Dans le chocolat.*"

"In the shit?"

"Way in it. But they won't find him. I wouldn't have done it if I thought he was stupid. He's not stupid."

"He may not be stupid, but he might get greedy."

"I don't think he'll be stupid enough to be greedy," Naomi said with a degree of finality. "Let's have the chocolate parfait, shall we? It's more important than worrying about an English bloodhound. We're going to be safe."

The parfait came with a mango sorbet and they had a serving of Spondi's specialty coffee from Giovanni Erbisti in Verona. They went afterward into the garden to drink their *digestifs*, sit under the trees, and talk. Sam noticed that Naomi had already found her groove after the death of her father and stepmother. She was mapping out her next phase of life with a formidable composure. It was, now that the younger woman saw it up close, quite unsettling and unnatural in some way. At first she had thought it was high spirits, or else discipline, an ability to overcome grief. But suddenly in the garden of Spondi she began to think that it was something else altogether. The way Naomi had stepped quietly from one life into another revealed a certain degree of premeditation. Naomi, she thought, had been thinking about this liberation for years, and when it had come—albeit accidentally and unexpectedly—she had opened the door offered and walked through it without hesitation. But also without fuss. It was as if she had planned everything down to the last detail and was therefore unsurprised when things did not fail to go according to plan. Imperturbably cold and clairvoyant. She was maybe much more like her father than either of them had ever been able to admit.

When they were finally back in the suite upstairs at the Grande Bretagne, Sam opened the windows and glanced down at Syntagma Square and the parliament opposite it. She suddenly wanted to be alone for a few minutes. A few anarchists, a few fires in drums, and by the steps leading up to the parliament a line of soldiers standing under the lamps, an insufficient line to hold a riot. She turned and saw Naomi already between the sheets in her T-shirt. They smiled at each other, and the older girl blew a strand of hair out of her own face and said, "There's going to be a very silly revolution tomorrow."

Sam came to the bed and sat at its far end, uncertain where she was going to lay her head. Things were not quite clear between them yet. The earlier conversation had not been laid to rest entirely, and Sam still felt that she harbored within herself the wariness of the hunted.

"It would be better," she said.

"It would, wouldn't it? It's always better to get it over and done with."

"Naomi, do you think—" she paused—"is it possible that Faoud killed your father and stepmother on purpose?"

Naomi took this in her stride, with her usual nonchalance.

"Anything's possible."

"That's what I thought. Pretty much anything."

"And what if he did? What does that change?"

"Nothing."

'That's right. When I was small my father had a horrible toast. He used to say, when he lifted his glass and touched yours, 'Here's to killing marmots.' I never knew what it meant, but now I think I do."

"I don't understand that at all," Sam said.

"It's a British thing, I guess. But as I said, I didn't understand it either. It just made me laugh."

"But why?" Sam said earnestly. "You mean the world is violent anyway?"

"Maybe."

Naomi reached out and touched Sam's cheek with the back of her hand, then keeled over slowly until she was lying next to her.

"But not us."

"What are we, then?"

"We're the noble ones. We're undoing the violence of others."

Sam's eyes were wide open, and she stared straight up at the ceiling where shadows merged. A part of her mind had split off.

"What have we undone, then? We're profiting from it."

"That's just an accident."

Naomi blew the strands of hair out of Sam's face now.

"One has to learn how to improvise. It's all a war, in the end. It's a war we have to win."

"Did we win yet?"

"Not yet. But we will."

We're drunk, Sam thought, and just babbling.

Nevertheless, it could be said that she had won something. She had won her independence.

"I feel like a bank robber," she said weakly, her eyes finally closing. "Running and running. But sort of happy."

"It's the running that's fun."

"But I have to go back to New York. Then I don't know."

Naomi turned on her back as well and she smiled, almost to the point of breaking into laughter. The kite-flyer almost losing control, but remembering at the last moment that her kite had to remain airborne at all costs.

She had hardly slept from then on, though the revolution didn't come that night or even during the following morning. When they were taking their mute breakfast together at their window the city below them refused to throw a single insurrectionary sound their way. It was only the seabirds prowling a wide summer-vacation blue sky who projected their cries downward while the protestors of the night before appeared to have gone to sleep in the middle of the revolt. Everything was therefore quiet. Sunlight lay on a pot of hotel jam and the girl's long fingers picking at things with a delicate indecision: Naomi shaded her eyes with one hand to look at her, admiring once again the undiminished fineness that she had relished the first minute she had set eyes on her at the beach at Mandraki. Sam was nearing the end of a long and fruitful innocence. But was it really a war they were in now, or had they already won it?

NINETEEN

N EAR LAKE BOLSENO, AS THE SUN FELL BEHIND CY-
presses that made him think of Hajez, Faoud passed
through a place called Valentano and then onto a road that
made its way alongside the waters past little camping grounds
and shuttered stalls with the word *Fragola* written across them.
Beyond the lake another road rose steeply along the edge of a
colossal ravine as it approached Sorano, a place that he was sure
was inhabited only by the old. When he got there at ten the
piazza was already empty and that suspicion was confirmed.
The village was a honeycomb of caves and abandoned houses
clinging to a great spur of rock, and when he got out for a few
minutes to test the air and to regain his sense of place he heard
at once the birds that gave Sorano most of its nocturnal life.

Close to the entrance of the old town a terrace hung above
the ravine that could be half-seen by the glare of the piazza
lamps. Water churned along the bottom, and he could see the
mouths of caves where the Etruscans had once buried their
dead. For a moment, leaning against the rail, he was compelled to remember Aleppo before the ruin. The impeccable
city where he had studied years earlier at the music school of
Frenchman Julian Weiss, master of the *qanan*. The nostalgia
came out of nothing but the sepulchral abandonment of Sorano
at a late hour. Houses carved out of the rock, thousands of years

compressed into simple walls and arches and secret doors. But the Syrian stones he would never see again.

Sovana, by contrast, lay at the bottom of a road that descended into an archaeological site. The road crossed a river and near to the waters lay the Codrington house, accessed not by a normal driveway but by a dirt track that wound its way through an orchard of quince trees. He left the car on the far side of the orchard, locking it and taking his bag. A footpath led to a tall iron gate that had to be unlocked. He had various keys from the car, and in the darkness he fumbled with one key after another until one turned and the gate opened. The house was low and very long, like an enormous stable, though it had two stories. Before it lay a bedraggled garden with pieces of statuary and a well. He went to the front door and negotiated the three locks one by one until he was able to push it open and walk into a hallway of flagstones, beams, and austere open stonework. Groping for the light switch, he turned on the overhead lamp and found himself in a restored convent with long white corridors and lines of cell doors. Parchment maps in frames hung on the walls, time-darkened religious paintings and strange wooden ladles, the instruments of forgotten nuns.

Closing the front door quietly behind him, he locked it again with a horizontal iron bolt and took his bag into a salon to the right of the hallway. It had been created from the former chapel, with arches rising above velvet sofas and a Renaissance dining table. The Codringtons had not departed hastily. The shutters were all bolted shut, the armchairs and tables were sheeted. In the heat of summer the rooms were cool because the outside air had not touched them in weeks.

He ventured upstairs with his bag and found that the former convent cells were now individual bedrooms, each one decorated differently. Some were painted rose, some green or yellow. But they were all adorned with antiques and wall tapestries. He chose the smallest one and laid his bag there, then went back downstairs and explored the vast Codrington kitchen, a place where the impertinent twenty-first century imposed itself in a score of German gadgets. He scoured the fridge and found nothing there. They had cleaned everything out before leaving, and even the freezer was empty. A little crushed, he tried the pantry and the cupboards. It was the same disaster. Impossible, he thought. Rich people didn't live in empty houses, even if they left them for weeks or months at a time. But the kitchen, in fact, had been very carefully evacuated and he couldn't find even a lonely can to offset the calamity. They had emptied it out and probably taken everything with them to Greece. Because the other side of the rich was their hidden and repulsive frugality.

He decided to sleep instead and deal with the situation the following morning. Going back upstairs, he crashed onto the bed in his clothes and let his gradually accumulated exhaustion overwhelm him. But it didn't take him into sleep directly. His mind, instead, spun with images of Istanbul. He hadn't thought about the city for a long time, not even when he was alone in the hut in Episkopi, but now it came back to him, that city of humiliations.

An adopted city was always held to a lower standard, but even by that standard Istanbul had been rough on him. Driven from a city of mosques by artillery, he had found his first consolation in the mosques of the Ottomans, where he could be alone. There was the Mihrimah near the Roman walls in the north, which was being renovated at that time and which was covered with scaffolds. One of Sinan's less-known masterpieces, it had been built for a princess of that same name and its marvels were entire walls made of windows. Even at dusk it was intense with light. It was a place in which to think about music, in which to dream his compositions; afterward he walked to the Kariye Church a few streets away where the Christian mosaics furnished the same inspiration. During the first winter, days of solitude could be spun out between these two places, his compositions coming and going inside his head while he never found the time to write them down. And it often felt to him that snow fell every day, though it couldn't have.

Through musical connections he found work tutoring the children of Turkish families, and several times a week he took a bus up to Ulus or Etiler or Bebek and entered houses filled with carpets on the quiet lanes that overlooked the Bosphorus where his pupils lived and where he taught them how to sing or how to play the flute. None of them had talent, and none of them improved. But as they failed to improve their parents came to the conclusion that the fault was his, and that he was not really a proper teacher. So one by one they let him go, without explaining why. He took a room near Kadirga Limani in Sultanahmet, a street of bakeries and *sut sahlep* vendors. The tenements nearby, above the railway lines, were filled with Africans and Syrians, and these were the alleys whose names he still knew by heart: Hemesehri, Alisan, Ismail Sefa. Those were his places of idleness and sorrow. Here he reflected that once he had wanted to be a master of the *qanun*; a composer, a teacher, or even eventually a professor in Paris teaching Arabic music. But it was dust now. Some of his fellow students from Aleppo had also fled to Istanbul, and together they went to the soirées of master Weiss who had taught them all in their destroyed city. Weiss had also removed himself to Istanbul to continue his career, and he could be seen on windy nights in the streets around Galata in flowing robes, a man of towering beauty and Sufic estrangement. Once a month Weiss played for his friends in an apartment right next to the Galata tower, and there Faoud sat in the background with other students and re-found the world that had once been his. The enchantment of the group. *When I am silent, I fall into that place where everything is music.* But he always left alone and without speaking to anyone. It was enough to listen to the master from a distance and to be close to the ghosts that connected him to home. But time passed, and it worked against him.

Whereas he had at first hoped to save enough to get a decent room, with the passing of months he gave up that hope and fell into grander but more impractical ones. Exodus and escape, flight to Europe. In the spring he drifted to the cafes at Ortakoy under the bridge, where the better-educated Syrians shared their coffees and conspired, three men per cup. There was only a Turkish friend of his father's who looked over him, arranging his tutoring from afar, while using him as ruthlessly as he could. His name was Mert and he worked in the tea business, but with fingers in matters less open to the light of day. But this man had always remained obscure to him. Faoud never was able to learn much Turkish, and his patron never invited him into his social circles, so his ostracism remained permanent. They used to go to tea together at the Ciragan Palace Kempinski hotel on the Bosphorus and reminisce about Faoud's father, since the two older men had known each other in Damascus. They had made money together, but Mert would not reveal how they had done it. There was merely a sense of obligation toward the son on his part. So they would chat and evade harder truths, and Faoud would watch the Russian tankers making their way to the Dardanelles as they had tea and wonder how he could escape on the same sea. It was to this enigmatic and unpleasant man that, in the end, he confided his all-too-common desire.

He could have stayed much longer if he had found the means. But there was no work and his family had finally gone bankrupt after losing all its assets. He was now just a ghost among ghosts. The Syrians begging in the street along Istiqlal had become unpopular, the war changed form, and the borders had taken on different meanings. The exiles began to be rounded up and taken to a new detention center, which he himself never saw. So then one day you wake and you know that your time is up, that God is no longer watching over you, and the Merts of this world can no longer save you any more than music can. Yet he could have stayed as a ghost. It was just that he no longer had much in common with the other Syrians and there was no one to talk to besides the other scattered music students, his now-homeless peers. He sometimes saw them at the mosques, and they shared a tea afterward, but it was conversation purely for its own sake. Many of them thought of him as a spoiled rich boy who had deserved his comeuppance; he looked at them as people with whom he shared a regrettable accident of origin.

But then what did Adonis, their shared poet, say about his own dead brother?

He was the god of love as long as I lived.
What will love do if I too am gone?

WHEN HE WOKE he decided at once to run a bath to civilize himself again. In the marital bathroom their toiletries, unlike the provisions of the kitchen, were intact and he wallowed in the bath for an hour washing his hair, his nails, his impover-ished skin. It was a long-overdue purification. Not the baths of Istanbul, not the hammam of Sultan Ahmet, but enough. Refreshed and powdered, he went in a bathrobe down to the kitchen. Fetching the service-station provisions he had bought the day before, he made a pot of coffee and a light breakfast of bread and cheese.

Through the gaps in the shutters he peered out at the orchard and the garden with its statues. There was a house nearby, but as far as he could tell it was a ruin. There was no way of telling whether the Codringtons employed year-round staff there, and it was too soon to fling open a window or venture out into the garden. He would wait until the late afternoon before deciding if he was really alone.

While he waited, he went through the house room by room, lingering among their possessions as if he had temporarily in-herited them. He went down to the cellars, where there were several rooms: one filled with bottles of wine, another filled with weapons, the third a room of magazines and books. The weapons room was very small and had a table at its center. Its surface was piled with boxes of bullets and shotgun cartridges. On one wall a Benelli Montefeltro Silver semiautomatic shot-gun, a Benelli Ethos shotgun, a Tikka bolt-action, and three Beretta Storm semiautomatic pistols. The old man seemed to have had a penchant for Italian guns. Perhaps he acquired them locally and had an Italian gun license in order. The shotguns were not locked into place, and he took down the Montefeltro with its glossy walnut grip and turned and weighed it in his hands. It was a good weapon, strongly built and finely tooled. The pistols too were contemporary models, light and easy to swing, virtually unused as far as he could tell. He laid them all on the table among the boxes and then loaded the Montefeltro and two of the handguns. There was no reason for doing so, but suddenly laying his hands on weapons allayed the impotence and fear that had oppressed him for months. It was purely symbolic as emotions went, but it was not unreal. A surge of animal confidence and a vague stirring of revenge. He didn't unload them when he laid the guns back down but left them there as if in readiness. It was like the moment that Jimmie came toward him in the other house, forcing him to act—because either you act or you are shipped back in a cage to face an anonymous fate that no one will care about anyway.

He went out onto a terrace on the first floor and looked down at the domain. The orchard was unmanned and it was clear that no one had come to the house all day. Obviously, the Codringtons had chosen a place where they would have no neighbors, where they would enjoy a rural isolation. He went back down to the garden, passed through the iron gate, and on via the quinces to the car. He paused for a moment to reassure himself. He was already thinking of how to change the car's plates, and he wondered about the garage up in Sorano. But of course they would know Signor Codrington and his opulent Peugeot. He would have to do it further on, in a small place where no one passed through. And then there was the question of money. He had about 140 euros left in cash but had already noticed that even rural Italy was much more expensive than Greece. It wouldn't last more than two or three days.

An hour after he had returned inside the house, someone came to the door and there was a series of knocks. At first they were gentle, hesitant disturbances, an unsure request as it were. But then came a second round that were a little more impatient. He went down to the basement and took the Montefeltro shotgun, still loaded, and crept quietly back to the front door with the barrel pointed toward the lock. The voice, a female voice, was calling, *"Signori, siete a casa?"* A telephone began to ring in an upstairs room.

It droned on for five minutes before falling silent. The woman moved away from the door, and he saw her shape flicker against the shutters of the main room as she tried to peer in. At length she walked off and he heard the iron gate creak; so she had a key to enter them. It must be a domestic, someone working the grounds in their absence or a friend entrusted with a key. He put the shotgun against the wall and thought over the implications. Someone must have told her, or suggested to her, that the Codringtons had returned from their holiday in Greece. And that someone must have known that it was not the case. It was a new element: he had an enemy. But then, more calmly, he realized that he had forgotten the more obvious explanation. She had simply seen the car. The car betrayed him here, and this simple fact resolved him to move on.

He decided to take all the weapons with him. He loaded them into the trunk of the car and locked up the house, leaving the keys in a flowerpot in the garden. He drove to Sorano in torrid heat, under a cloudless sky.

TWENTY

A T TWENTY PAST TWELVE THAT DAY THE VALLEY BELOW
Sorano baked in a silence that was broken only by the
sound of water tumbling across riverbed stones. At the back of
the village was a platform with rails where the carless alleys
intersected, and from there Rockhold could look down at the
dozens of caves that spoke of a past older than the present religion. He gripped the rail, because the heat made him a little
faint, and let his ears and eyes do his work: far below, on a small
bridge over the stream, a girl was lying in a swimsuit, still and
camouflaged as a stick insect and unnoticed by the other eyes
above her.

He could not quite bring her into focus, even after he had
lifted his sunglasses for a moment, but he thought he recognized her from the Eastern European staff at the Hotel della
Fortezza, where he was staying. The hotel was built into the old
fortress that loomed above Sorano, and he had checked in there
late the night before. Cat-like, she was probably asleep in the
sun or quietly absorbing the voyeuristic attention of strangers.
He lowered his sunglasses back onto the bridge of his nose and
caught from afar the hiss of the cicadas. Earlier in the morning
he had glimpsed one or two English bohemian residents padding through the labyrinth, but they didn't seem to belong to
Jimmie's crowd unless they were avant-garde artists whom he

could collect. Nevertheless it wasn't difficult to imagine him and Phaine strolling arm in arm under these endless vaults or having lunch in the sweet piazza with its town hall. He walked back there now, measuring his steps and humming a bit of *La Traviata* to himself. It wasn't such a bad mission, traveling from hotel to hotel across Italy. It had not yet occurred to him that Jimmie wasn't just playing truant from his own hectic existence. There were two cafes in the piazza, and he chose the one nearer to the entrance to the pedestrian zone because everyone at the hotel said it had the better ice cream. He sat there and got his *macchiato*. He looked over the cars parked in the piazza, which he had also inspected on his way down, and saw that they were more or less the same cars as had been there an hour earlier. On the terrace with him were a few old-timers, clerks from the town hall, a young male tourist in a nice shirt and two girls he had seen earlier, also at the Fortezza. He leaned back and checked the messages on his phone.

From London, Susan had asked him if he wanted her to cancel all three cards; the search had been issued for the car as well, but nothing had come back. He thought, I'll have to go down to the house right now, perhaps they're there after all. That would be the most welcome surprise under the circumstances. But then his expenses-paid jaunt would be over and that would be a bore. Perhaps he could delay things a day or two.

He leaned over to the tourist and asked him in English if he had a light for the cigarette he had pulled out and was waiting to use.

"I don't smoke," the man said in the same language, but with a velvet accent.

"That's the best policy, I suppose!"

"I'd advise you to stop."

The words were said with a lovely smile.

"Too late now." Rockhold laughed.

He lowered the cigarette and then finally put it away. It was sensible advice, all the same. The man saw this and said, "No, I didn't mean that. Please smoke, it doesn't bother me."

"My wife agrees with you." Rockhold sighed. "But for some reason cigarettes make me feel healthier."

"Do they?"

"It's hard to explain. By the way, do you know the way to Sovana? I have to drive there."

The man looked out across the square and pointed to the garage on the far side.

"It's down there, I think. It's about two kilometers."

"Thank you very much. I should walk it for my health."

"You can walk. It's not far. But uphill on the way back."

"Uphill?" Rockhold echoed.

"A steep climb on a bad day."

That wouldn't do, but he decided to walk it all the same. To hell with uphill climbs, but pity the aging, unexercised heart. By two he was at the house, to which he had his own key from the office in London along with the number of the woman who looked after the grounds in their absence. He let himself in through the iron gate and then rang the bell at the front door. There was no car parked outside, so it was clear that the Codringtons were not there, not in any case at that moment. He called the woman and she answered. In good English she promised to come down at once. He let himself into the house as well and left the door open. Then he entered the salon and saw the sheeted tables and chairs and the atmosphere of abandonment. He understood at once that they had not been there.

He walked around the vaulted rooms while waiting for the woman and then he happened upon the room where Faoud had slept. The visitor had tidied it up after himself, but it was still obvious that someone had been there, because on the floor there were breadcrumbs and the pillows were dented. He looked at them closely to see if there were hairs to pick from them: there were three to pocket. Just as he was filching them, the woman arrived and he went down to see what her story was. They talked outside in the garden because she didn't want to go into the house, and there was an eager indignation somewhere in her voice, but not related to himself. She said that she had seen their car the day before parked by the orchard, and that it had appeared out of nowhere, unannounced. The Codringtons always called her two days before they arrived.

"It was the Peugeot?" Rockhold asked.

"The same as always. My husband says he saw him driving in during the afternoon?"

"There was only one?"

"They weren't together. There was only one driver. My husband says he was driving erratically."

"Did your husband see Signor Codrington?"

"No, he didn't. He saw a black man driving the car."

"I'm sure he didn't see that."

"My Roberto has an eagle eye, sir."

"That man drove in here and left the car in the orchard?"

"He must have."

"It's unlikely to have been a black man, Signora Tassi. But at least your husband says he was alone."

"He saw what he saw."

She drew herself up defiantly.

"He's not lying, Signor Rewkhol."

228

"I'm not saying he's lying. I just mean that sometimes it's hard to see things correctly."

"*E cosa vuol dire quello?*" she burst out.

"I'm afraid I don't speak your lovely language, Signora Tassi, you'll have to forgive me."

He was so polite that she relented at once.

"It's an impertinent thing to do," she said, "coming back here in their car."

"He must have stayed in the house," he muttered.

"Of course he stayed in the house."

Rockhold began to think backward. The shoe shop in Fasano had said it was a young man who bought the shoes. The car had arrived home with only one driver. The man in the cafe in Sovana had a nice smile and idle eyes. Everything hung together on one thread. He suddenly swore, because he had left the car in Sorano and he would have to climb back up there; it would take an hour at least. He asked the signora if she could drive him up there, but her husband had taken their car to Orvieto for the day.

"You didn't walk from Sovana?"

"I did, madame, I did. My heart cried out for it."

He set off back to Sovana with a wild feeling of failure and irresponsibility. Halfway there he lost his breath and sat on a stone wall to let the sweat dry. He called Susan and asked her to leave the cards untouched for twenty-four hours. He needed one more clue, one more place-marker, because he was now sure that the man who was driving the car would make a mistake larger than the ones he had already made. When he arrived back in the village he went through all the cars parked in the square but was unsurprised to find that the bird had flown its open-air cage. He therefore went up to his own car parked at the Fortezza, paid the bill at reception, and then sat for a few minutes in the lobby, reading the maps he had brought with him. He would have to guess which of the two roads the man had taken, and in which direction, but almost immediately, and without effort, he knew it was north.

AN HOUR LATER, on the autostrada to Florence, Susan called him from London to tell him that a Codrington credit card had been used an hour earlier in a hotel just north of Siena. It was a wine estate called Badia a Coltibuono, not far from Gaiole in Chianti.

At the dead center of the afternoon, the sun blazing down on thousands of totemic cypresses ("Planted by the English," he always said to himself), he stopped in Radda and stretched his legs along a panoramic view, climbed up to a cold little church, and sat on the steps to continue his conference with his assistant. The stony calm of the Tuscan villages in high heat; the birds swarmed around him as if attracted to his internal energy.

"How many charges were there on the card?"

"Three."

"The hotel—"

"Yes, a charge for 110 euros, which has to be the room. Then two small charges for food and drinks, I think."

"So he must be there now, then."

"He made the last charge an hour and a half ago."

"Almost there," he said tensely.

"He'll be there for the night, so there's no hurry."

"Look at the website for the estate. How is it arranged?"

She had already done it.

"It's not really a hotel," she said. "The rooms are in various places spread over the property. There's a tower with three units. Then there's a separate house. Then four rooms in the main house."

"We can't tell which room he booked or what kind?"

"No, we just have the charge. It looks like he got a tower room, because they cost 110."

"Can you call ahead and book me a tower room?"

He waited on the steps for her return call and shooed the curious pigeons away. Waiting was a thing he hated to do, and he did it badly. He put on his panama and put together a plan for the evening. The usurper would show himself eventually, but he would have to go about things carefully, with a subtle touch. But where, then, were his friend and his wife?

Susan called back and told him that the tower was fully booked and that he would have to stay at one of the houses farther down the road. It was as good as she could do.

"Book it. Tell them I'll be there in half an hour."

"What about the Italian police?"

"Not yet. Let's wait until tomorrow. I'm not sure yet. I want to wait."

He thought that maybe he could ferret out more information working by himself and in secrecy.

He got up and went back to the car parked by the panorama and felt himself brimming with formless melancholy and unease. They were almost certainly dead, then. Carjacked on the road in southern Italy. The bodies could have been buried anywhere; they would be impossible to find without a detailed confession. That, in a few seconds, was what it had come down to. The entire scenario, the working hypothesis, changed and grew vaster and darker. It did so among slopes of vines and avenues of cypresses, in a humanizing sunshine that made everything

231

under it look preordained for happiness. But, of course, it was an optical illusion. Everywhere is dangerous, he thought, everywhere where human beings exist and multiply and continue to breathe.

The road in the direction of Montegrossi twisted its way toward a junction, and there he found the first sign for Badia a Coltibuono. The estate's main complex lay at the top of a hill, and as he parked there he saw that it was actually a small medieval hamlet of some kind taken over by the winery. He went along its cobbled streets and found the reception. They had his booking; a young woman would take him to the house in her car, and he was to follow in his.

They drove in the two cars out into the estate on gravel roads. His room was a mile from the winery and the reception, and they passed the tower on the way. There were three cars parked there, but he would have to return there later to see if the Codrington car eventually appeared among them. The track then ran through woods and sloping vineyards before arriving at a stone farmhouse with a few outhouses around it. He would be alone in the house, the other units were not yet booked, and he could drive up to the winery to have dinner in the restaurant. The woman left him there and he went up to the room, leaving his bag in the car, and took out only his swimming trunks, which had gone lamentably unused on Hydra. He went back down to the edge of the vines, which rolled serenely to the horizon. He warmed up in the last of the sun's rays and then went to the indoor pool for a quick swim. Under the greenhouse glass panes the water was tropically warm, and after three righteously strenuous laps he lay on his back on the surface and stared up at the darkening sky. He had a sense that he could nail his man without his knowing it, until it was too late for him. If he could find the Peugeot he might finally call in the Italian police and the matter could be wrapped up. He was already in contact with an old friend in the Italian force, though he had not disclosed the nature of the matter. Everything would fall into place at the last moment.

He went back up to his room and took out the small Glock pistol he was licensed to carry, looked it over, made sure it was fully loaded, and slipped on the shoulder harness which held it snug and unobtrusive against his chest. Even under a light-weight cotton jacket it was unnoticeable. Then he returned to the courtyard and his car. The sun was setting and the Albanian and Serbian workers in the vines were heading off. At the winery the tables were set up at the restaurant and a few guests had ventured out onto a large patio area on the roof. Rockhold had a sudden inspiration. He stopped at the restaurant bar and asked the man working it if Signor Codrington was booked for dinner that night.

"He's on the terrace upstairs," the man said.

Rockhold went into the courtyard and up a flight of steps to the terrace, which was spacious and made of two levels. At its far end was the panorama, the distant vision of Siena, the dusk. Here a man stood alone, facing the city, his arms folded, isolated from the other guests. From behind it was hard to say if it was the same man he had seen earlier in Sorano. It could go either way. Tempting fate, he stepped out onto the terrace and sat on one of the benches as swallows swooped around the eaves and into the nearby vines. The Italian dusk was always a place of sibilant swallows. He watched the well-heeled foreigners drift back into the restaurant until it was just himself and the stranger on the terrace. The man began to stir as if thinking of leaving, but as soon as he did Rockhold was quietly gone. He had decided that he wanted to observe him. He was curious about him.

He therefore went down to the restaurant, procured a table in an obscure corner of the room and turned his chair away from the other diners. Resolutely relaxed, he ordered a plate of *gnudi* with ricotta, a deboned and roasted guinea fowl and some roasted potatoes. He added, naturally, a bottle of the Badia a Coltibuono Riserva. The room soon filled with wealthy Russians, exactly like the hotels in Hydra, though one had to imagine that their buying power was now on the decline. It was otherwise with the Chinese there; they ordered Riservas from the 1980s that had to be brought up from the cellars. Rockhold drank half his own modest bottle before turning to check out the other tables one by one, but the man he had seen on the terrace was not there. He had not taken a table even briefly, so he must have left without Rockhold's noticing him go. It was a slip on his part, and he paid the bill quickly in order to make up for it.

The car park above the winery was right against the vines, and the roads were still visible in the half-light. There was a thin pall of dust above the downward-tending track along which the guest residences lay, as if a car had just driven there. He was a little wine-groggy—another careless mistake—but as soon as he was in the car his senses sharpened. He went down the hill and then parked the car to one side of the track in deep forest and walked down to the tower on foot.

The track ran between two majestic vineyards before ending in the forecourt of the ancient building, a tower from the Middle Ages. There was only one car here, but it was not the Peugeot. The upper rooms were occupied. He went up silently and explored the landing that connected the two doors. From one room came the sound of Italian television and a rustling of papers; from the other, nothing at all. Disappointed, he went back down to the parking area and from there out to the terrace, filled with sofas and cushions, and he sat in filtered moonlight thinking it over. It made little sense. He wondered if the impostor had been aroused by some instinct, as impostors often were.

When he returned to the parking area, the vineyards were dark and the track itself was difficult to see. But he was halfway to the car when he saw a pair of headlights barreling down toward him. He stepped aside into the undergrowth and the blue Peugeot swept past him at high speed, swerving to a stop by the tower. He was sure that the driver had seen him—he fancied that he caught the white flare of his eyes for a split second—and that the driving was nervous and frenetic. From the undergrowth he saw the door open and a man step out onto the gravel. He decided not to follow, however: the exit to the road was behind Rockhold and so all he had to do, in theory, was wait.

He got back into his car and turned on the engine. But he kept the lights off since they would be seen from the tower. As he began to reverse up the hill, he saw the man from the Peugeot approach the gates and stare at him. He was clearly unsure, puzzled. He advanced a few paces and then stopped. There was, obviously, some dumb confusion between them. Rockhold had reached a clearing where he could turn the car, and he drove off to the winery at the summit where any car already inside the estate would have to pass in order to gain the main road. There he waited while wondering if the man was going to retire to his room and sleep away the night. He was uncertain one way or the other, and caught in his confusion, he called Susan.

"Cancel the last card, my dear. I think I have him."

"Yes, Mr. Rockhold. I'll cancel it at once. But are you calling the police?"

"Soon. I want to talk to him myself."

"Do you think that's wise, Mr. Rockhold?"

"I didn't say anything about wisdom, Susan. I said I wanted to talk to him. I want to get a sense of him."

Clearly astonished, she made no reply.

He said, "Don't worry, I'll call them soon. Within a few hours."

He sat back in the car and waited. Somehow he knew that he would not be there all night, that things would erupt. He was not disappointed this time. When the winery had closed and the last guests had drifted away from the restaurant the Peugeot came up the long track and appeared with its lights off. It crawled slowly and quietly across the car park and reached the downward dip to the surfaced road. There it hesitated for a moment before rolling over it and out of view, and almost in the same moment Rockhold drew out of the car park just as quietly, with his lights also extinguished, and followed the tail-lights down to the road where the cypresses cast their shadows horizontally across the tarmac.

TWENTY-ONE

FAOUD DROVE WITH THE LIGHTS OFF UNTIL HE WAS AT the bottom of the hill, then turned them on. Confused in a mountainous and unlit landscape, he decided to follow the signs to the autostrada, which would take him up to Arezzo more rapidly. Within minutes he was within sight of a gas station near a junction, with auto-pay pumps standing forlorn in a hot wind. He stopped there and looked around, then turned off the lights and walked around the pumps. He was aware how disheveled he now looked, as if a sharp decline had overtaken him. His shirt had long lost its poise, and his stubble was not a flattering five o'clock shade. He felt exhausted and unloosened from within. There were credit-card machines and no one to man them; he took out his last card and decided to take the risk, since the machine could not swallow it anyway. He had a third of a tank left and not enough cash to fill it. He slipped the card into the slot, selected his fuel, and waited for the authentication. It was refused.

He tried a second time, and a third. Growing impatient, he cursed and snatched the paper receipts and tossed them into the wind. They whirled away from him toward the office, and he was left with nothing but a third of a tank and a useless piece of plastic. Putting the card back in his pocket, he strode over to the windows and peered through them into a shuttered room.

He rapped on the glass, but it was futile. This area lit by lamps and, as he realized now, under surveillance from four cameras was not the place to throw a tantrum. He calmed himself, returned to the car, and drove back onto the smooth and empty highway into Arezzo.

It was brightly lit with streetlamps, and in the rear mirror he saw, far off, a ghost of a car following him with its lights off. At first he ignored it and then wondered why its lights were off. He slowed, and it seemed to slow as well. The alternative was to accelerate, and he pushed the car to eighty and let it coast into the outskirts of the town.

The map was of no use in navigating Arezzo, and as soon as he was in the old center he was lost in an infuriating maze of lanes. There were a few bars still open with crowds of teenagers, and he had to pick his way through them slowly. He came out on a wider street that curved around to the railway station. He went past it and onto a highway with roundabouts that clearly led out of town, passing through a suburb and on northward to Bibbiena. Within minutes he was back in the rural darkness, but moving much faster and not concerned about conserving his precious fuel.

In fifteen minutes he had passed Bibbiena and he could no longer see the ghost in his mirror. Instead of following the main route eastward he swung left onto a much smaller road that shadowed a river, the Arno, of which he had heard long ago in a classroom somewhere. Stopping here for a moment, he got out of the car and listened for the motor of the pursuer in the dark, but there was nothing but the sound of pines ruffled by wind. By the road was a sign for a monastery, which he assumed must be secluded. He wondered about it. If he turned off there, anyone following him would be thrown off his trail; the road up to the mountain was narrow and unlit, a surfaced path to nowhere. But the trees near the road glittered with fireflies. He resolved to try it.

It rose steeply and soon he was winding his way through forests, the air rapidly cooling. By the hairpins there was a faint light falling from above the trees, as if from a partially obscured moon, and by it he could see steep banks of ferns rising from the road and the shafts of ancient pines. The road rose until it reached the monastery, a somber complex built in a clearing next to what must have been a glacially cold river.

He parked behind the main building and saw that all the lights were off before he silenced the engine and decided to stay the night. Listening for the sound of any approaching car, he waited for some minutes before feeling satisfied that he was truly alone. He then walked behind the monastery, where a path ran along an old wall with vegetable gardens in the wide ditch behind the dormitories.

On the far side he found the river whose sound he had heard straightaway, a bridge, the white gleam of the water far below. There was a path that rose up the side of the mountain and disappeared out of view. He went up it with one of the pistols in his pocket, taking his steps slowly and making sure that he made no sound. He came to a saint's shrine built into the mountainside, and from there he could look down at the curving road along which he had just passed. He was safe for the night, and as soon as he knew it he went back down to the river and leaned on the wall of the bridge to gather his wits. He had one piece of bread left and some sliced cheese, and by morning he would be up against the very different wall of hunger.

He wondered if the monks gave alms or took pity on people who turned up at their doors. But there was also the risk of his being reported by them. The plan was to sleep in the car and leave before first light.

But the night was hot and windless and the forest was cooler and more comfortable than the car. He lay in the ferns next to the river and slept for four or five hours. His father came to him in his dream. The old man was in one of his Parisian suits, but also a keffiyeh. He was eating an orange with a knife, and he stood under the pines asking his son how many nights he had left on earth. One, two—maybe not even that.

"Look at you," he said. "You are not even a vagrant. You have not come far at all. You are a disgrace and you know it."

When he woke the stars were still out and shining with indifferent splendor, but lights had come on in the monastery. The monks were chanting as he walked back to the car. One of them had come out to see whose car had parked among them during the night, and the face was mild and unsuspecting. "Are you lost?" he called out in Italian, but, not understanding, Faoud waved and smiled back and got into the car. It was almost six and the morning promised a pure, torrid summer day.

He drove slowly down a different road from the one he had used the night before. There was a Banca Monte dei Paschi, but it would not be open for hours. A cafe was open and he had enough for an espresso. He felt the eyes upon him, the mild surprise at his odd appearance—the nice clothes spoiled by too much wear—and the glances down at his unwashed hands. Driving a Peugeot 506. He had enough for one last blood-orange *spremuta*, and he drank that too, his hands shaking and his throat so dry that it contracted. He could feel that things were winding down and that he had no way to escape the net that was drawing in around him. When he went back onto the single street running through Tosi, the sun was almost up and the land beyond the village had suddenly appeared as a soft green carpet of gardens and vines and hazed ridges. He took the downward-spiraling road into the sun and rows of cypresses against the road cast long shadows into the grass. Along this high road, with its views to the right across the valley toward a distant freeway, the villages offered random targets—pharmacies, stores, small restaurants—which might have tempted him had they been open.

The next little town was called Pian di Sco. As luck would have it, there was a fancy bakery with a window filled with what looked like wedding cakes. Two women inside. It was as good as any other target. He parked opposite it, took one of the polished shotguns from the backseat, and calmly crossed the street to enter the shop.

The sun was in their eyes, and they squinted to see who had come in. He was very polite. In English he asked them to give him the contents of the cash register, and then he leveled the barrel at the woman standing by the till and waited for her to open it and empty it. It took a few seconds; they said nothing whatsoever. It was about three hundred euros, a good enough haul. She slid it across the counter, and he took the notes with a quiet "thank you." Then he handed back a twenty-euro note and asked for a handful of cakes. They were bagged for him with the same silent efficiency, and he thanked the women a second time and told them to keep the change. Then he lowered the shotgun, walked out of the shop, and without undue haste got back into the car and drove on.

The road ran over a high ridge with vineyards sloping down to the right, wineries posted at the road, *agriturismi* and cellars and a thousand olive trees basking in a still-refreshing sun. It was not yet nine o'clock.

At Castelfranco, the road pitched down and swung around and rose again. A road without shade or overbearing trees, raised above the world and bright with the promise of wine, that feared and despised temptation. He drove quite fast, eating the cakes from the bag until he was no longer starving. It was impossible not to be in a better mood, to feel slightly uplifted.

At the turn-off for an ancient church he found a line of cars waiting for no apparent reason. At first he assumed it was a red light, but when he darted out of the car to investigate the matter he saw that it was not. It was an accident. Two cars had collided and swerved to either side of the narrow road. The occupants were unharmed, and they sat also on either side of the road, smartly dressed as if on their way to a wedding party. He sauntered up to the scene and saw the glass shattered all over the tarmac, and two young girls, sitting on folding chairs in their satin skirts and dresses, with expressions of disbelief and sly mischief. They seemed to find the whole thing a lark.

On the far side of the accident another line of cars stretched up the hill. The police had not yet arrived, and he thought of their inevitable and imminent appearance and realized that he was trapped.

He walked unhurriedly back to the car and removed the weapons in the blanket he had wrapped them in and slung his bag over his shoulder and walked off toward Gropina, which looked to be a kind of ghost village, but decorated with pots of flowers. Only now did a car draw up behind his, effectively shutting in the Peugeot, and he was above the road by the time two others drew up behind that one. Disputes and flaring tempers seemed desirable from his perspective. Before long, however, he heard the distant approaching sirens of the police, but for whom they were coming was as yet unclear.

He found the Gropina *pieve* and walked on until he was once more in the fields. There was no one there, no inhabitants to track him. He passed a copse to his left and the air became suddenly hot, like the air of a quarry, and the drone of bees came out of the edge of the shade. The track dipped back down to the main Setteponti road, and he could have continued and simply walked on in the same direction. But he didn't know from which direction the police were coming. He left the track therefore and passed into the lines of vines. Beyond them lay a thicker wood where the leaves seemed to be in a dark sweat. By the time he got there the sirens on the far side of Gropina had become loud and then they were shut off. He hurried into the wood and took out both shotguns and laid them at his side.

THAT MORNING ROCKHOLD was woken in the hotel above Donnini where he had taken a room for the night. The Villa Pitiana was originally a noble's villa, but now it was a threadbare hotel barely able to keep up with itself. Susan was calling him and the phone's ringing brought him back to consciousness, but as it did he looked up at the lofty ceiling and had no idea where he was. The night before he had lost the Peugeot somewhere near the town of Poppi and, furious with himself, had decided to stay on the same road in the hope that the following morning would give him a second chance. And so it did. He stumbled to the shutters and threw them open. A sunlit landscape appeared, a cool morning edged with coming heat. Susan told him everything that had happened that morning, which she had heard about only minutes before.

"A robbery where?"

He paused the conversation to order some coffee from

downstairs and then sat by the window in the sun, a lizard getting its warmth back.

"Pian di Sco?" he went on, unfolding his map on the table and looking for the tiny settlement. The police had been summoned but were making their way to a different place down the road, where an accident had happened. She had heard it from their contact inside the Italian police.

"What time was that?"

It had been an hour ago.

"So they're already at Gropina. Maybe it's not him."

But he knew it must be. Leaving everything behind and grabbing his room-service coffee in the lobby before it arrived in his room, he left the Villa Pitiana and drove along the sinuous road that overlooked the valley.

The road to Gropina was not so easy to find, and when he was finally on it he called Susan for updates. Eventually he, too, came to Pian di Sco. There was a police car parked outside the bakery, but no commotion. He called his Italian colleague in Florence. The police had found the abandoned Peugeot, but its driver had vanished. There was an accident at the scene that they also had to deal with. Confusion reigned, and when he himself arrived there he found the same people gathered around the two crashed cars that Faoud had seen. The police were taking evidence and four officers were walking slowly through the lines of vines to the right of the road. Rockhold parked in the verge behind the line of bottlenecked cars and walked first to the Peugeot with the English plates that he had, at last, found. A policeman stood there, and they shook hands. They had been told who he was, but their English was limited. The doors of the car were open and he peered inside. It was evidence that should not be touched, and so he merely walked around it and examined the mud-flecked surface of the metal. He was told that detectives were on their way, they would be there within two hours. The suspect had escaped on foot. The robbery had been reported by the owners of the bakery, and it was unusual for the area that the police had reacted with such admirable efficiency.

"Escaped?" Rockhold said.

"Ran away. We're looking in the fields."

Then he moved on to the shattered pieces of glass and introduced himself to the officers taking notes there. It was surprising to him that absolute priority would not be given to an armed robbery in a cake shop only a few miles away. But they were locals interacting with locals; they all knew each other and insurance claims were at stake. Things had become heated between the two car owners and shouting had erupted. The police tried to calm them down, and Rockhold wandered off to the hamlet above the road, where something told him a man would go if he had to escape. But they had not posted any men there. A question of manpower and confusion. He walked up to the little church, dark and ancient on its platform overlooking a sea of vines, and then moved through the lanes, coming almost immediately to the end of Gropina.

But at the edge of the olive groves an old woman stood with a bucket and a rake, and as he walked past her she pointed to the wood farther down the path. It was a silent gesture, and he took it gratefully. Ahead of him the somber trees echoed with cuckoos.

As he came through the vines and into the first clammy pools of shade inside these same trees, a shot rang out and something seemed to whizz past his left shoulder. Almost without remembering it, he saw that he was himself holding his

Glock in one hand with the barrel pointing carelessly downward. He would have crouched in the following moment, but almost instantly a second shot rang out, this time from something bigger and more purposeful, and the shotgun slugs hit him in the chest, sending him rolling backward into the vines in a silent stupefaction that held his tongue. He lay on his back, trying to breathe and gazing up at the sky, which seemed, in some surprising way, to have suddenly released him from its grip. The man within the wood, seeing him fall, himself stood up, shouldered the shotgun that he had just used, and turned to move deeper into the wood. He had recognized Rockhold from the square in Sorano at once.

He got as far as the olive groves that surrounded a large house nearby, from where the road could be seen. Police cars swarmed along it now, and the men from them had begun to fan out through the vineyards with dogs. Naturally, they had heard the two shots, and were now making their way toward the wood with the pack leading.

He came to a path with high cypresses and with more forest beyond it. To his right the police moved up through a steep vineyard and the dogs barked furiously. There were cries and shouts: they had discovered the dead Rockhold. Faoud slipped across the track and into the new woods and began to run stealthily through the olive trees beyond. Eventually he dropped the bag and retained only one shotgun and one pistol. He came to another house, and here there was a swimming pool brilliantly lit by the sun. A woman was lying next to it, and in a moment she had seen him. She had raised her head, her mouth had opened, and a short scream had been uttered. He darted up the slope above it, vaguely conscious of the dogs also darting through the trees below. They brought his fear back.

One of them appeared right behind him; he turned and shot at it with the shotgun, missed, and then resumed his run. But the pack caught up with him as he came to the edge of yet another copse, and there he turned on them with the pistol and fired off three rounds, scattering them and giving him time to settle behind a tree and reload the shotgun. It was midday before the police had controlled the area and set up their cordon and begun to talk to him through a loudspeaker. But he had already decided not to play games with his honor.

They waited until nightfall before moving in. During the afternoon the fields were peaceful, birds swooped in blustering gangs upon the vines and the silver-backed olive leaves, and Faoud lay on his side remembering the grave of Ibn Taymiyyah, which he had once visited in a parking lot in Damascus when he was a boy. That was courage, if you thought about it. The theologian who rode out of Damascus in the year 1301 to confront the Mongol invader Ghaza Khan and accuse him of being a bad Muslim because he had taken it upon himself to wage war on other Muslims. To face down a conqueror with words and remonstrations. If you meant what you said, you could confront whole empires. Death was far from being the worst thing that could afflict you. Being a slave was more bitter, and being a heretic was darker still. Remembering which, he aimed his shotgun with a calm calculation as the dark blue figures came edging through the vines. He wondered how long it would take for them to kill him, those soft officers of European law who had probably never fired a weapon in their lives. It might last well into the night with all the advantage on his side. They, after all, cared about their lives: it was a tremendous, perhaps fatal, disadvantage.

THE
MILLIONAIRES

TWENTY-TWO

ROCKHOLD'S FUNERAL WAS HELD IN THE SUSSEX VIL-
lage of Poynings, hidden in a fold of the South Downs a
few miles from Devil's Dyke. It wasn't far from where the Rock-
holds had long lived, and his wife had reserved a place for them
in the small cemetery behind the church years before.

Of course she had realized that, to begin with, it would be
occupied by only one of them. But she had never imagined that
it would be so soon, and under such circumstances. The Codringtons came down from London as a group, staying for a few
days at the Metropole in Brighton: Jimmie's brother Rupert,
his nieces and nephews, and Naomi, who had returned from
Greece for the formalities. It rained all week and the service in
the chilly church was one that Jimmie would not have liked—
so said his brother. The priest who knew him well extolled his
virtues; the little crowd was silent. Rockhold's body was con-
signed to the earth in the shade of the Victorian yews with the
chalk hill behind it, its crust filled with the Iron Age relics he
used to collect on Sundays with his metal detector. The gathering afterward at the Plough Inn was awkward. Rockhold had
worked for the Codringtons for thirty years, but few of them
knew who he was. He was Jimmie's secret, and Jimmie had still
not surfaced nor ever would. The secret, therefore, endured and
grew. The survivors did not know what to say or think about

Rockhold. They didn't know the stiff, petite widow in her black pearls, with her air of accusation and fury. They didn't know what his virtues really were. Only Rupert knew about him.

He took Naomi aside and they went out into the drizzle of the lonely, steep-pitched lane that ran outside the pub. He suggested that they drive up to the Dyke together and have a talk.

"I think it would help to get away," he said. "You look a little shaken."

"Better than stirred."

He almost smiled.

"Quite."

It was the end of the day when they got there, and the cafe at the summit was barely open. But the summer rain had stopped and they walked together down the open hillside with its grassy fosses. In their funereal dress they looked, she thought, like suitable ambassadors from the afterlife in a place where she had always thought that ghosts were legion.

"Jimmie used to take me here when I was very small," she said. "You can see the sea on a clear day."

"So you can. Not today, though."

There was just a layer of horizontal light where the sea lay. They came to a halt among the stiff flowers of gorse, the grass rippled by wind. The skylarks trilled so far up they couldn't see them. Rupert was a rugged man, more rugged than his brother, but in the end peas and pods yielded their results and she could see that the two men were made of the same stuff. They were both half self-made and the same bitterness lay at the bottom of both. Rupert, the younger man, had looked up to his elder sibling only until a certain point in his life. Was that not always an irreparable loss?

"I'm glad you came to the funeral," he said, not looking at

her. (The view was an excuse for both of them to avoid each other's eyes.) "I believe you met Rockhold once, did you not?"

"He came to Greece to interview me."

"Would you call it an interview and not an interrogation?"

"It was both, in a way. I didn't mind him. He had his reasons."

"I'm sorry they haven't found your father and stepmother. I had a rather long interview with the Italian police—"

It had taken place in Rome. He had gone down there with his wife, stayed at the Savoy, and the police had come to the hotel every day to brief him. It had been more surreal than one might have expected and he had sat through the whole thing quite passively. They told him that the migrant had, in all likelihood, carjacked Jimmie and Phaine's vehicle in southern Italy, killed them, and buried them somewhere along this route from Brindisi to Rome. That was the likeliest possibility, anyway. Now that the suspect was dead there was no one to ask and the theory had to remain suspended, as it were, in the air. It was true that the couple had made no mention to anyone of their intention to drive back that week, and when the police had asked Naomi about it she had simply told them that her father and stepmother were prone to such improvisations. Rupert himself had received an e-mail earlier in the month in which Jimmie had expressed his desire to do so—as they did every year. It was only slightly surprising that he had said nothing to Naomi.

"He did mention something," she said quietly. "I can't remember when, though. He was quite impulsive anyway, as you know—"

"Indeed he was. It was part of his force."

"It didn't do him much good," she said sourly. "He would have been better off being a bit less impulsive."

"I can't disagree with that one. But you're sure he said something to you about leaving for Italy?"

"Yes. He was getting tired of Hydra."

"Were the two of you arguing? I mean, do you think that was part of him feeling tired of it?"

She flinched a little but didn't turn.

"How should I know? He kept himself to himself. All I mean is that I wasn't surprised that they left without saying anything."

Was he really free as the wind? Rupert thought.

She wondered what her uncle knew about her, if anything; over the years they had had very little contact. Not enough contact, in fact, for him to fall into an easy suspicion of her. It occurred to her that most of what he knew might well have come from Rockhold. Would that make it close to the truth, or far away from it? He explained all the intricacies of the estate now that there was a presumption of death. It was about what she would inherit, which was in essence the house in Hydra, the house in London, and a large block in the company shares. It was a standard arrangement for an only child and nobody would contest it. Indeed, the only person who could realistically contest it was Rupert, and he had no intention of doing any such thing. It was the only compensation for such a horrifying trauma, and he knew that Jimmie would never have put such things into his will if he had not meant them. There was just the question of Phaine's share of that same will. He had granted her the house in Italy, but since she was presumed dead as well they would have to come to an arrangement. Personally, he didn't care much himself. Perhaps something for the nieces and nephews, then, though they were already very well provided for. She might give it a thought.

"So we're assuming they're dead?" was all she said.

"I'm afraid they must be at this point. The Italian police said they would carry on looking. They're combing all the roads, but between you and me, it's an all but impossible task. They're not going to find them. I know it's hard."

"That's the hardest part."

"Not knowing where they are?"

"Yes. It's obscene."

"I would agree with you. But there's always a chance they'll get lucky."

"Who was the suspect?"

Rupert felt like smoking, but it didn't seem to be a good moment for it. He stroked his chin and wondered what to say.

"They have no idea. He had no ID. None whatsoever. One of these bloody migrants. There's no way of knowing where he came from. Even the fingerprints led nowhere."

"A nonperson, then?"

"Yes, you could say that. A nonperson to us, anyway. A person to someone somewhere."

"And we can't even guess his nationality?"

"No. No way of knowing. The police more or less said it was a closed case. Of course, they'll run fingerprint checks for a while, but I expect it'll go nowhere. He made a grab for the car and it got out of control. They even said it didn't mean he was a criminal. Just desperate."

"He didn't have to kill them."

"We don't know—like I say, it might have just spun out of control. If you steal someone's car, it usually does."

"I can't believe," she said, "that no one at the ferry terminal remembered them crossing."

"But they did. They remembered them perfectly. That's the funny thing with people. They remember things perfectly even if they didn't happen."

"People are morons," she said bitterly.

"That they are," he said, and laughed. "It's an undeniable fact."

"And what did the authorities in Italy do with his body?"

Rupert was slow with his words, as deliberate as he could be. There was something odd in her tone.

"They cremated it after a week, I believe. There wasn't much else to do. I think they did the right thing."

So they've all disappeared without a trace, she thought.

It was slowly dawning on her that she was now very rich on her own account, and it was curious that this obvious fact had not occurred to her at all in the previous weeks. It was like a new fact that had suddenly dropped into her lap courtesy of Uncle Rupert. She was a millionaire now. How did nice left-wing millionaires behave?

They went on their quiet rampages, which often were conducted purely inside their own heads. But they might also burn a few barns in the real world. They might look for a little vengeance.

"Are you going to stay in London?" her uncle asked. "It's a very nice house. It must have a few memories for you too."

"It has a lot of memories. But anyway, I don't know. I may go back to Greece. London drains everything out of me. I can't stand the place."

"Fair enough. What will you do on Hydra?"

"What I've always done—nothing and everything. Maybe I'll paint the house. It would be therapeutic."

"I daresay it might."

Rockhold had once said to him long ago, "That girl is a piece of work. She is Jimmie's negative image." He smiled to remember it. But what did it mean?

They walked back to the car.

"There's a family gathering in the restaurant at the hotel tonight, if you feel like coming. The kids will drink champagne and all that. If you don't want to come, I'll understand."

"I'm a bit exhausted now. The funeral was too much."

"Yes, pity about poor old Rockhold. He was always a bit zealous to my mind. Do you know what I mean?"

"Not really. Zealous?"

"Yes, a bit of a fanatic. Not that that's a bad quality in a man like that. What did he grill you about when he was over there?"

"My childhood, mainly. But strangely, it didn't feel nosy. I rather liked him. He was just worried when Jimmie didn't return his phone calls. His curiosity seemed completely normal to me at the time, and it still does. That was his job, after all. I couldn't resent him doing his job."

"True enough."

"Besides, he paid for dinner."

Rupert smiled, and she did too.

In some way, he reflected, he had cleared the matter up and he had done it without a ruckus. He congratulated himself. They drove in his Jaguar along the looping roads contained within wire fences on the way back to Brighton, and as they came to the first traffic circle, a silver light broke over the sea as it came into view. The sea of the Normans, she thought, not my sea. There's no blue to it.

That night she stayed in her room at the hotel. From her window she watched, gin in hand, the rollers exploding against a dark shingle beach and a hurricane wind tearing at the fairy lights strung across pale turquoise lampposts with dolphin motifs. Even summers here were wintry on certain days. Her thoughts were already back in Hydra. Her isolation returned after a long, nervous day filled with meaningless pretense and chatter, and with it came her doubts and her guilt—however ephemeral—and her hatred of her family. It wasn't that they were insufferable; it was that she hated them for what they were. The emotion was straightforward and natural. In the center of this sudden turmoil and returning hatred was the thought of Faoud's cremation. The ashes must be somewhere even now, stored in a place where a person could pick them up eventually. What if she did so, just because she expressed curiosity to the Italians? *I want to have the ashes of my father's killer.* Wasn't there a certain logic to it? But she would never do it. The box of ashes would remain unclaimed and eventually someone would dispose of it on the quiet, unless a family member heard of the events from afar and came for them. It wouldn't happen. There was something orphaned about Faoud, an unmistakable abandonment. Certain people don't come back from the dead in other people's minds—but nevertheless he existed in hers.

The following day she took the train to Victoria and a taxi to St. John's Wood. Her father's mews house there never looked as if anyone ever lived in it, despite the confusion of his study. They had gone through his papers already and someone, without her knowledge, had obviously gone through his hard drive as well. Perhaps it had been Rupert. She wondered if he had talked to the Rockhold widow in that knowing and wheedling way of his. Rockhold must have talked to his wife about his comings and goings, his suspicions. It was impossible that she knew nothing. Perhaps she had let slip a thing or two. Things that he thought about the girl he was investigating. Things about the visitor at

Episkopi and the Four Seasons that he could have easily found out about. Troubled by the possibilities that she would never be able to verify, she lay in her old room from schooldays—still filled with her cherished and stored school textbooks—and traced in her mind the paths of Hydra, the steps and squares and landings and the little churches high above the port, and especially the one near her house, the chapel of Agia Paraskevi. Since she was little she knew when it was open (it was usually closed) and she knew the story of the obscure saint whose face was painted above the door: a Greek woman of second-century Rome whose name means "Friday" and who was tortured by being forced to wear a steel helmet filled with nails. She was later decapitated after causing the idols in a temple of Apollo to disintegrate. It was her favorite building on Hydra, though it was not much frequented by Greeks.

A long shade was almost always drawn down from the top of the door to the ground, in the Greek way, and the waste lot opposite it was a mass of flowering weeds. Nearby stood ruined stone arches covered with teeming vegetation, paths that went nowhere. They were houses that the old had left years before and that no one had yet reclaimed. The prickly pears leaned out precariously from the walls as if colonizing yet more space and pools of odorous shade had formed under the trees: she roamed through every street in her mind as if looking for a mistake she might have made, a false turn somewhere in the past. One can only calculate a certain number of things. Mistakes are inevitable.

She opened the church door and went in. There was only an old woman alone in the dark, waiting for her reply from heaven. She knew the old woman somehow, she almost remembered her name. She had been young when Naomi was a little girl.

So time passes and destroys them. Then she woke and heard the English rain on the mews. Above her, directly above in his study, she heard Jimmie padding about as he always did. He went to the door and opened it, and a light came on in the hallway outside her room. She sat up and gripped the sheet on either side of her, and for a moment she doubted that events had unfolded as she had imagined. But his foot never creaked on the first step downward. He hesitated, as if mocking her, and the result was that her terror did not abate. It went on until she recovered her normal breathing and she remembered that, unlike Faoud, he had not been cremated.

TWENTY-THREE

A T THE END OF AUGUST THE CLEAR BLUE EVENINGS IN the port began to grow more unstable and sudden winds blew out of nowhere, bearing a veil of haze-like cloud. The elaborate awnings of the cafes flapped and shuddered while the waiters grappled with ropes as complex as nautical rigging, and with expressions of sedate anxiety. The late-summer crowds looked up and wondered if the fine weather would continue uninterrupted into September as it usually did, or whether it would now decline and force them to carry a light sweater in the evenings. Often Sam would sit there with Toby, sipping the tsipouro that Naomi had taught her how to drink, and she too would look up at the haze enveloping the sun and wonder if it was sand falling onto them after crossing the Mediterranean from Africa. She could feel it in her hair, on her lips. It was not the first time that summer, but it was now more pronounced, the grit more salty. Her anxiety simmered constantly. But perhaps it was also just her imagination. Since Naomi had left the island, her days had become more languorous and more self-absorbed. And she had her new boy.

"We're leaving in a week," she said one evening, when the little storm was blowing and the waiters were rushing back and forth in front of the Porto Fino bar, trying to catch napkins as they flew through the air. "It's all right, though—it feels like time. It's overdue actually. Are you all booked for the return trip?"

"We're going to London for a few days—Dad has some work there. Then back."

"Naomi says this place is like a tomb in winter."

"I can imagine."

"Are you going to come back next year?"

He looked genuinely surprised. "Next year? I hadn't even thought about it."

"We could come back just by ourselves."

"That would be cool."

"Let's think about it."

"Yeah," he said. "We'd probably run into Naomi all the time, though, wouldn't we?"

Sam's face lost its brightness for a moment, but she recovered.

"Would that matter?" she said quickly. "Do you not like her?"

"She's all right. But you're different around her."

"I am?"

"Yeah, kind of. You start kind of acting like her."

She wanted to say, "So what?" because it was not, of course, the first time that this had been pointed out to her.

But instead she merely said, "She's older and interesting. Maybe I do change a little. It's not that surprising."

"I never said it was. But imagine a whole summer here just by ourselves. It would be so much better."

"Maybe we should go to Spetses instead, then."

He laughed. "Maybe we should."

He went on to ask her if anything had been unearthed about the Codringtons, but she shook her head and brushed the question off. She was under orders from Naomi to say nothing to anyone.

They walked hand in hand through the port to Xeri Elia, the place where famous people once strummed their guitars under the trellises, with its twisted whitewashed trees and its outdoor tray of iced fish. They sat under the plumbago and ordered aubergines imam and *fasolia*. She had learned to read Greek characters by now and she spelled out every item on the menu for him, who could already read them. Stuffed tomatoes: *tomat-tes gem-istes.*

"I love the way," he said, "they use the word 'partheno' in the phrase 'virgin olive oil.'"

She read slowly: *"Partheno elaiolado."*

"How beautiful is that? 'Virgin olive oil' just sounds silly."

She said, "Let's have a drink and toast to us."

They made it Babatzim with anise.

"Slug it back," he ordered.

It felt good on the throat.

"I don't want to stay here forever," she said when her head had cleared, "but then again, sometimes I want to stay here forever."

"You don't feel that everywhere."

"You can say that again. It takes a special place to make you feel like that."

"I feel it here from time to time. My parents don't, I don't think. They can't wait to get back to the States now."

"I think we should come back next year and not tell anyone."

"Deal."

They moved on to Manolis for dessert. It was just around the corner, and she loved the downstairs room with its dozens of pictures of ocean liners and schooners and old Greek frigates, if that was what they were called. They gorged on rice pudding and then sat at the two tables outside in the alley and drank ouzo. It was the most beautiful part of the summer. These lazy nights with Toby with no one to distract her, and the roiling tensions and dramas that Naomi's presence seemed to create entirely absent. Even the "event," as she called it to herself, had become abstract and unreal. Certainly, she was forcing herself to forget and erase it. But it was more than that. She was edging closer to the idea that—quite out of the blue—she had stumbled upon the boy she would eventually marry. This enormous event suddenly eclipsed the other one, and she felt superstitiously that one had led to the other. It was not fortuitous. And it was this idea that kept her sane. The idea, and the constant presence of the boy with the soft buzz cut.

She spent most nights at his house and her parents no longer seemed to mind. They had eventually asked about him and then invited him around for dinner. It had been a surprisingly relaxed affair on the terrace, and Toby had sagely groomed himself impeccably for the occasion, showing up in an oxford button-down and subtly stylish slip-ons. His family standing was thus discreetly advertised, though she was ashamed to admit that she noticed or even cared. He talked well through dinner, and he and her father got into some spirited and erudite exchanges in the finest WASP tradition. So much the better.

Mr. Haldane: "Of course, although Pinochet was a rat Chile's economy also improved with the reformed pensions scheme. I won't and can't deny it. That's the paradox."

Toby: "So you credit the Chicago School with some successes?"

Mr. Haldane: "I'm ashamed to concede the point, but yes." And so on.

"How's Princeton?" her father asked eventually. "Hated it there myself."

"It's fine for now," came the suavely offhand reply. "I might go somewhere else for grad school, though. Maybe somewhere in Asia."

"Oh?"

"I'm doing Japanese as a minor. It would be cool to spend a year or two over there."

"A shame you can't get your MA here on Hydra," her mother said. "The beautiful places are always the most useless."

Sam bit her tongue. Inadvertent profundity was always the worst kind, especially coming from her mother. Nevertheless, they drank a lot of coffee in a hot wind and it was glorious. Her father was intellectually revived and irritated, her mother gave her an approving eye that clearly referred to the young man, the bell from the little church up the road tolled, and they wondered who on earth went there at that time of the evening. The maid brought out a bottle of sweet liqueur of some kind and a companion bottle of Metaxas, and small thimble glasses were rapidly filled and emptied.

From time to time Sam's thoughts wandered—out to sea, out into the winds where the other girl still existed. It was Toby who caught her eye moving outward and away from the faces around the table. He knew at once what it was, but he had enough discretion not to bring it up later. They played cards after the table had been cleared and, unsurprisingly, Toby turned out to be a good player, better than any of them. Her mother was extremely pleased. She asked him about his parents, their house in Hydra. Were they the usual bohemians (though she phrased it otherwise)?

"No, my father runs a drug company. We're not really the

265

creative type. Anyway, I think a lot of the artists have left now. It's gotten too expensive. There must be another island they've moved to without telling anyone. When I find out where it is I'll let you know. But I don't think you'll want to go there."

"Oh, but I will," Amy burst out.

Sam took him down the steps afterward and along the path toward Kamini. They sat on a wall and kissed and reviewed the odd evening. They both knew that he had performed well, but that it was of no importance to either of them. She was already imagining how their relationship would be on home soil, thousands of miles away, surrounded by their common language. It seemed to her that it would be better, finer. And in some way easier. Her certainty about it was still growing.

"Let's go swimming tomorrow at Vlychos," she said before he left. "Come and get me around ten. I want to sleep in."

"I'll come and have your mother's pancakes, like she said."

"She'll love that."

There was lightning at the horizon later that night. She lay awake, letting the wind pour through the open windows and scatter pieces of paper around the room. After midnight there was a text from Naomi, the first in more than two weeks.

I'll be there soon. Will be on the mainland at Ermioni. When are you leaving for New York?

She didn't answer immediately. The idea of Naomi returning filled her with dread, but at the same time there was the companionship and the complicity, the easy exclusivity that they enjoyed between themselves. These were things she missed. But she wasn't sure and she decided to sleep on it. In the morning Toby came with oppressive punctuality at ten and they walked to Vlychos in a terrible heat with their bathing gear. They climbed down to a rough beach and swam out into the pale-lime water up to the edge of the dark shelf. She thought he had been up all night for some reason, and she hadn't slept particularly well herself. When they were back on the beach she snuggled up against him and they enjoyed what would likely be the only moment of cool in the day.

"I'm so looking forward to air-conditioning again," she said.

"You can live without it."

"I really can't. If we come back next year, let's stay at the Bratseras."

She rolled onto her back and stretched out her arms until her fingers were driven into the loose shingle. She was even more sure that a fine, invisible sand was falling through that clear sky onto her body.

FOUR DAYS LATER, Naomi sent another text. She asked Sam to get the morning ferry to Ermioni, a short crossing on the SeaCat, and to meet her on the dock in the middle of the village. Twenty minutes west of Metochi, it was the alternative landing on the mainland for day trippers. Reluctantly, Sam agreed. She could see why it would be a better idea not to be seen together on the island and Naomi knew that she was leaving at the weekend. She took the fast mid-morning ferry and came into the quiet and lovely bay of Ermioni, a place she had not visited during her time on Hydra, and there on the quay among a few fishing boats—but no obnoxious yachts—stood a thin and feverish Naomi in a blue-and-white-striped T-shirt and espadrilles. She looked changed. It was not for the better, but she was tanned and fit-looking nevertheless and Sam had the immediate feeling that she had already been in Ermioni for a number of days. So she was observing things from a safe distance.

They hugged and there was a sudden moment of tears as Naomi took her hand, as if taking charge of them both and pulling them into a patch of sunlight.

"We need coffee and sweets!" she cried.

Next to the port ran a single road. On the far side of it were the cafes and tavernas, most of them still closed. They found a bakery called Drougas with stools on the pavement, cool in the shade, where they sat with slabs of *bougatsa* filled with custard and covered with confectioner's sugar and cups of Ipanema coffee. Bare-shouldered, they touched lightly; the frisson was still there. Naomi recounted the most recent events in London.

She told everything truthfully because she thought it was better that way. It was a way of expressing trust in Sam, because the latter would only react badly to a lie. The truth would make her loyal, even more loyal than she already was. She then said that she was renting a forty-euro-a-night room on the same waterfront and that she would stay there until the Haldanes left for America.

"So the investigator is dead?" Sam said.

"It seems like everyone is dead. It was all an accident."

Naomi's eyes were dry, but Sam thought she probably cried it all out of her last week.

"It doesn't seem real," Sam murmured.

Naomi agreed. "It doesn't. But it is."

"And your relatives went along with our story."

"They had no choice."

Sam nodded. "That's how it is. They have no choice. But you can't go back to the house."

"Why not? I don't believe in ghosts. I can't sell it."

"Why not?"

"The risk is too great. Someone might get it into their heads to dig up the garden."

"So you'll keep it."

"Of course I'll keep it. I'm going to live there. I'm going to repaint it."

"And live—"

"Unhappily ever after. I guess you won't visit."

Sam shrugged. "Probably not."

"I'd be sorry not to see you again."

"I would too," Sam said.

"But it might be for the best."

Naomi cut a strip of *bougatsa* and held it up to Sam's mouth on a fork.

"Eat, mummy says. *Que será será.*"

They walked along the road that led eventually to both Naomi's temporary digs at a place called Xenophilia Ganossis and a peninsula covered with pine groves. It was the site of the ancient city of Hermionis, long vanished. The path went around its perimeter, the cliff to the left plunging down through fragments of ancient wall to the water. They passed a pile of dark stones. It was a Temple of Poseidon worn down to its elements. In the woods there were more stones, unmarked and unvisited, slabs laid into the ground. Collared doves called through the trees, and at the tip of the peninsula spearlike agaves stood at angles against the brilliant glare of the sea. At the far side of the water the mountains were layered against each other, dark with their own forests. They sat on a bench and looked out across the water. It was a moment of complete confusion. Sam thought she might say something about Toby, as if it was relevant, but she couldn't bring herself to do it. But perhaps a farewell was in order. She didn't know. What she wanted to know was whether she was safe and the future was secure. Her future now depended in some measure on Naomi and her ability to keep up the secret. Mutual blackmail, she thought, but it was a vicious thought that wasn't even necessary. They both knew what to do. But what was not decided was how long it would last. There was no possible term that could be set to the secret—and so it would last forever. That implied a bond that would also last forever. It was calamitous and sweet. Realizing it, then, at the same time, they turned to each other and there was the horror in their eyes, as bright as all the other buried feelings.

"It's going to be horrible to be away from here," Sam said, half truthfully. "But I can't come back. There's no way."

"I know."

But Naomi was smiling, she was forgiving. "We'll find a way to meet again one day. Maybe in London if you ever come there."

"I'd like that. But you know how it is."

Sam had already begun to imagine a future without Naomi at all. They would never meet again, and it would be a relief that they didn't. A summer was just a summer, and its dead bodies should remain confined to it.

Naomi took her hand.

"I know how it is. I'll be here anyway. I'm going to take up painting. I may as well. It's what I always wanted to do."

"You told my mother you weren't a painter."

"That's right, I did. But I wasn't lying. I'll make myself into one."

"Is that what you wanted all along—a room of your own?"

"It's a cliché, but why not?"

"Or just a place where no one can look up your lies?"

"They're your lies too," Naomi retorted. "They're ours. Anyway, why shouldn't I want a place where no one can look up my lies? It's what all human beings want, in my opinion."

"It's the last thing I want."

"Then you're a very special person."

"I'm not special. I'm just gullible, apparently."

"You're still a fantastic liar—a virtuoso, in fact. I think you enjoy it. So that makes two of us."

The subtle malice made Sam recoil a little, but she calmed herself. She realized now that she knew nothing about Naomi or her past, let alone what tortuous road had brought her to this spot at this moment. It was all unknown, a shadowed story that was not her own and which she had probably misinterpreted. But she let Naomi embrace her and suddenly they were locked together in silence, baked by the sun, half blinded by the sea, and it was a long time before they disengaged and Sam laid her head on Naomi's shoulder.

"You know what the Greeks used to say?" Naomi thought aloud. "Love makes the time pass and time makes the love pass."

Turning her head, Sam could see the low-clinging pines on the rock shelves, moving slightly as the wind disturbed them. Their sound was familiar, but it was deeper than she remembered and more relentless. She could have changed all her plans in one instant, but the instant came and went and she did not.

TWENTY-FOUR

IN NEW YORK, THE LAST DAYS OF HEAT PASSED SLOWLY for Sam as she caught up on her reading for the next semester. Her parents and her brother went up to Maine to stay with her grandparents, and she stayed in the city at the family apartment in Morningside Heights. After the jet lag had cleared she was able to assess everything and refind her bearings. Gone was the blinding Greek sky and the sun that pierced your mind to the core. Here it was deafening cicadas and a moist, cloying heat with no wind. She got up at first light and ran along the river, her mind cooled by the low forests on the far side and the mechanical motion of the other joggers.

She had the freedom to see Toby as much as she wanted. During the exhausted late-summer days, with the city emptied out, they laid the groundwork for a relationship that might last for a long time, longer in any case than she had expected on Hydra. In the cavernous apartment overlooking the river they made dinner together with their own groceries and watched movies or made sorties to bars that Toby had personally discovered and which he wanted to pass on to her. They went often to Sakagura on East 43rd Street in the basement below a garage and sat at the long counter with plum blossoms where Toby could practice his Japanese. It was not especially young or hip, but she liked the fact that he knew such places and knew how to handle himself inside them. In the second week of September, her parents still away, he asked her if she had heard from Naomi. His own parents were back in the States and they had finally heard something about the terrible events in Italy with the Codringtons. It defied explanation.

"I heard about it too," she said. "It doesn't seem possible. I can't say they were nice people—but I only heard Naomi's side of things."

"My parents liked them well enough, though. You can never tell about families. They're incomprehensible from the outside."

"It's true. Man, mine too—"

"But Naomi didn't seem upset beforehand?"

"She thought they went away for a trip. There's nothing suspicious about it."

"Either way I'm glad we're here now," he said. "Away from her."

"I know what you mean."

He looked down and saw that her hand, as it tried to lift a *masu* brimming with sake, was causing the liquid to tremble. He reached out and lowered her hand for her.

"You're upset," he said. "Let it go."

"Not really upset—"

Her lower lip went slack and he sensed a crisis suddenly developing.

"I don't know what it is," she went on.

"Let it go all the same."

She picked the *masu* up again and it was steady. He did likewise and they touched boxes. There, there, his eyes said.

That night he slept over at her apartment. He thought back to the first night they had spent together on Hydra and the way her face had contorted in her sleep before waking with a scream. He had thought about it ever since. It was a clue to something that he knew he shouldn't investigate. But press Sam a little and she withdrew. She could not be hustled into confessions, and it was clear by now that she didn't believe in them.

When the semester began and her parents returned she began to spend her days and evenings in Bobst Library on Washington Square, sitting close to the glass walls at one of the desks at the end of the stacks and reading with hours-long concentration. It was her last year doing comparative literature and she was reading the French Romantics. The days grew darker, and when Toby was in town from Princeton they went to places in the East Village and then went to his parents' pied à terre on East 63rd—the Carhargans spent most of their time in Maine now, and only occasionally visited the city. Slowly, she came to know them: they all had Hydra in common and it made it easy to bond. Over the winter she came three times a week and the hospitality was returned in the opposite direction. Toby soon appeared at her parents' dinner parties when he was down from Princeton, where he was shown off like an adorable trophy who might, by the miraculous alchemy of time, turn into a son-in-law before a single gray hair had appeared on his head. This was, in fact, exactly what happened, and much more quickly than she had expected.

He proposed that first winter six months before her graduation. Dizzy and alarmed, she panicked, asked for more time, then accepted within a week. Her mother was ecstatic; her father demurred a little, then gave in with unconvincing jollity. The parents met together at a restaurant with the three children and the introductions were made. She was aware that as she and Toby sat together with their parents in the dining room of Ilili in the West Village they looked as perfect as a young couple could look in the first flush of an enviable marriage. She thought, Our future children are already visible like beautiful ghosts to the people around us.

It was too perfect—and yet didn't people in perfect situations always think "It's too perfect"?

"I must say," Andrew Carhargan said as the waiter opened a bottle of Musar at the table, "I think it's an extraordinary coincidence that we were all on Hydra at the same time. I'd say that was as good an omen as one could want. I hope you'll consider getting a house there every summer from now on. What do you say, Jeffrey?"

"I'm in! I think Amy and Chris are too?"

"I think next time I'd rather be in the port," Amy said.

"We can help you with that, can't we, Elizabeth? I'm surprised we didn't see you at Sunset at all. We've been going there for years."

"We liked our cook," Jeffrey said blankly. "It was also a long walk there and back. My leg—"

They all knew that they were all acquainted in one way or another with the Codringtons, but it was a subject that could not be broached without unpleasant associations and awkward questions. So it was left untouched, though its presence could still be felt. Under the table Sam felt Toby grasp her hand and hold it, as if to steady her through the dinner, and when they were on to the *raki* at the end Toby's father asked them where they were thinking of buying a house.

"Brooklyn," they said together.

But Carhargan seemed to be still thinking about Hydra, and failed to follow up on the subject of Brooklyn real estate.

"All the same," he suddenly said, "you must have seen the Codringtons fairly often while you were there. I suppose you know the story?"

"Once or twice," Jeffrey admitted. "But we didn't become friends in any way. Did we, Amy?"

His wife shook her head, and yet her eyes, to Carhargan's keen perception, suddenly sidestepped to the right.

"They're a funny couple," he said coolly, now interested in their reaction. "Or should I say were? They're presumed dead, as I'm sure you know."

"It doesn't seem quite real," Amy said.

"I never thought Codrington was very real in the first place, to be honest with you. He was a braggart and a blowhard. They told me he had a hard life, though."

"Oh, in what way?"

Carhargan shrugged. "I don't really know. It's just what people say. Someone told me he was a mercenary in Angola back in the day. But we all know islanders gossip all the time. Some of the neighbors say—but what does it matter? I'm gossiping now myself."

"What?" Amy burst out, but quietly.

"Nothing, nothing. I shouldn't talk about the dead. They didn't deserve to be murdered, if that's what happened. I suppose we'll never know. I'm sad about it, to tell you the truth. We had some jolly times back in the day. The story was that Phaine's family were once friends with Onassis. Can you imagine?"

At the end of the following summer the young couple moved into their house in Brooklyn Heights and they settled into the lives they had planned for themselves. During the winter, however, she began to feel restless.

One week in December it snowed for almost three days without stopping. She put on her snow boots one afternoon when Toby was out and walked down to Prospect Park, along the slushy length of Flatbush Avenue with her podcast drowning out the noise of traffic. The park was nearly empty, soundless under the snow, and she walked deep into it until she was alone with the crows and the icicles. Choking and sobbing, she suddenly felt that someone was following her. She took out the buds from her ears, and when she turned she saw two figures indistinct in the falling snow, each moving in a different direction until only one was left. It was a man in a long coat moving toward her along the same path, blurred and lumbering as if he was as blinded as her. She moved on, but now almost running. She came into a grove of black, dripping trees and she wondered if she should call Toby.

It's just hysteria, she thought, and resolved to not call him. Instead she walked back to Grand Army Plaza at the entrance to the park and sat there waiting for the man to exit from the park as well.

When he did, she stood up as if to confront him and she saw—as he walked past her—that there was indeed something familiar about him. Something in the gait, in the loose, limber insolence.

He strode off down Flatbush and she followed him. The snow was heavier and it became more difficult to keep up with him. When he reached the Atlantic Terminal Mall he crossed the street where a small strip of halal stores stood behind banks of black snow. He went inside one of the butchers and she arrived at the window herself. The shop was full and she couldn't see him in the crowd. There was a line by the cash register, so she pushed her way past it and into the long, narrow store. The butcher's counter lay at the back behind two plastic curtains. Here there was also a small crowd, and two men working at the counter with meat saws and cleavers. As she parted the curtains, the smell of blood hit her and she put a hand to her nose, stumbled into the hot room, and looked quickly into the faces. She glanced at their coats but couldn't say if any of them were his. The eyes turned upon her were glacial and old. She went back to the front of the shop. As she did she saw a tall young man slip out of the door and she rushed back out into the street. But it was too late; he had merged into the sidewalk crowds.

When she got home she wanted to call Naomi. It was out of the question, but she wanted to ask her if Faoud had really died or whether there was a possibility that he had not. Even a tiny possibility. It was different from a total certainty.

But she never called. She thought for a while of telling Toby everything, but it was already too late for such a gesture to mean anything. It would cause her nothing but anguish.

"I think I was followed in the street today," was all she said at dinner that night. "Some guy followed me out of Grand Army Plaza."

"He did?"

He asked if she knew him.

"I wasn't sure. He seemed like someone I knew. Maybe from school."

It was as much as she could tell him to get a part of it off her chest. She went to bed early in a difficult mood and, sensing it, Toby left her alone. She opened the bedroom window a little and let the room cool with the radiators hissing against the walls and lay in the four-poster listening to the snow. Looking back on it, the day seemed empty and yet filled with riddles. The young man in his elegant long coat and woolen hat, the onetime sweep of the eyes with which he had picked her out sitting on the bench in Grand Army Plaza: a shiver of attraction, terror, and a certainty that had filled her. How did she know that Naomi had told her the truth, anyway? Maybe she would go to Prospect Park again the following day in the hope that she might see him again. Maybe he, too, went there every day. There was just the question of whether she would leave the house for no reason on any day of the week in the years to come and go wandering, blindly looking for a man in a crowd. She didn't know. She wasn't at all sure that she wouldn't.

TWENTY-FIVE

WHEN THE HALDANES HAD LEFT AND MUCH OF THE summer crowd had gone with them, Naomi crossed over to the island with several boxes of house paint that she had bought in Porto Heli. She already knew the exact color schemes she would impose upon her new property and how she would go about executing the plan. She knew which color every wall would be and she would lovingly paint it herself. In her mind she had rehearsed the redecorations hundreds of times since she was a small girl. It would be, as she had told Sam, a return to the house her mother had created but with the addition of her spirit and taste. Together they were the true custodians of the house, not the impostors. The tins of paint were her instruments in this act of restoration.

The port had returned to its presummer normalcy. The large yachts had slipped away and the cafes around the docks were back to their leisurely ways. By the Pirate Cove, the statue of the lion and the hero with his handlebar mustaches looked almost lonely, resigned to yet another interminable winter, though winter was still far off. She found a donkey driver, left the boxes with him, and went for a quick coffee. She wanted to look around. A few familiar faces, but no one came up to her or asked her where she had been. The noble discretion of the Greeks. But even if they had, she had prepared herself. A gritty wind blew through the awnings, and she yearned to be back at Mandraki among the prickly pears and the lizards.

Naomi didn't know what to expect at the house. In the end she had asked Carissa to stay on and look after the place until she returned. The maid had refused, though she grudgingly agreed to clean the house a final time before she left for her homeland. Naomi paid the driver and they unloaded the boxes in the cool salon.

The place was immaculately neat. The shutters were closed to keep out the heat and the floors had been recently polished. There was a smell of pine and wax. When the driver had gone, she closed the front door and unpacked the cans of paint, lining them up according to which room they would be used in. Having done this, she went to the kitchen, poured herself a glass of wine from the fridge (it was stocked to the hilt), and went to lie down in Jimmie and Phaine's bedroom.

She lay on the bed and drank, slowly and introspectively. She laid out a plan to clear out this room first. She wouldn't keep anything. The clothes, the pictures, the rugs, the photographs—it would all have to be annihilated.

When she had drained the glass she got up and opened the shutters. The room was dusty and suffocatingly sour, and she aired it as she began to collect the things gathered on the mantelpiece and the bedside tables. She piled them on the bed and then went back down to the kitchen to fetch some plastic garbage bags.

She cleared out the bathroom and then the cupboards. As she was doing this the thought suddenly came to her that she needed music. One couldn't cleanse and purify a house without music. So she went back down to the salon and put a record on Jimmie's ancient sound system. It was the soundtrack to *High*

Society. She turned the volume up as high as it would go and returned to the bedroom to begin her labor in earnest. For an hour she bagged the contents of the room and then dragged the bags down to the living room. She put them all in the garden shed and then poured herself another glass of wine. She took the glass out onto the terrace and drank it with a fierce feeling of vengeance. They would never have imagined how easy it was for her to expunge them from memory. It was as easy, in fact, as repainting a room. It was the hour of the swallows and the bell of Agia Paraskevi was ringing.

She set down the glass on the parapet and stared at the parched hillsides with their near-vertical walled enclosures that seemed to have been built by spiders. Soon she heard someone passing below the outer wall, the slow shuffling of the old, but no one rang the doorbell. She returned to the upstairs room with two cans of paint, one pale green and one a canary yellow. Opening them, she tested the brand-new brushes, laid down newspaper on the floors, and began to paint the largest wall.

The work went smoothly, the music pulling her along. She worked in bare feet, enjoying the stray drops of paint that fell onto her skin, and she finished the wall by early evening. She was alone and yet she didn't feel entirely alone. The garden grave was so close, a mere step away, and there they lay peacefully under the trees without a complaint in the world. Slightly tired, she laid down the brush and went back downstairs while the paint dried. There was a soft chill in the air now, the first cool evening breeze of autumn. She poured out the rest of the bottle on the terrace and enjoyed the wine with her feet up on the wall. She now estimated that it would take her about four days to repaint the house entirely and another three to rearrange all the furnishings and decorations according to her plan. So a week could overturn a decade of misrule. She would spend the rest of the night finishing the master bedroom and then begin the salon the next day.

Farther down the hill, in the grand sea-captain houses that were empty for half the year, the longer-term expats and the wealthy Greeks who also liked the off-season and therefore stayed longer, speculated around their dinner tables about the stories now circulating concerning Jimmie and Phaine Codrington. The news had broken out, but quietly and without fanfare. It was not a rumor, but it played like one. Jimmie, they recalled, had never been much liked. And the unliked are more easily forgotten than the amiable. Their deaths are also more easily passed over with a shrug, however violent and mysterious they have been. The unspoken consensus was that they had it coming to them, as if karma existed even here, far from the landscapes of Buddha. What interested them supremely was that their bodies had never been found. Who could be blamed for that?

No one went up to call on Naomi, though they all knew that she had inherited the estate and had decided to stay on Hydra. It was her right, after all. It was not that she was disliked either, it was that no one—more enigmatically—knew who she was. Even though they had known her since she was a child, they didn't feel comfortable exchanging more than pleasantries with her. People sometimes saw her walking down through the sunlit alleys of the old port, but few knew what she was doing with her time on the island. Her eccentricity kept them at bay, and it seemed to them that the older she became the more eccentric she appeared to be. The English in any case were always distanced from the Hydriots. They lived in slightly different spheres and both sides acknowledged the fact. Peaceably, they left each other alone, and so with time they left the English girl alone as well. On the terrace of the Xeni Heli, under the plumbago, the old seadogs playing backgammon watched her flash under the shade, bright and young and alien, a beautiful animal indeed—*ena omorfo zoo*—and they had no theories about her.

She walked down to Mandraki in the dry cool of the mornings with a portable parasol, as she always had, and swam alone on the far side of the headland by the Mira Mare. She took books with her and read under the parasol, as if she would do this for the rest of her life, and at dusk she walked slowly back to Mandraki to have a drink at the taverna next to the resort. It was there one evening during the first cold days, overlooking the bay, as she was drinking her tsipouros in a pair of mittens, that she saw a familiar rowing boat coming slowly toward the wrecked and tousled beach of the Mira Mare.

It was the girl rowing, with her measured oar-strokes and her sense of knowing at all times who was on the shore. She must have rowed all the way from the most remote parts of the island, diligent and cunning in the way of the sea, unafraid of the gathering dark. Around her the sea looked feverous and almost black, as if its energies had fallen back on themselves and were brewing below its surface. She pulled the boat onto the mixture of sand and debris and pulled her leather satchel out of it. There was no one at the resort and the wind that blew through it was already cold as soon as the sun dipped below the horizon. She glanced around, saw the idle seaplane with its dust-covered floaters, and came along the beach until she was through the small gate that gave onto the path. There she caught sight of Naomi seated outside at the taverna with her solitary glass and her bowl of chopped ice, and she recognized her at once. The

English girl who loped through life with a mental hunchback. The girl who was possessed some days—you could see it in her white eyes.

She gave Naomi a cool *Yassou* and sat at the same table. She seemed to know the old couple who owned the place and they came out with a paper mat and a glass for her. The girl was thick with salt, and she poured a little water onto her arm to show how much had accumulated on her skin.

"My clients," she said, "have all gone for the winter. I thought you had too. I didn't see you for a while."

"No, I decided to stay on. I'm not going back to London after all."

"You've become one of us?"

"In a sense. I always was, anyway."

"I can see you look much happier."

"Do I?"

"You look like a grown-up finally."

Naomi offered her a toast.

"Death to death?" the girl said. "I've never heard that one before."

The best of all toasts, Naomi thought. One could cheat death in a certain way, or one could sidestep around the death of others. Doesn't everyone feel immortal in their deepest self? It didn't matter if it was an illusion, the intuition was still there and had to have a kernel of truth to it.

"Do you have any weed?" Naomi asked after their first round.

"I'll make it free, as a welcome gift now that you're a citizen of Hydra."

She unwrapped a plastic bag on the table and laid flat on the surface a low mound of golden fluff. She had with her a

285

metal pipe and she filled it with the weed, then lit it and set it going. The smoke was blown quickly away, revealing nothing to Naomi, but the remainder that made its way into their lungs made them high almost immediately. They sat back and swilled the tsipouro to increase the effect of delicious lostness, and the water in the bay began to turn a darker violet as the light retreated.

"By the way," the girl said, a great slyness in her eyes but no trace of judgment, "what happened to the Arab boy who I used to see on the far side of the island washing his hair in the sea? I always gave him a free hit. I liked his eyes. Do you know who I mean?"

"I think I saw him get onto one of the ferries," Naomi said.

"Ah, I thought so. At least the police didn't get him. He had a look of freedom about him."

"Freedom?"

"Something like that. That's why I felt sorry for him and gave him a free hit. He was always charming."

"Yes, he was a charmer."

She's right, Naomi thought, that freedom and charm are the same thing.

They lit a joint and the owners brought out a plate of olives, some bread, some oil and salt, and some sardines. The simple and eternal food of the ancients, Naomi thought.

The wind soon picked up and the girl returned to her boat, pushing it back into the bay, and raised her oars. Naomi could hear her laughing in the dark, half stoned, unconcerned, and soon she had slipped away as quietly as she had arrived, and Naomi recalled that she didn't know her real name and never had. She was just the girl who rowed around the island with weed, half stoned and enchanted on a feverish sea. Life was full of such people. One didn't know anything about them, even though they occupied a position of utmost importance in one's life for a time. They were like shooting stars, flaring up for a brilliant moment, lighting up the sky even for a few lingering seconds, then disappearing forever.

ACKNOWLEDGMENTS

I WOULD LIKE TO THANK Konstantin Kakanias and Dimitrios Antonitsis for their irrepressible company on Hydra, and for showing me so much of the island they love.

ABOUT THE AUTHOR

Born in England, LAWRENCE OSBORNE is the author of the critically acclaimed novels *The Forgiven*, *The Ballad of a Small Player*, and *Hunters in the Dark*. His nonfiction ranges from memoir through travelogue to essays, including *Bangkok Days*, *Paris Dreambook*, and *The Wet and the Dry*. His short story "Volcano" was selected for *Best American Short Stories 2012*, and he has written for the *New York Times Magazine*, *The New Yorker*, *Condé Nast Traveler*, *Forbes*, *Harper's*, and other publications. He lives in Bangkok.